Forbidden Quest

She eased his hands from her shoulders, stood, stepped over the side of the tub. She dried herself with the new blue bath sheet, a gift that must have cost him a day's wages. When he left the tub, she dried him, trying to ignore his rationale when he spoke.

"In your country I am black—not a good thing to be. And I am poor with little chance to change that." He took the towel, roped her waist, drew her to him, his voice and his eyes softening. "In my country I am not poor enough to notice. If I give up art and music and go back to school I can be anything. I will go home, Cally. I will do those things. When I am a fine pink Jamaican gentleman, you will come to me. You cannot love me more there, but maybe then you will tell me."

He braided her hair, erotically texturizing the six-hour ritual, just as before. He bathed her again and made love to her.

The pall of reality and their approaching separation hung over it all.

Visit our Web page for latest
releases and other information.
http://www.genesis-press.com

Genesis Press, Inc.
315 3rd Avenue North
Columbus, MS 39701

Forbidden Quest

Dar Tomlinson

Genesis Press, Inc.
315 3rd Avenue North
Columbus, MS 39701

First Edition

To Mikie, with me through every word.
I'll forever miss you.

Chapter 1

*C*arolyna Sinclair held the phone to her ear, listening to rock music on the other end as she watched Hugh Masters move about his impeccable kitchen. Coffee dripped, toast popped, juice cascaded into crystal. All in perfect sequence. Carolyna thought of the already made bed upstairs and listened to the washer churning out last night's sheets.

A voice came on the line. "It's here. I can see the crate out my window, sitting on the dock. The dock foreman checked the label. Looks like it's yours all right."

"Carolyna Sinclair Design?"

"Yes, ma'am. All the way from Rome."

"Thank you. I'll come for it. Today."

Carolyna rubbed the receiver on the borrowed terry cloth robe she wore, removing makeup residue, before hanging up. "I have to go to Savannah, Hugh. Apparently, the freighter off-loaded Jessica Renfro's Louis XIV desk without a waybill and sailed away. I should go. It might rain."

She scribbled on a conveniently placed desk pad imprinted, Hubert Wilson Masters A I A, Architect.

Hugh glanced at the makeup residue on his blue robe, then moved his gaze back to hers. "If the desk is crated it should stand a little rain."

She fingered the makeup smudge. Abandonment had flavored his lovemaking the night before. He had devoured her, lovingly. Yet, this morning a smudge on his robe caught his eye. Hugh was neat to a fault, but trying. Orderliness was an admirable trait, she reminded herself.

His attire made her ask, "City council this morning?"

"City planning. My first meeting. Wish me luck."

1

"You won't need it. They're fortunate to get you." Cooling toast, warming juice, the aroma of coffee passing its peak nudged her, but her stomach fluttered anxiously. She glanced at her watch. "I'll get dressed. I should be on my way to Savannah."

"What about breakfast?" His blond brows arched.

Hugh was thirty-seven, nine years her senior. He sometimes employed the same parental tone with her as with his twelve-year-old daughter, Katharine.

"You can't drive sixty miles on an empty stomach," he said.

Actually she could and often did. "I don't feel hungry." Pressure could have that effect. Or, depending on the source, pressure could also make her ravenous.

"How often do we get the house to ourselves, Cally? When you can stay the night and Katharine is away?" Patience oozed over his tanned face like honey over wheat toast.

"Not often." Katy's absence had contributed to the quality of last night's intimacy. That and the setting: Hugh's own bed. "I'm worried about the desk . . . but I'll take time to eat."

She eased into a chair. Catching her hair at the back of her neck, she twisted it into a thick rope. When her scalp stung, she released the coil onto her shoulders. It was a habit, a ritual almost.

He brought the toast and joined her at the table. She forced herself to eat the breakfast he'd prepared, knowing she was fortunate, all things considered, to be engaged to Hugh. He represented marked strides toward her goal: restoration and absolution from her first marriage.

The meal was sparse but elegant. When she reached for the raspberry jam, he retrieved it with diplomatic dexterity.

"Let me." He measured a scant teaspoonful onto her Wedgwood plate.

She scooped the dab up with her spoon, swallowed it, eyeing him with mock defiance.

Smiling, he deposited a double amount on his own plate, replaced the top, and placed the jar beyond her reach. "It's good, but full of sugar, sweetheart."

"Hugh, have you ever studied the lush women in Rubens and Renoir art?"

He looked as though she spoke a foreign language.

"I'm beginning to think a continuous obsession with being thin . . . hipless, thighless, bellyless . . . is futile."

"Not with discipline."

"When I compare my body to those figures and think of your compulsion to keep me thin, I sometimes wonder if you have a fear of females." She smiled, striving for diplomacy, yet truth. "I think you shy away from the idea of the flesh and power of a full grown, take-charge woman."

He laughed, but she saw his mouth tighten a little. "That's ridiculous. I just know fat is unattractive. Spoils an image."

"I'm starving," she muttered, pulling the coveted crusts off her grainy toast, nibbling them. "Last night left me hungry." Or was it more a feeling of emptiness?

"We need to discuss something that disturbs me," he said.

She met his gaze over the rim of her juice glass. "You're about to issue a mandate, aren't you?"

"I hope you won't take it that way."

"I hope I won't have to." She glanced at her watch, familiar irritation seeping in. "What have I done now, Hugh?"

His firm mouth pinched. "Nothing yet, I hope. Olivia Steinberg called me yesterday. She said you're shying away from taking their job because you're considering moving to the city."

"To be near the Renfro project. I spend so much time—"

"Hearing that from a near stranger was a shock. It's embarrassing. Olivia wouldn't understand an engaged woman living away from her fiancé. She and Prentice are an old-line Southern family with old money . . . just the kind of doors your mother and the senator can open for me—you and me."

His ongoing pursuit of elite clientele, his insistence the two of them work together as architect and designer, sometimes made her feel like bait. "The Steinbergs are New York Yankees of Jewish descent, Hugh. You've gotten them confused with the old-line WASP Georgia natives you usually court."

His brows knitted. "Whatever gave you the idea to move, Carolyna?"

He buttered a second piece of toast, reopened the jam. Cally's

3

mouth watered.

"Jessica Renfro offered her guest room to me until the house restoration is finished. I spend so much time there and on the road—"

"That's a sacrifice we'll have to make."

"We?"

"If we were married, now, would you be considering this moving venture?"

If there were many breakfasts like this one, she might be. "It seems a feasible solution. But I didn't mean to upset you."

"You have to think, sweetheart." He put down his fork, leaned back in his chair. "We have to discuss these things."

She drained her juice glass, wishing for more, but orange juice was on Hugh's limited amount list, for her. "And this is a discussion?"

"Doesn't it seem like one?"

She left the question hanging. "I don't know if I'll be able to add the Steinbergs to my schedule. At the moment it just doesn't seem possible. I've examined it from every angle—"

"We have all the business we can handle, right here on St. Simons and Sea Island. Savannah shouldn't even be a factor. Until you're finished with the Renfro house, you'll have to manage your time better, sweetheart."

"There's no time to manage—but, you're right, Hugh. Why didn't I think of that?" She reached for his glass, drained it. "Almost a lovely breakfast. I have to get dressed."

❦

When she stood in the back door, briefcase and keys in hand, he said, "You will be back in time for dinner at the Gradys'?"

The Grady house, in the old elite section of the island, had been their first joint project as architect and interior designer. The Grady guests would be prominent, invaluable to Hugh's career. And hers, she reminded herself.

He smelled wonderfully bracing. The familiar fragrance of Bijan soap, shampoo, and cologne took the edge off her irritation. She tried to remember he'd been through a lot before her, just as she had

4

before him. She had to believe he would mellow in time, learn to trust her and her judgment. She leaned back to look into his eyes, mossy green this morning. In the bright sun, the brown tips of his pale lashes were as pronounced as the worry line in his brow. The streak of gray running back from his brow contrasted nicely with his sandy hair. He gathered her tighter, and she wished his kiss stirred her more.

"I don't feel right about this trip today," he said.

"Why today? Savannah is in my regular repertoire."

"I feel vulnerable—like I might not get you back, somehow."

"I could be back on the island in time for extracurricular activity if *you* could be available." She pressed into him, met his gaze. "As in making love . . . in the afternoon."

"I'll be happy if *you 're* available for dinner." But he granted her a smile. "You can use the extra time on your hair."

His remark pricked like a needle. Her tolerance ran dangerously low. Pulling her hair up, twisting it, had been the plan. Nothing elaborate. "What do you suggest?"

"Cutting it." He kept smiling.

It had been much shorter when they met. "Sometimes, Hugh, I wonder if you approve of me . . . at all." She walked toward the Volvo station wagon.

Hugh accompanied her. "I know I'm critical at times, Cally. Bear with me, please. I'm just aware of your potential." He opened the car door, his manicured hands gripping the metal for a moment. "Drive safely. I don't want to lose you."

As she entered the Torras Causeway, leaving St. Simons Island, she thought of recovering the lost desk, but Hugh Masters and their impending marriage took top billing in her mind. His chameleonic traits vied constantly in her reasoning, often as she lay in his arms at night assuring herself Hugh had the substance good husbands were made of. On such nights she considered a lifetime attempting to measure up to his expectations, then weighed that against the less than satisfying scenario of her life to date. Hugh always triumphed.

Her parents, particularly her mother, had to be taken into account. Geneva Sinclair regarded Hugh a savior, absolution for her daughter's botched first marriage, the ideal mate and son-in-law.

Geneva was hinting at withholding Cally's pending inheritance from her maternal grandfather to keep her on the straight and narrow. Her father, retired Senator James Wainwright "Wain" Sinclair, was hell-bent on mentoring Hugh right into Washington, by way of local island government and then the Georgia legislature. These were heavy considerations for a conventionally bred-in-the-bone genteel-familied Southern woman. When she weighed these factors, her pending marriage to Hugh always won.

She juggled her cellular phone and dialed Santa Barbara, then opened the sun roof. Heavy salt air teased her nostrils, moistened her cheeks. Squinting into the blue deep-water glare, she waited out five rings before a machine answered. The voice was throaty, matching Jessica Renfro's blonde California image.

"Mrs. Renfro, it's Cally Sinclair. I've found your desk. I'm on my way to Savannah to inspect it and get it delivered. I've considered your offer to let me stay at the house until it's finished. That would be convenient, and I've decided to accept. I'm not sure when I'll be moving in . . . but I will. Oh—I'm also thinking about your housewarming party. I promise it will be wonderful."

She hung up, realizing Hugh's declining her offer of intimacy when she returned to the island added time to her work day, easing the pressure. Now, she considered a different concern: the rejection itself. Rejection seemed a shaky basis on which to begin a marriage.

That troubled her.

Chapter 2

*W*hen she arrived near noon, the Savannah dock seemed deserted. Sea gulls ambled away, scolding, as she circled the crate. Hearing a different noise, she whirled around, startled to find herself face to face with a tall black man.

"Hey, girl. Does this big box belong to you?"

"Excuse me?" Didn't he know he shouldn't call her girl—no more than she should call him boy in this age of political enlightenment? "Were you speaking to me?"

He made a show of looking all around, tiptoed unnecessarily to look over her shoulder. He shrugged elaborately, smiled innocently. No one else here, his expression said.

He wore Reeboks, she noted for no discernible reason. Scuffed and worn, but extremely clean. She glanced around warily, afraid. She eyed her car, tried to remember if she'd locked it, preventing a swift escape. Down the pier, men were eating, laughing, their voices coarse. A foghorn sounded in the distance, through blistering sun and humidity.

"This *is* my . . . box. Where did you come from?"

"Jamaica." He almost sang the answer. His blinding smile didn't fade. His teeth flashed impossibly white. "And you?"

She ignored the question. "Are you a longshoreman?" She needed assistance. Someone who would help her claim the crate.

"I am a *long* shoreman." His lips pursed around the word "long," and he measured horizontally with his large hands.

Heart hammering, her mind darted futilely, searching for any off-color connotation. She settled on the fact that he stood extremely tall, and that alone had been his meaning.

"That is a joke, girl."

His melodic accent was . . . Creole. No. He'd said Jamaica. The "t" was hard, the "a" softened nicely. He spoke meticulous English

7

with a cadence that required concentration and often left her a few words behind.

She circled the crate again, adopting a business air, not exactly sure what was needed in the way of help. He followed in her footsteps, his shoes squeaking a little against the creosote dock planking. He moved with animal grace and appeal.

"This box is almost ending up lost, girl."

Not sure if she'd heard insolence or concern in his voice, she spun to determine just what he was about. She'd had twenty-eight years of personal conditioning to prejudice, had inherited centuries of traditional white domination. Now, she scrutinized him for disrespect but saw only a guileless smile. His skin was rich caramel, taking on an amber glow here and there, where the sun caught a moist sheen of perspiration. The sheen was sweat, actually, the uniform indigenous to the area. Although he appeared harmless, he also appeared to have no business on the dock but to be unmotivated to leave. His presence intimidated her to the point of sweat pouring from her own arm pits, trickling down her skin beneath the thin cotton dress.

She made a determined effort toward the business at hand. A crack in the plywood, not quite broken through, indicated a significant bump somewhere along the way. She had painstakingly selected the desk in Rome. Now, its possibly marred glory surfaced in her mind as she ran a finger down the crack.

"Your box is broken?"

The question was songlike. The elongated "o" in "broken" stretched the word, caressed it with an arresting inflection. She found it difficult not to stare at him. His hair was brown, shot through with copper glints. He wore dreadlocks—cornrows, actually. They were a modest chin length, immaculate, each one sealed with colorful, beaded bands. He was a black man.

Yet he wasn't, quite, judging from the lightness of his flawless skin. She had seen movie stars—George Hamilton for one—with tans darker than this stranger's. His face was lean and classic, as though chiseled by a sculptor who, loving his craft and subject, had given him prominent cheekbones, a slender nose, and lush carved lips. Heavy but precise brows and luxuriant lashes framed improbable, deep-water blue eyes. She fought against the urge to look into them deeply, and lost.

He brazenly stared back.

His long, muscular stature brought to mind all those art classes she'd taken in college—hours of drawing forms. All the hours of mixing colors made sudden sense, too.

"Has anyone ever . . . painted you?" she heard herself ask.

"Sure, girl." His smile was wide, genial. "God painted me brown. You know?"

Perspiration ran from her forehead onto her singed cheeks. "I was an art major. You have wonderful—never mind," she stammered, her second major, English, suddenly wasted.

An empathetic smile broke out. "Oh, yeah, girl. I, too, am an *artiste*."

Did she see, or only imagine, humility in his expression now? Approaching the dock, she'd seen a lone figure with a wide-brimmed straw hat in the distance. The artist had been seated on a stool before an easel, back to the street. She'd assumed the artist to be a woman.

"I am drawing your box." He indicated the easel, where a pelican pecked at the hat that now lay on the ground.

"Whatever for?"

He shrugged, smiled. "A feeling, maybe? Who can know a thing such as that?"

She pulled a copy of the waybill from her briefcase, along with copies of the canceled check, documented phone tracers, and correspondence. She had come prepared to fight, and he was the only one around.

"I must have this desk. I have all the supporting documents. My name is on the crate." Garbled in red paint, smeared a little, misspelled. But, Sinclair was plain enough.

He folded his arms, cocked his head. The beaded hair-bands clanked softly in the noon quiet. A small hoop earring and a tiny gold stud glimmered when the sun caught his left profile. He waited for the rest of her speech.

She fished again, came up with her driver's license and a business card. "See, it's me." She spoke loudly, a conscious attempt to lessen any cultural or language barrier.

He frowned, backing up a step. "Very nice picture. *Very* pretty girl." There was no language barrier. His English was perfect, melodiously honed. He passed the license back.

The hard "t's" in "pretty" gave his compliment credibility, even if he didn't know *he* shouldn't call her that—not in Savannah. Grimacing involuntarily, she studied the grim, typical license photo. He was apparently adept at flattery. She handed him a business card, her nail pointing out Sinclair. She nodded toward the crate with an expectant expression, not yet recovered from her original impression that he worked on the dock.

He laughed. Not an unpleasant sound, but rancor played along her spine, aggravated by oppressive heat and humidity.

"What's so amusing?"

"You are named after the state—Carolina—but it is spelled wrong. You know? You have this fancy card with the wrong name. You could sue your printer, girl. I am a witness."

Momentarily amused, she envisioned a guilty printer being dragged into a courtroom, protesting. She jerked herself back, feeling foolish. A welcome breeze stirred her hair and brought with it the smell of tar-coated pilings, bracing her. Over his shoulder, a few clouds gathered on the horizon. It could rain at any moment in semi-tropical Savannah.

"Carolyna is . . . I was named after my grandmother. It was her middle—" Flustered, she pulled up short from detailing her ancestry to this brash artist—*long* shoreman, whose eyes rested on her tolerantly. "I'd love to chat, but I have to get this desk released. I have to have it." She attempted to level him with her gaze, dismiss him. "Today."

"Hey, girl. Be calm." He raised his hands, palms out. "This box is here for a week. Where is it going now that you have found it?"

His face glowed with unguarded amusement, and she was sorely tempted, now, to address him as "boy." As unattuned as he was to political correctness, she suspected he wouldn't care.

"I believe you can risk one more night," he said.

"No. I can't. This desk has to be taken off this dock today. It has to be—" She thought of Hugh's mandate that she be back on the island for dinner, then of the storage she had hoped to avoid. "It has to be delivered tomorrow."

"No problem, mon—girl." He shrugged. "*I* can do that." He pronounced "can" the way Jack Kennedy did in all those historical documentaries Hugh watched.

"You?"

He nodded, his smile glimmering. "Sure, girl. I can take your desk home with me."

She took back her papers. Her heart raced a little when he pocketed her card. Hugh's frequent warning of her too-trusting nature echoed. She pushed away a vision of his tightening lips, his furrowed brow, and attempted to act responsibly.

"I don't know you," she said firmly. "This desk cost a small fortune."

"You can come too."

Her body surged backward, her cheeks flaming.

His smile turned kind. "No. No." His palms raised again. Cream, creased with milk chocolate. "I can get your box cleared through my friend." He nodded toward the men down the dock. "I will take it home with me. Today. You can come to see where. Tomorrow I will deliver. If not—you will know where to bring the law. Lock me up forever. Throw away *da* key," he mimicked wryly, arching one brow.

"Why would you want to babysit this crate and deliver it?"

"Money?" He executed his most elaborate shrug thus far.

"Oh."

"Oh, yeah, girl. Money. The necessary evil."

"Do you have equipment—a truck?" Her throat warmed as word connotations loomed suddenly overt, because he was black. "I planned to call a delivery service."

"I have a van. It would welcome this box nicely. I could sleep in the van, too, be on guard, if you like. Don't worry 'bout a t'ing. No problems." He smiled encouragingly.

"I still don't know you. This desk is valuable."

"Not to me, girl."

Of course. Where would he fence a Louis XIV, gold inlaid desk?

He pulled a heavy gold chain from beneath a purple T-shirt

11

logoed JAMAICA JAM. His long, slender fingers worked the chain up his body, lifted it over his magnificent head. A fat, intricately engraved locket dangled from the end of the chain.

"*This* is valuable. You keep this, girl. Tomorrow I will bring your desk. We will exchange treasures." He held the locket out to her.

She didn't take it. "What time will you finish drawing?"

"No more drawing today, if you like."

He would forsake an afternoon's work to deliver her desk—a dalliance, if he earned his living as an artist. It fit the Southern legend of slothful blacks. With time management like that, no wonder he considered money evil.

"What time normally? If it isn't too late, I could wait and see where you take the desk—as you said." Dinner plans crowded her mind. And, considering Hugh's morning critique, she had to do something different with her hair. Inwardly, she bristled. Crimp it? Braid it, maybe? Like this strange young black man, smiling at her so guilelessly? It might teach Hugh a lesson about criticizing too freely.

"I quit whenever I like, girl. An artist can work anywhere. No problem. I paint here only to visit my friends." He indicated the men down the dock. Getting to their feet now, they milled around. Lewd comments accompanied by the acrid smell from the nearby Union Camp paper mill echoed off the torpid water.

"My main friend can release your box and help me load it."

"What time?" she asked dubiously.

Seeming to pluck a time from the stifling air, he announced it formally. "Three o'clock."

"I'll come back." She took the locket, wondering if he would protest and if she was actually going to trust this stranger with her client's desk. What had stirred her confidence that much? And was it confidence or a hesitance to end the association? No wonder Hugh kept such a tight rein. "May I have your address—and something to show you live there?"

"I have nothing to show that. Would I steal your desk between now and three o'clock? It has been here—"

"For a week. I know. I'll be back at three. I won't have much time. Do you live near here?"

12

"No way, girl." He looked happy to denounce one of Savannah's most rapidly deteriorating neighborhoods. "But not far. I will load the desk now. My friend comes."

Her gaze followed his to another black man approaching. No coppery cornrows. No sing-song speech, she'd wager. A Savannah black man. Massive and stout, dark, swaggering. The kind she'd been warned about as a child, taught to fear. She shoved the papers back into this stranger's hand, dug for her keys.

"Thank you." She turned, looked back. "What's your name?"

"Paul Michael Quest." He fastened his improbable blue eyes on her, lips twitching. "Paul is from my father. Michael is from my great-grandfather. Quest is the story of my life."

She tried not to smile. "I'll see you at three."

The car phone shattered her afternoon reverie on the drive back to the island. Hugh informed her he had invited a potential client for cocktails, not to his house but to hers. Hugh had drawn the plans for the refurbishing of "the cottage," her parents' palatial home on Sea Island Golf Club's sixteenth fairway. It sat empty in the non-elite summer season, except for their displaced daughter, Carolyna, this summer. Now, Hugh wanted to show the cottage off.

Irritation nagged. What had happened to her early morning gratitude for having him, for the impending marriage?

Traffic slowed for construction. She pulled in behind an old Chevy. The head of a toy dog bobbed in the back window, mesmerizing her, making her a little dreamy.

There would be cocktails with strangers, now. Those fluffy-pastry, special occasion hors d'oeuvres she'd been saving. Dinner with even more strangers, along with Hugh's courted benefactors, the Gradys. Tonight would call for the perfect dress for her—if one existed. Heat rollers for her hair. Perfect smiles, polite conversation. The projected evening took on a jaded connotation.

She reminded herself that hers was an enviable life, from any angle, and she had veered from it only for that brief time with Turner Cole . . . .

13

She shoved Turner's face to the back of her memory and welcomed a renewed spirit of gratitude and understanding concerning Hugh.

She had to remember, his stability was her sustenance. Their professional talents complemented, meshed, and produced wonderful results. She was as hungry for success in her field as Hugh in his. He had broken the surface into local government, pleasing her mother. Wain Sinclair had the power necessary to pave the way to Hugh's higher political aspirations as well as Wain's aspirations for him. Cally had but to settle back and watch it all fall into place. Never before had she tried this hard at anything.

Traffic came to a standstill as the detour trailed through a small town. Tourists in stretchy polyester milled about the front of a Black-Eyed Pea Restaurant, stalking the early dinner special. Her mouth watered. Her stomach rumbled. Halfway through her fat-gram allowance for the day, and dinner to go.

A scrap of paper peeked from the corner of her Day Timer. She retrieved it and read the address. The image of a battered black van of unidentifiable make with surreal depictions on the side panels, ran through her mind . . . Jessica Renfro's desk tucked inside, an exuberant driver with braided locks.

Cally had followed the van down Bay Street to a decaying three-story Victorian house near downtown Savannah. Paul Michael Quest had honked as he pulled to the curb in front of the house, waved jauntily, and watched her drive away after she wrote down the address.

She examined her cavalier departure from the conservative character she was trying hard to form after her first marriage. Today's renewed disregard for caution haunted her. In her care-laden day, how much had this intriguing stranger's carefree demeanor, his kind concern, to do with trusting him so unwisely?

Would she ever see Jessica Renfro's Louis XIV desk again?

She fingered the locket in her pocket. Something foreign quickened within her at the thought of seeing Paul Michael Quest.

Chapter 3

"Oh, no!" Cally's moan hung in the cottage's grand entry.

She thrust Turner Cole's letter to the back of a stack of mail she'd retrieved from the hall table. Eventually it came up again. Turning it over, she inspected the back of the envelope and imagined Turner's tongue licking the flap. She shivered.

He was in Mobile. Not far away at all. She replaced the remainder of the mail on the table and climbed the stairs to dress for dinner, Turner's letter clutched to her breast.

Half an hour later, she back-brushed her hair and fluffed it around her shoulders. Standing at the bath vanity, she froze the arrangement with hair spray as she studied a duplicate of the engagement photograph Hugh kept on his dresser. It had been taken the previous autumn for their announcement in the society sections of the Sea Island, St. Simons, and Savannah papers. Her hair hadn't been long then and she'd worn it in a simple bob, cupping at her nape.

Lowering her hairbrush, she thought of the dress she had worn the day the engagement photograph was taken. She had driven all the way to Atlanta, chosen the dress carefully, only to have Hugh disapprove. She didn't inquire why, preferring to operate in naïveté. The resulting photograph was a perpetual reminder of having failed to please.

Then, based on her five-foot-nine height, there had been the issue of her standing behind or sitting on the arm of Hugh's chair. Hugh had argued down the photographer's preference, and she had stood in a crouch behind the chair. Marriage to Hugh could never be fraught with quandary; he was capable of manning the wheel of any ship.

Door chimes put an end to reflecting. Cally took one last, not too hopeful, look in the mirror and went downstairs to handle the latest onslaught of potential clients.

❦

She and Hugh stole a moment during cocktails at the Gradys'. Handsome in a navy suit, striped shirt, and club tie, he leaned a shoulder against the carved mantle. He smelled wonderful again. Chanel this time.

Cally took a shrimp canapé from a nearby table. Exercising his best smile, he removed the morsel from her fingers, put it back on the tray. Anger flared. An inner voice warned, *Be still, Carolyna. Hugh is controlling and it hurts. But, be still. He's a perfectionist, but he loves you. He'll mellow. Consider the age difference. Consider . . . whatever the hell it takes to be still.*

Hugh said, his voice smooth, kind, "What did the new people think of the cottage?"

She glanced past his shoulder, across the room, saw their hostess's wrinkling brow. "Hugh, don't tell them I can work on their house. I told you—"

"The *nouveau riche* Renfro project. I know." He smiled.

"Mercy, Hugh. What do you think you are? Old money?"

"You're waving your hands again, Carolyna. And spilling your drink. Do you have a headache?"

"It's been a long day." When he waited for more, she said, "There was a letter from Turner when I got home."

He looked past her shoulder, nodding, holding his empty glass aloft. A white-coated butler swooped in, took it from him. "What did he want?"

"Want?"

"He always wants something. What was it this time?"

"An ex-wife's understanding, maybe," she murmured into her glass. "I don't know, Hugh. I didn't open the letter."

"You threw it away. I'm glad, sweetheart."

"The letter is on my pillow. I didn't want to spoil my mood. I'll open it when I get home."

"Home." He accepted the fresh Scotch from the waiter, very dark, one ice cube.

She wearied, finally. "I made my bid for your attention this

16

morning. You were preoccupied. I have to get up early for Savannah, and I want to sleep in my own bed tonight. You're welcome there. In fact, I'd love to have you."

"I could watch you read Turner's letter and then put the pieces back together. There wouldn't be much point after that, would there?"

They were fighting over Turner again. "I suppose that depends on where your priorities lie."

"The age-old bid for intimacy." His lips tightened. He half turned away from her, held his arm out to draw in a fellow guest. "Sylvia. Come and get acquainted with my fiancée. Carolyna did the interior on this house."

She winced. Hugh affected Southern charm but the remnants of his Midwestern upbringing betrayed him. A true Southerner might have said, "Let me make you acquainted." Not enough years remained for the conversion Hugh sought, unless she helped.

Hugh pulled her close. His arm circled her waist, his fingers drifting surreptitiously up her rib cage to the slight swell of her breast. "Darling, you've met Sylvia Trent. The Trents are considering a winter place on the island. You can tell her all the pitfalls to avoid."

"I'm not so sure I'm qualified." She spoke only loud enough for Hugh to hear.

⁂

Much to Cally's satisfaction and surprise, the black van pulled to the curb before the Renfro house the next morning. The vehicle loomed out of place in Savannah's resplendent Columbia Square. Paul Michael Quest's regal carriage and graceful stride as he approached the house nudged her recall of yesterday. He didn't strike her as formidable in her own environment.

Surrounded by hammering from the porch, the shrilling of a power-sander in the kitchen, the clunk of the painter's roller in the foyer, she awaited Paul Michael on the spiral staircase that ascended from the entry toward a sky dome and a second-floor ballroom. A stirring, vague but distinctive, lifted her spirit when he stood in the

17

open doorway, smiling, shrugging. His copper locks and caramel skin glowed in the pure morning light.

"Hey, girl. I will have back my locket now."

Strangely a tremble, Cally rose from the step, went forward. "Hey, boy. The desk isn't in the house yet."

His eyes fastened where the locket dangled against her breasts. She closed her hand around the heavy gold piece. Her fingers noted once again the rough solder sealing the locket.

"We had a deal," she said. "A desk for a locket." And why was her heart pounding?

His eyes, soft sapphires this morning, met hers. "I will need help. It can be you. Then every little t'ing going to be fine."

"I don't recall that arrangement."

His smile broadened. "You look very strong. Very healthy."
She flushed, suddenly self-conscious, the way she'd always been around her parents' black gardener, and without a word followed him down the crumbling brick walkway.

"This is Ebony." The van's tinted glass had obscured the girl in the passenger seat. Paul Michael wrestled a crude walkboard into place and hopped lithely into the van. "Ebony is strong, too. No problem."

"Nice to meet you," Ebony said, her hand brushing Paul Michael's derriere before making its way to Cally. Her speech was slow as cold molasses.

"Carolyna Sinclair." She hoped her perfunctory handshake camouflaged her busy eyes. Ebony was short, powerfully, tightly built, and named for her skin. Her teeth were blinding, her full lips Chianti dipped.

The desk was already uncrated. Cally tried not to imagine how that had occurred, only hoping for its unmarred grandeur.

Paul Michael extended a hand. Cally declined, attempting to climb into the van herself. The steep step up didn't accommodate her straight skirt. Cheeks flaming, she eased the skirt above her knees and allowed him to draw her up and into the van. His hand was large, warm. Never having touched a black man before, she felt short of breath, culpable. She chanced meeting his eyes and found them beautifully benign.

Following instructions, she and Ebony helped lift the desk onto a dolly, then balanced the load as Paul Michael backed down the walkboard with the treasure. Cally tried not to think of Jessica Renfro asleep in California, of her tolerance and trust.

Ebony and Cally duck-walked behind the desk until they reached the set of six shallow steps. Deserting Ebony, Cally hurried onto the porch to coach anxiously from there.

Paul Michael stopped to rest, glancing over his shoulder toward the porch. "The locket is almost mine."

His smile was soft, companionable. Cally assumed the intimate tone was for Ebony, assumed the trinket belonged to her, possibly the reason she had accompanied him.

"If there's no damage," Cally countered sternly, dubious of the crude operation. "Mind the steps. They'll be difficult."

"You are a hard woman, Carolyna Sinclair."

He began backing toward her, his shoulders displaying a ridge of hard muscle. The backs of his arms and legs tensed every time he executed a hardy pull on the dolly and mounted another step.

She pulled her gaze away and stood by the door, cringing, trying not to feel guilty over Ebony's strained breathing. Rather, she concentrated again on Paul Michael's conscientious maneuvering. Her confidence rose. She held the door steady as he rolled his burden through.

"And where would you like this fine desk in this soon-to-be splendid house, Carolyna Sinclair?"

"In here." She led the way into a room off the entry, the most nearly completed room in the house. When the desk stood upright again, padding removed, gleaming in all its glory, she released a pent-up breath. "That's wonderful! Thank you." She turned to the girl. "And you, Ebony."

Paul Michael and Ebony exchanged looks, and the girl wordlessly left the room, as though they'd rehearsed. Cally heard Ebony stomp down the wooden steps. Eventually, the van door banged closed with shattering emphasis that suggested she'd left under protest. Paul Michael's smile dimmed slightly.

"Gracious," Cally murmured, their eyes meeting.

Construction resonated around them. A breath of wind wafted

through the open door, across the entry, through the house. The breeze caressed all it encountered—her hair, the edge of her skirt—then ebbed, electrifying rather than soothing her skin.

She looked at him in silence. She'd always considered herself large, but he was so tall, so rangy, he was almost intimidating. His grace and courtesy prevailed, however, counteracting the Southern fable of belligerent black men.

Reaching behind him, he tugged his shirt from his waistband and extracted a small sketch encased in a zip-lock plastic bag. He handed it to her. She opened the bag and took out a slightly wrinkled, impressionistic pencil drawing. It depicted a huge Gentry crane unloading a container from an oceangoing vessel moored at the Savannah dock. In the foreground was Jessica's crated desk, insignificant in scale but recognizable.

"Your box, Carolyna Sinclair."

Loud silence echoed the noise around them. Her cheeks warmed, flamed, she was sure. She felt guilty for having distrusted him on the dock. "How nice. Thank you."

Still disconcerted, she reached for a drop cloth on the floor, and he hastened to help her cover the desk, their hands brushing. A current ran up her arm, through her body.

Abruptly, she stepped back, pulling a pen and a half- completed check from her skirt pocket. Only the amount remained blank. "How much do I owe you?"

"No problem." His hands came up, palms out.

Her eyes fastened there. Goat's cream today, with cinnamon streaks in the lifelines.

She said, "We had an agreement, and I insist on paying you. Is fifty dollars a fair price?"

"Just to have my locket back would be fair."

He spoke so quietly she had to listen, to concentrate on his full, sculpted lips. Her cheeks sizzled. "Oh—I'm sorry."

She lifted the chain over her head, handed him the locket. Suddenly feeling naked, she clutched the drawing to her breasts.

Paul Michael put the chain around his own neck, smiled. A vision of Ebony's wine lips crossed Cally's mind.

"Fifty dollars?" She reminded him, prepared to pay more.

"Free this time. I want only to help a pretty lady." He added, "Yes. A very pretty lady," making her wonder what in her expression had prompted that. His touch on her shoulder, no more than a suggestion, turned her to face the mirrored wall. "Black men are not blind men."

She stared at her image, rumpled from the drive from the island, the humidity. Her hair stuck to her head, pulled back, clipped at her nape. But her cheeks glowed, and she saw something in her eyes . . . she saw energy.

She met his mirrored gaze before facing him again. Suddenly a decision she had wrestled with throughout the morning was made in the blink of an eye. "Would you like to work for me?"

He showed guileless surprise and delight. "I would. Then everything would truly be fine."

"Would you have use of the van—is it yours?"

"It *is*," he declared and then added, "now."

"Do you have a driver's license?"

"Oh, yeah." Pridefully, he produced one that seemed to be loose in his pocket.

"This isn't you." It took no scrutiny, for there was no resemblance, and the names were different.

He shrugged. "The license comes with the van. No problem, girl. I am a good driver. Very slow. Very straight. Every t'ing will be fine."

She didn't want to know more or consider her rash offer, much less her decision to proceed. "Could you deliver for me once a week? Every Wednesday?"

"I could." Satisfaction shot through his electrifying smile. "*Every* Wednesday." He snapped his long, slender fingers, raised slightly on the balls of his feet. "No problem, girl."

"You have my card," she reminded, and he nodded. "If you could call me on Tuesday night I'll give you a list of places to drive by on Wednesday morning for pickups. We could meet here around noon for the delivery."

"Awl . . . *right!*"

Touched and relieved by his exuberance, she couldn't help smiling. "Are you sure about today? I really want to pay you."

21

"Very sure. Have a very nice day, Carolyna Sinclair."

Ebony wasn't in the van as Cally had imagined. She waited on the front steps. Cally stood by an open window, watched and listened. Outside, Columbia Square lay quiet except for the rasp of locusts. A car negotiated the intricate turns, and a horde of tourists swarmed into the hallowed Isaiah Davenport House.

Paul Michael sank on the step beside the girl. From Cally's vantage, his smile seemed apologetic.

"Just who *is* this woman, P.M.?" Ebony's voice, haughty and sultry, floated in the open window where Cally stood. Ebony's face was hidden, but her back was pencil straight.

Paul Michael draped his arm loosely around her shoulders. "A pretty lady who needs my help?"

"Get real, boy. She could hire the city of Savannah."

Smiling, he shrugged and took his hand away.

"Did she pay you, bro?"

"Not this time."

"*This* time? What you mean *this* time, fool?"

"She hired me. I have three jobs now."

"Three illegal jobs," Ebony fired.

Cally tensed.

"More money, Ebony. I can take you someplace." He kept smiling. "Someplace that is not Jamaica Jam. Where do you want to go, girl?"

Ebony folded her arms, stared at the street. "We won't be going places for long, P.M. You'll be too busy bowing and scraping to your honky boss."

Cally's body and mind lurched.

"Why do you want to talk that way, girl? Did your mother never tell you? A lady should—"

"Just listen, Paul Michael Quest. You ain't a real nigger. You ain't seen the things I seen. Remember, I told you."

"I'll remember, Ebony June Johnson. Every little t'ing going to be all right."

Ebony stalked away, got into the van. Paul Michael stayed seated on the step for a moment, his powerful hands dangling between his knees, head bowed slightly. A concern Cally couldn't quite name, an unidentifiable empathy, settled on her. Then he seemed to rally, rose, and jogged down the walkway.

Suddenly lonely, Cally watched the van leave the square.

$\mathcal{C}hapter$ 4

$\mathcal{C}$ally scanned the ocher wall of the doctor's office, reading his many certificates. Again. Philip Ballentine, Ph.D. Licensed Clinical Psychologist. Four framed diplomas from the best schools kept company with numerous awards and commendations.

"Is everything all right, Carolyna?" Dr. Ballentine asked kindly, scrutinizing her across his cluttered desk. "The receptionist said you insisted on coming in today."

"Was that the way I sounded? Insistent?"

"To her, apparently."

"Friday seemed too far away. My mother is pressuring me to pick out wedding invitations. My father is always off on some political bent and never spends time with her, so she's frustrated. Bored maybe. She's made two trips in from her summer home in Vail, but I keep putting her off."

Dr. Ballentine rocked a little in his chair. "And?"

"She's worried about my sister. She hasn't heard from her. She blames me for that, says Lucinda followed in my wanton and foolish footsteps."

"None of this sounds new, Cally."

She looked out the window onto a spreading forest pine. A bird, a sparrow, looked back, then fled, probably having read her thoughts.

Slowly, she pulled an envelope from her bag. "I got another letter from Turner yesterday."

"How is Turner?"

Beyond the window a siren wailed in the distance, and in the outer office someone laughed raucously. Inside Cally, the doctor's question called up regret. "He's broke. Lonely. He's injured his hand. He's dropping off the tour."

"The golf tour."

24

She nodded. "If that had happened when we were married, maybe we'd still be together. The pressure of Turner trying to advance from the Nike tour to the PGA tore us apart."

"How do you feel about that? Still being together."

"At the moment I feel I left a lot on the table concerning Turner."

"At the moment."

"I always feel fragmented when I get a letter. I can handle the calls. He makes me laugh. But seeing it . . . his feelings . . . written down, it affects me. The moment will pass. Almost."

Dr. Ballantine looked encouraging, and she said, "I've been thinking of Turner lately. How it was with us. How . . . it happened."

He waited.

"There was never any substance to our marriage. We never really knew one another. I think he appealed to . . . my base instincts. We had sex on our first date." She smiled, her throat flushing. "It was so good I wished we'd gone out sooner."

A very clear memory had surfaced last night, roiled, consumed, left her sleepless. She tried to hold it down, keep it in its proper place, in the regrettable past. But the recall was like Turner. Tenacious. "I'm captivated still by our intensity. I miss that. Even at the end when we detested one another . . . almost . . . the energy was so intense."

She looked out the window again, at the pine. "Nice, gentle Episcopalian girl that I am . . . I'm not supposed to miss that energy. But I do."

"That's understandable, Carolyna. Is this causing you distress? The fact that sex is important to you? That *is* what you're telling me? Isn't it?"

"Yes, sex is important, and, yes it distresses me."

"Why?"

"I've been to opposite ends of the spectrum now. With Turner and with Hugh. Neither has made me . . . ."

"Happy?" He waited and got no reply. "Are you saying you don't enjoy being with Hugh?"

"I do. It's just that everything has to be so perfect, to line up so precisely. It's almost as if our intimacy comes last."

Dr. Ballentine's silence prompted her to say, "Turner wants to

25

come here. He wants me to send him money. He thinks he can get his job back if he can get here."

"How do you feel about that?"

"Like I can't afford to take him on again."

Dr. Ballentine nodded, smiling tolerantly. "Regarding the trust fund the two of you squandered."

"Yes. I'm not sure I loved Turner . . . I just wanted him. And the more they didn't want me to have him—it wasn't the done thing, marrying the club pro. Excuse me, the *assistant* club pro. The more they didn't want me to . . . ."

"But this is your decision, Carolyna. Just as that was."

Rebellion. It was so simple, she wondered why she was here at all, sitting across from him, seeking what she knew so well.

"Living on the road was hell. I left him and came home for a while, and in my absence, he found someone to take my place." The tightening in her throat, the dull ache in her chest, were familiar sensations. "And I eventually found Hugh."

She left the chair, strolled to the window. The bird was back. It had been a wren, not a sparrow.

"No," she said. "I don't want Turner to come here."

⚜

That night she lay in Hugh's embrace, both of them feeling the strain of her lack of an orgasm.

"I've been giving you a hard time lately." Hugh traced her lips with the back of his manicured nail, trailing his hand across her shoulder. "Haven't I?"

She saw—or wished for—gentleness in his mossy eyes. She caught his hand, kissed his fingers, tasting herself. "Sometimes I worry, Hugh, that I may never live up to your expectations. Sometimes they're daunting."

His lips tightened, then slackened again.

"I want to be what you want," she said. "I want our marriage to be the best it can be. I just don't know if I'm qualified to—"

"You are. We'll compromise. I'll try to . . . ." He appeared to grope for words. "I know the pressure you're under over the trust

26

fund, sweetheart." He pushed himself up, dragged a pillow behind his head, and smiled at her. "We'll work together, Carolyna. There will be plenty of clients. We'll live off my earnings, and you can replenish the raped fund in short order."

Cally became aware of a gentle rain tapping at the window. She pulled the sheet over her breasts, tucked it. The feel of fine linen against her skin failed to soothe her.

"What would that prove, Hugh?"

"What do you have to prove?"

"My individuality. My own worth . . . separate from you."

He frowned. "I'm demanding, but I'm working on it, although that may be hard to see."

She wasn't sure they were speaking of the same things.

"My first marriage was virtual hell," he said. "Sometimes things you do remind me. It sets me off."

His creased brow, his drawn lips, gave her an opaque view of the memories he'd given only a blurry account of. Each of them was dragging an abundance of scars to the relationship.

"I'm not Debra," she said quietly.

"And I'm not Turner, but the possibility that he and that glitzy, vagabond lifestyle could be what you really want, bothers me."

She had revealed the contents of the letter to him, withheld her thoughts. "I was different then. I didn't know *you*."

"You know me now and you don't seem happy, especially considering your threats to move to Savannah."

"They aren't threats. I'll be moving soon."

"I choose to think that won't happen, but you're definitely sympathetic to Turner and his plight. One way or the other, he's always on the fringe. An available alternative."

"I choose not to think I can be completed only by a man." She sat up, her heart heavy. "I'd like to think you respect my individuality, that you've heard what I've told you."

"I'd like to think I'm the man who *can* complete you, Cally. You're the woman I'm counting on to complete me. I'd like to think Turner isn't a threat."

She caught her hair up, twisted it in a long rope at the back of her neck, releasing it once she felt her scalp ache.

"Indulge me in my grief over my failed marriage, Hugh." She allowed Paul Michael Quest to enter her mind, relived the feel of the heavy locket against her breasts, pictured again the drawing he'd given her, seeing his kind and gentle gaze behind her closed eyes. "I assure you *Turner* is no threat."

Chapter 5

*T*he ringing phone, jagged and jarring, ripped through Cally and Hugh's lovemaking in the diffused light of her bedroom a few nights later. She stiffened with relief for the call, regret for the timing.

Hugh raised his head, his eyes glazed. "Let it ring."

"I can't. I have to answer. It's about the Renfro house."

"Christ, Cally. It's midnight." He eased his body pressure on her but increased her emotional tension.

"I know." She sat up, gripping the sheet against her with one hand, reaching for the phone with the other. "Hello."

"Carolyna Sinclair! It is you, girl, and it is Tuesday." Music and laughter provided backdrop for the effusive announcement.

Her heart pumped wildly, unexpectedly, startling her. "Paul Michael Quest. Actually, it's closer to Wednesday."

His laughter blended with the raucous background. "You believed I was not going to call."

He was right, but she wouldn't give him that satisfaction. "Why would I think that?"

Hugh sighed heavily, flounced onto his back, stuffed a pillow beneath his head, settling in.

"Do you have the list, girl? Give it to me quickly. If you don't get your sleep you can't help me unload tomorrow."

"No."

"No, you can't help me?"

"I don't have the list. But I'll get it."

Hugh raised on one elbow, his large, smooth hand coming down on her turned hip, half caressing, half protesting.

She leaned away, toward the new business at hand. "Can you hold on, Paul Michael?" Placing the phone on the table, she made a move to get out of bed.

29

"Carolyna, for goodness' sake."

She grabbed the receiver, covered the mouth piece with her hand. "I have to go downstairs, Hugh. Please hang up when I'm on again." He would wonder about the call now, prodded by her sharp directive. "Paul Michael?"

"Yeah, girl?"

"Hold on," she murmured and grabbed Hugh's shirt to cover herself. She felt the hovering tension as she hurried out of the room.

She positioned herself behind the senator's immense desk in the downstairs study. "Hugh?" The bedroom extension clanked in her ear. "Paul Michael? Are you there?"

"Yeah, girl. I am ready."

"Scrooge & Marley Antiques first. Then Savannah Galleries." Silence. "Kenneth Worthy in Lafayette Square."

"Oh, yeah. Lafayette Square." He sounded relieved.

She laughed. "You're not familiar with the other stores."

"Yeah, girl. But I learn fast. Then I never forget."

Painfully aware of the time being taken away from Hugh, she walked Paul Michael through the list, complete with directions. "I've called each merchant and they're expecting you. Otherwise they wouldn't release—"

"I know, girl. These things cost a small fortune."

His ability to mimic her so delicately—his audacity—should have been grating rather than engaging. "Do you think you have it all? The list?" There had been a rash of "yeah, girls" throughout the instructions.

The laughter at his end was muffled now, as if he had put a hand over the mouth piece. Ebony's face flashed in Cally's mind. She heard him say something indistinguishable, then he was back, loud and clear. "Yeah, girl. I have it. You can go to sleep now."

"Paul Michael?"

"Yes, Carolyna Sinclair?"

"Will you be . . . how do I know you'll be there?" She knew nothing about him. The late hour, the raucous background on his end of the line was cause for concern. The job he had agreed to required him to get up early, be clean, sober, sincere. Her business image was at stake.

He fell into his alternate character. "Don' worry, girl. Every little t'ing going to be *awl* right." He hung up.

She cradled the buzzing receiver against her breasts for a moment, rocked back in the senator's leather chair and smiled into the luxurious surroundings. Agitation had plagued her throughout the day. It hadn't lessened with watching Hugh prepare dinner while she perched on a stool in Geneva's kitchen and sipped wine. She had offered bogus, ebullient dinner conversation and melded into the sexual progression of the evening, but she had taken her vague disquiet, along with Hugh, into bed. Now her agitation was gone.

"Carolyna, I need my shirt." Hugh stood in the arched double doorway to the study, clad in his pants, shoes, and evident irritation. His upper body was bare, his jacket and tie draped over his arm.

"Oh . . . Hugh." She placed the receiver on its cradle with a slap, stood and pulled his shirt together in front, covering suddenly unwarranted nudity.

He advanced into the room. "Who was that?"

She kept the desk between them. "Paul Michael Quest."

"Right. What does he have to do with the Renfro house?"

More and more. "Nothing. He's my new delivery service."

"Tell him not to call in the middle of the night again."

"I can't promise that."

The grandfather clock in the corner ticked loudly. Lamplight haloed Hugh's body. She waited for his decision to stay or go, sure now of her own lack of desire. At last his eyes met hers, his resignation relieving her.

He leaned to kiss her cheek. "I have to go. Katharine is alone. Good timing on the part of Mr. Quest."

Cally released her breath slowly, silently. If they had made love in the time she had stolen to talk to Paul Michael, Katy would still have been alone at this moment. And, after making love, Cally would have the familiar sensation of emptiness, and Hugh would still have left her.

Tonight, it didn't seem to matter.

Two weeks later, Cally leaned against twin columns banking either side of the newly-repaired front porch of Jessica Renfro's English Regency mansion. She nibbled a cold chicken breast held in greasy fingers and flexed her bare toes luxuriously. The chicken bucket sitting on the porch separated her from Paul Michael. His bare feet rested on the step next to hers. His toes were long and slender, the nails perfectly kept, his veins vulnerably close beneath his fine skin. With one foot, he kept time to an imaginary rhythm she was not privileged to share. Her eyes took in the shiny seam of a small, jagged scar on his shin and then reluctantly shied away to gaze onto Columbia Square.

Across the square, an automatic lawn sprinkler switched on, perfectly synchronized to drench a maid whose hair matched that of the enormous chocolate poodle she attempted to drag down the walkway.

Cally took a chicken thigh, ripped off the skin and tossed it into a nearby heap of scrap lumber. The sweet fragrance of honeysuckle and confederate jasmine tangled with the aroma drifting from the cardboard bucket with Colonel Sanders' portrait on the side.

An unfamiliar sense of contentment wrapped around Cally. Tossing the stripped bone into the same rubbish heap, she wiped her hands on her thighs, smiling at Paul Michael. Cooling sweat trickled between her breasts inside her T-shirt, and her cut-offs clung to her backside. Her Nikes had long since been discarded, socks stretched to dry on a sunny lower step. She had come dressed for the occasion, Paul Michael's third delivery in as many weeks.

"Good chicken. I'm glad you thought of it." She fished for another breast, sucked the fingers of her left hand, one by one. "Finger licking good."

Their eyes met, locked longer than proper before she tore her gaze away. She felt his eyes on her still, lingering, palpable. He waited, she knew, for her to return his gaze. Inside she quaked, warm and filled with wondering, a reaction becoming more difficult to deny.

He smiled finally, bit and chewed, teeth flashing in his sweat-shiny face. His skin was buttery caramel in the clear light. His eyes invited names of colors to run through her designer's mind. Azure.

She discarded it. Indigo . . . lapis lazuli. She settled on sapphire once more.

"Hey, Carolyna Sinclair." He'd caught her looking at his eyes again. "You think I am a freak. Say it, girl."

As recently as a week ago she would have shifted her gaze, sputtering an apology, cheeks flaming. Today, she met his stare, laughing softly. Unable to envision any living creature more beautiful than him, she had ceased denying it to herself and had begun to enjoy, to envision the impossible. Today, working inside the house—lifting, heaving, straining, carefully placing, carefully covering—every time he'd looked at her, his gaze was so intent she felt he leaned forward, entered her.

"On Sea Island we'd call your eyes deep-water blue."

"In Jamaica we call them a blessing." He smiled with a touch of irony. "These eyes belong to the *pinks*. A pink is a very good thing to be in Jamaica."

His hands—satiny, nails clean, the skin beneath like rich cream—manipulated a chicken leg. Again, Cally watched too long. "What is a pink?" she asked, pulling herself back from her phantasies. The color pink seemed farfetched, highly unrelated to the character he portrayed.

"A pink is a Jamaican registered on the census rolls as white. That is me, girl." He shrugged, tossed his cleaned chicken bone to join hers, then rummaged in the bucket. "In your country it is different. If there is a drop of black blood, you are black. In my country, if there is a drop of white blood, we are privileged to call ourselves white. But our pure black brother calls us pink." He gazed at her. "Do you understand this, girl?"

"I'm pretty quick, actually. I believe that translates to you being elated with your drop of white blood."

"Yeah, mon." Grinning, he recovered. "Yeah, girl."

"Please call me Cally. All my friends do."

"Cally Sinclair." His smile dazzled. "The boss lady. Please call me P.M. If you would like that."

"P.M." She tasted it, tried it. Ebony called him that. "I'll think about it."

He smiled, nodded, hair bands jangling softly.

33

"Where does your drop of white blood come from? Are you a family fable . . . or scandal?" Did he know the stories of the Southern plantations, the mulatto slaves fathered by white owners, the tragedy of parental denial, the quandary of belonging to no race?

"It is no scandal, girl. In Jamaica everyone tries to be white, to be more like our English forefathers. I never knew my maternal grandmother, but I am told my blue eyes come from her. I got lucky." Again he smiled with that touch of irony. "Some day I will father lucky pink babies."

Her throat warmed at the thought, something tremulous invading her lower mid section. She quelled the sensation, denied it again. Finishing the chicken, she tossed the bone, then employed a Wet-Wipe on her fingers with finality.

"We need coffee now. Iced coffee. With lots of cream and lots of ice." She dotted her forehead with the damp towel.

"Coffee will make you black," he said softly. "Ebony tells me whites here believe that. Do you believe that, Cally?"

"No." Abruptly irritated, she reached for her sun-dried socks, began to pull them on. In Ebony, his precious drop of white blood would be lost. The week before, she had pleasantly missed the girl. Her surly manner and judgmental obsidian gaze unnerved Cally. Ebony had watched shrewdly as Paul Michael got paid in cash, at his request. Cally imagined his pay going to various unsavory events or purchases orchestrated by Ebony.

"Where *is* Ebony today?"

"She is not here. Not today." He narrowed his eyes for an instant, so briefly Cally could have imagined it. But it was a way he had, she'd come to realize, a bid for emphasis, eagerness to convey understanding. "Ebony is a working girl," he said quietly.

Did he know the unsavory connotation of the term? If not, if the label was guileless, she wondered if he considered *her* a working girl, too. The afternoon, since his arrival, had been extremely laborious but satisfying.

"I could take delivery another day—other than Wednesday. If Ebony has another day off, she could help. Then *I* wouldn't have to work so hard." She managed a smile.

"No problem. Wednesday is going to be all right. And hard work is good for you." He pushed the half empty bucket toward her. "You are skinny, I think. Be strong. Eat more chicken."

She patted her stomach, ran her finger inside the tight band of her shorts. "I can't."

She slipped her feet into her shoes, tied them. In her corner vision, the sun glinted on the gold in his ear and turned his hair to copper fire as he reached for his socks and shoes. The locket swung, glimmering, into the sun and then banged softly against his broad chest. Again, memory of its feel against her breasts rushed back.

"You have to eat, girl." He inched the bucket closer. "Sickness ride horse come, take foot go away."

She straightened, leaned against a column. "I'm sure that's significant . . . somehow."

"Jamaican proverb. Easier to get sick than to get well."

"Profound." She extracted a wing from the bucket. "One more." Tearing skin away, she guiltily recalled the soft, clingy dinner dress she had planned to wear. "Paul Michael?"

"Yeah, girl?" He glanced up from lacing his shoes, cocked an eyebrow.

"You told me, that first day, that 'quest' is the story of your life." A distinctive name, Quest. One he could have devised and chosen, as he'd chosen to be white on the Jamaican census. "Would you tell me about that? About your quest?"

Without hesitation he said, "To find my mother. She was once living in Savannah. I have come here to know her."

"Know her?" Cally searched for the emotion behind his words. His classic face was void, a mask. "You mean . . . ?"

His shrug was less jaunty than usual. "I am twenty-six years old. She left me the day I was born." His tone dipped toward bitterness, his voice hardening. "I have never seen her. I have never heard her speak. I do not recall her touch."

She risked a quiet prompt. "Left you?"

"With my father. With my *grand-mére* and my aunties."

"I'm sorry." Her spirit dampened. "How sad for you."

A muscle just beneath his temple pumped wildly.

Suddenly she wanted levity, missing it, craving it for him—for her. "Actually, mothers are sometimes severely overrated."

"I will find mine." He looked at her, his eyes resolved as he fingered the locket. "My *grand-mére* gave me this locket. If I do not succeed, I am to bring it back to Jamaica and we will open it together. The secret of my mother is inside."

"Mercy, Paul Michael. How in the world do you keep from smashing it and looking inside?"

"*Grand-mére* asked me to open it with her."

"Still . . . ."

"I love my *grand-mére*. I honor her. But, I will find my mother. Everything is going to be all right."

His tone was at odds with the outcome he projected. His smile returned, but not so genuinely, making her wonder if she'd ever view it quite the same way as before.

He picked up an antique doll chair beside him, turned it slowly in his hands, studying it intently. While unpacking, they had discovered one leg loose, almost dangling. Cally had been daunted, Paul Michael unperturbed.

"I can fix your chair, girl. No problem."

Mesmerized, she watched his forearms change from supple to rigid and back as he slowly turned the delicate chair in his long fingers.

She saw a workman stare as he passed from the yard to the house. Chafing under the disdain she sensed, a true barometer on Savannah's racial climate, she wished for Paul Michael's naïveté. He appeared unaware, or perhaps unaffected. She was supposed to care enough for Savannah tradition not to sit in the harsh, judgmental light of Columbia Square sharing chicken with him, sharing interests and concerns. She wanted to care, but he was foreign and engaging. So . . . gentle, so thorough. She had allowed him to take her above and away from the prejudice.

She rose from the step, suddenly wary, guilty. "If you can fix the chair, I'll be grateful."

His head jerked up and he stood, reacting to her change of mood. "I can do that. No problem."

He bent, scooped up the bucket and replaced the top, cupped the container in his arm. Swinging the chair from his long fingers, he said, "You know where I live. You can come for it."

"There's no urgency. Bring it next Wednesday."

She dug in her pocket for the cash she had gotten that morning, having calculated his number of stops and their agreed amount for each. Depositing the bills in his open hand, she met his eyes. The moment lengthened, deepened, neither of them looking away.

"I *could* come Saturday morning," she heard herself say. "Hugh plays golf." Always the same foursome, the same tee time, the same Saturday ritual. She added, "Hugh is my . . . fiancé."

Paul Michael's smile could only be described as tender now. Tenderness coupled with an understanding of the reason for her change of mind. She wanted to deny that reason but couldn't.

"Would Saturday be all right?" she prompted.

"Don' worry, girl," he said softly, tolerantly. "Saturday is no problem. Saturday is going to be very fine."

"I'll go on calling you Paul Michael . . . if that's all right?"

His beautiful lips curved in a smile. "Goodbye, Carolyna Joy Sinclair, my friend and beautiful boss. Until Saturday."

"Cally."

"Cah-*lee*," he said carefully.

"Cally." She doubted she would ever hear his soft "a" hardened, emphasis eased from the last syllable, an inflection with a caressing sound. Sometimes in the middle of a sleepless night she heard him say "Carolyna," and said it aloud, imitating him, her tongue caressing the back of her teeth. Nice.

❦

Cally made her way back to the island in the waning day. Ensnarled in that same traffic detour, in that same little town, she tried to rationalize the feelings Paul Michael roused in her. Drawn to him, she became whole in his presence. His voice, his gentle manner, soothed a nameless, ulcerous wound in her being. He exuded a positive aura she desired to embrace even as she questioned his hope, his air of certainty.

She suspected he owned very little yet was content within himself, a creed she coveted and craved to emulate. She knew only that he seemed as beautiful inside as out. She was complacent yet

37

exhilarated in his company. When he went out of her presence, she felt lonely, deprived. Their association was improper, had always been, would always be.

Nothing in the impropriety made her longing less real.

Chapter 6

*O*n Saturday, Cally stood doodling on Hugh's desk pad, drawing little circles around his name as Geneva's voice droned in her ear. "Hmm," she said into the phone, watching Hugh move efficiently around his gleaming kitchen. No wasted effort. Hugh was at home here.

He appeared crisp and fashionable in an ice-blue Ralph Lauren polo and madras golf slacks, but Cally saw the ever-increasing suggestion of a roll between his belt and rib cage. She shifted her gaze, feeling like a voyeur.

"Yes, Mother. I *am* coming into town but I can't stop by. I have a full day—lots of errands." The idea of picking up the antique doll chair from Paul Michael hovered in her mind with sheer delight, like birthday parties with ponies when she was a child. "I know we have to do the invitations—no, I haven't chosen a wedding dress yet, but—" Geneva protested and Cally rolled her eyes, shrugged elaborately, grimaced at the phone.

Hugh's mouth tightened as he poured mimosas into Erté champagne flutes. Last night hadn't seemed that special to Cally . . . but his daughter *was* gone for her annual visit to her grandparents in Chicago. Privacy lent the predictable uninhibited air to Hugh's affections.

"I have to go, Mother. Hugh's made breakfast for me. I'll call you later about choosing a dress."

She replaced the receiver after swiping it on her robe. "I'll take the robe home and launder it. No problem."

Hugh kept his gaze averted as she took inventory of the table.

"This is beautiful, Hugh, but I don't have time to eat." Her eyes settled where his blunt fingers wrapped the five depictions of womanhood that adorned the stem of the Erté crystal flute: lover, wife, mother, professional, and confidante. Nonentity had been omitted. Meeting his gaze, she clinked glasses with him, drained hers, and ascended the stairs to dress.

He eyed her closely when she returned and stood in the door, ready to leave. Tensing under his gaze, she recalled her reflection in his cheval mirror upstairs. The cornflower blue cotton dress hung loose and full just above her knees from a yoke that gathered across her sparse breasts. She'd pulled her hair into a severe top-knot, allowing a few tendrils to dangle. She had dressed for comfort and coolness.

"You resemble a pregnant *Precious Moments* doll," Hugh said.

She turned away, knowing she would never be precious in his eyes, nor pregnant with his child.

In the tree-sheltered drive he said, "I don't see why you have to be on the road to Savannah on Saturday. All of the social deviates come out on the weekends."

"Social deviates and Carolyna Sinclair, whose fiancé just happens to play golf every Saturday morning." Sudden recall of all the years the senator had chosen to spend his time away from Geneva, and therefore Cally and her siblings, lessened the pressure of Hugh's disapproval. "Don't worry. I'll be careful. Maybe I *will* find time to visit with Mother and make her happy about the invitations."

"Somehow I feel this compulsion to be in Savannah really has nothing to with the Renfro house or your mother—or wedding invitations. Especially today."

Déjà vu nagged. Standing in this same spot the morning she'd gone for Jessica's desk, the day she met Paul Michael, Hugh had confessed feeling he might never get her back . . . somehow. She wasn't certain he'd ever had her in the first place.

She offered an appeasing smile. "I could be back in time to make you forget those ungrounded feelings."

"I have dinner reservations at the club with the Steinbergs. Just be back for that, Carolyna."

Their parting seemed staid, repetitious. As of late, she found it difficult to connect Hugh's unrelenting priorities to her. Just once, she would like to come first.

She pulled the Volvo to the curb behind the black van and looked at the massive house perched on the grassless lot. Sorrowful colors, her mind whispered. At the turn of the century, Savannah's Victorian houses had been painted somber brownish reds, olive greens, pewter grays. Somehow, Paul Michael's battered rusty-red dwelling had survived, color unchanged. To Cally, his vibrant nature seemed inconsistent with his solemn habitat.

Shrill cries and masculine commands in a vacant lot across the narrow street drew her attention. Alighting, she locked the car and stood watching teams composed of young and old, male and female, blacks and whites, chase a soccer ball across the trampled ground.

Cally spotted Paul Michael on the edge of the crowd in which dark, scantily clad Ebony engaged in a kicking frenzy with a red-haired little boy. As if Cally had called out to him, Paul Michael turned, saw her, waved his arms in the air. His coppery braids gleamed in the sun as he motioned his head in invitation.

She folded her arms across her chest, settling against the Volvo.

Shaking a protesting child off his arm, Paul Michael broke from the crowd, calling consolation over his shoulder to the child. He scooped a tattered T-shirt from the ground, pulled it over his head, waiting out a passing car.

A pungent odor preceded his approach. "Welcome, pretty Cally."

He stood panting, his chest heaving, drawing her eyes. Sweat rolled from his hair, down his bare arms, circled his waist, staining the band of his brief shorts. As her eyes fell on the minute gap between his otherwise perfect teeth, she felt a comforting sense of familiarity.

"I see I'm interrupting." She glanced at the game field. Legs apart, hands on hips, Ebony was watching them. Cally could feel her disappointment, but Paul Michael only shrugged.

He stepped around Cally and walked backwards, smiling, motioning her to follow. She stood her ground until she gleaned his intent and followed him to the shade of the house. He kicked off his shoes, peeled off his socks, and drenched himself, delightedly, from crown to toes, with a water hose. Bending his head to the stream, he drank, his deep-water eyes lifted to hers until he turned off the spigot and dropped the sun-bleached, pink rubber hose back to the ground. A small white dog came running, lapped from the puddle the shower had created.

"I'm sorry I'm late," Cally said.

"No problem. Good things are worth waiting for." His eyes ran over her gently, lingeringly. "Your dress is very nice. Pretty blue."

The now familiar hard "t" sound made his praise special, negating Hugh's hurtful observation, his rigid face.

"You hair is pretty that way. You are a Jumeau doll."

"How do you know about Jumeau dolls?"

He shrugged. "My *grand-mère* has one. I always believed my mother gave it to her. *Grand-mère* told me only it came from France. She never went to France. Do you know, girl?"

"Yes," she murmured, her gaze seizing the wet, glistening locket, then going past his shoulder to Ebony. "I won't keep you. Ebony's waiting. Do you have the chair?"

"I have it," he assured her, turning to look at the field, then back. "But you have to come upstairs. There is something you must see."

"Upstairs?"

He nodded toward a triple flight of rickety steps that clung to the side face of the peeling structure.

Her heart thundered in her ears. "I don't . . . think so."

"I think *so*." He bent for his shoes and socks, his face almost stern. "No need to be afraid. Come and see, pretty Cally."

He grasped her hand, led her up the steep, weathered steps, smiling tolerantly as she murmured time limitations.

At the top of the stairs, they entered through a squeaky screen door. A parrot cried, "Awk! Come in. Awk!"

Paul Michael urged Cally forward.

She let her eyes adjust to the softer light. Then, bathed in the surprise of a gentle cross breeze, aware of Paul Michael's warmth and hovering presence, she surveyed his quarters. Bob Marley music supplied the quiet backdrop for her observations.

The octagonal-shaped single room was spacious and lofty with a high dome ceiling. Each section of wall boasted a large curtainless window to usher in the cool wind from the Savannah River, just blocks away. A multitude of strategically placed electric fans hummed and whirled a mesmerizing rhythm.

"I had a fan once . . . when I was at summer camp," she said, cast back in time. "I loved lying under it."

He nodded, smiled knowingly as she advanced into the room.

Foliage of every size, shape, and variety, healthy and verdant, filled the room. Some bloomed with profuse color. "So many plants!" Her surprise and pleasure surfaced, flowed. "I love plants—you do, too, I see."

"I do, girl. They are from the restaurant. They get sick and put out to die. I heal them. I make them beautiful."

Her eyes sought his healing hands, and for a moment she allowed their imagined touch. "The restaurant?"

"Reggae Ruby's. I cook there some nights. I like cooking very much. It is not real work."

"And Jamaica Jam?" She looked at the logo on his shirt front, then back to his mellow blue gaze.

"A riverfront night club. I play steel drums." He assumed a stance to beat an imaginary rhythm on illusory drums, crooning with heavy Calypso inflection the theme from a television commercial. Then, laughing, he pantomimed playing a saxophone, a trumpet, a guitar.

"Mercy. I'm impressed. I had no idea."

"No problem. Now you know." He added, "You can bring Hugh Masters and come to see me."

The unlikelihood of that assailed her mind.

He guided her to the kitchen area, boasting an old iron sink, an undersized once-turquoise refrigerator. A rickety pine table near a window held a hot plate and toaster oven. Aged, chipped enamel pots dangled above the table from ceiling wires. Peeling terra cotta pots of greenery sat on a makeshift counter.

"Herbs," he said. "From Jamaica."

Listening to his resonant voice, she was suddenly struck by the improbability of being there, a tourist in the misplaced world of Paul Michael Quest. She tried to ignore Geneva's image in her mind. She tried not to think of wedding invitations or unchosen dresses.

"Some of these herbs I know the names, some not—or how to use them," he confessed. "But my *grand-mère* sends them. I grow them. Do you like herbs, girl?"

"I don't know." It was a new and foreign concept.

She surveyed the room, an immaculate space, crammed in orderly fashion to form comfortable, chaotic harmony.

Straw bottom chairs, painted garish colors Cally had thought she detested until this moment, surrounded a bright-white kitchen table. There, a mayonnaise jar cradled a past-its-prime bouquet. Nearby, a curtain screened what she imagined to be a toilet. An oversized claw-footed tub, antiquated shower mechanism intact, jutted into the room with a regal air.

A simple set of free weights explained the muscled arms and legs in his severely lean body. Convenient to a tattered chair and ottoman, crude crates offered paperbacks, a boom-box, and cassettes. Bob Marley wailed plaintively, softly. Designating his bedroom, mute, motionless fans surrounded a tie-dye covered mattress centered on a sisal rug. Quickly, she pulled her eyes away from the mattress.

Art canvases cluttered a large table. An easel boasted work in progress of thickly layered oil, undisciplined strokes of brooding colors. Varieties of finished art dangled from the ceiling, wafting in the cross breeze. Jessica's doll chair perched in the center of the art table.

"You really are an artist." Cally steadied a swaying depiction of a child holding a cat. Soft, blurred pencil strokes contrasted the work on the easel. "All of this is wonderful."

He looked pleased and a trifle shy. "I draw character portraits at Factors Walk for the tourists. Very cheap. Very good. I take a cat as bait. All the little children and the pretty girls come. You can come, too, and make me very happy."

She crossed to an object in the crate shelving. The highly lacquered hardwood box had the checkered black and white look of a square soccer ball. She raised quizzical eyes to her host.

"It is a Chinese puzzle box." He took it from her, held it gently, turning it in his long, slender fingers. "It holds a treasure. If you can get inside without causing damage, the treasure is yours forever."

A cat mewed, brushed Cally's legs. Paul Michael scooped the animal up, held it close. Cally's eyes were riveted there, Paul Michael's gentleness initiating an undeniable ache deep in her barren middle.

"My main man, Ziggy Marley," he said.

She smiled, nodded to the box, prompting, "Is there a puzzle formula?"

"There is. The secret lies in connecting touches." He ran a finger from square to square, ever so lightly. "Touching one place brings the easing of another place, and that one reveals another." He shrugged. "If you are patient, you are granted full entry and gain treasure."

"Like life." Taking back the box, she ran her fingers where his had been.

"Oh, yes. Like life . . . or a beautiful woman who, with gentleness and patience, opens layer by layer." He looked across the room, out the window, then to where his fingers worked the cat's back. At last he looked at her, their eyes locking.

"That's sweet, Paul Michael." Her husky tone betrayed the impact of his look. "Is it a Chinese proverb, or Jamaican?" She forced a smile, coloring the question with levity to counter the intimacy of his disclosure.

"Mine," he said quietly. "The proverb is all mine."

His eyes still held hers, and she felt as though she might drown. At last, reluctantly, she turned away but felt his gaze follow her across the room.

She concentrated on goldfish he called Princess Diana and Major James Hewitt swimming in a giant pickle jar on a window sill. The parrot, untethered on a newspaper-skirted perch, cawed, "Awk! Pretty girl. Pretty girl, awk!"

"Pierre. He is a rainbow lorikeet," said Paul Michael.

Cally considered the feminine traffic frequenting the room and her new knowledge of how her host entertained. "You live in a menagerie."

"I like warm living things. You know, girl?"

Having no suitable reply, she circled the area, her leather sandal heels clopping softly against bare wood floors. She moved, he moved, sensing her interests, perfectly choreographed to her intentions. He bounced a little on the balls of his bare feet.

Cally stole a glance, accepting how young, how guileless he appeared. She felt older and jaded. Then, suddenly, she didn't. A sensation of energy, vigor, one associated with his nearness, his warmth and intensity, rushed through her.

She stopped before a framed poster to read aloud. "As many languages as he has, as many arts and trades, so many times is he a man." She met Paul Michael's anxious eyes. "Emerson," she murmured. When he nodded, smiled happily, she asked, "How long have you lived here . . . in this room?"

"Almost a year." His smile turned tentative. "My visa has been renewed once. I will return to Jamaica soon."

A grave sense of loss descended, regret for his imminent departure and the wasted time when she hadn't known him or this place. "And you've been able to do all of this in a year?" Her eyes, her spread palm, encompassed the room.

He shrugged. "It came with the van and the license."

A van, a license, a space, could be inherited from a friend. This intriguing element was Paul Michael Quest. She surveyed the circle again, taking in much more than her consciousness could perceive or would allow.

"Now you know I am poor, but clean and educated. You do not need to feel sorry for me." His darkened-copper brows arched. "Am I right, Cally?"

"I will never again feel sorry for you." She wondered what else she had unwittingly revealed. "You wanted to show me something. What is it?"

"Come." Placing his hand on her shoulder and carrying the cat, he directed her to a cloudy mirror above the sink. He held the cat next to her face, and they stared at the triple reflections.

"Carolyna Sinclair has Ziggy Marley's eyes."

She looked into the cat's yellow, gold-rimmed eyes, took him, then turned back to the mirror to compare again. Paul Michael was wise to show her the eyes. Simply being told would have left her dubious.

"A perfect match," she murmured, stroking the cat's loose, rumply back. He rumbled in his throat, vibrated against her breasts.

"Perfect," Paul Michael echoed.

He turned to pull out the purple kitchen chair, easing her and Ziggy Marley into it. "I have coffee."

From the refrigerator he produced a glass of mocha colored liquid, added ice cubes, and set it before her. For himself, he filled a pink mug from a battered electric percolator and leaned against the sink.

"Blue Mountain coffee," he announced with flair. "The finest in the world, hand-picked from three thousand feet above the sapphire seas of Jamaica. My *grand-mère* keeps me supplied."

"It's wonderful." Lots of cream and ice, exactly as she had wished for on Wednesday when they ate chicken on Jessica's porch. His kindness, his attentiveness, touched her soul. "Are those pictures of your family?"

Small, framed photographs filled a lace-covered, altar-like wall shelf, interspersed with a hanging portrait of Haile Selassie and a pen sketch of a conspicuously Jamaican Jesus complete with dreadlocks under the crown of thorns. The initials PMQ were scrawled in the corner.

When he set his pink mug down and crossed to pick up two family photographs, she asked, "Are you Rastafarian?"

"No, girl." He smiled tolerantly. "This scary hair is for Jamaica Jam. No ganja, for sure. No rum, either. I am not radical. I am just me. Paul Michael Quest."

His claims prompted her inquiry, "Are you Christian?" She accepted the pictures he passed to her, depictions of a mature man, an older woman. Looking up, she caught his elaborate shrug.

"I am deciding—still sitting on the jury. Jesus was a gentleman. Much power, but he kept it harnessed. Something I would very much like to be and do."

"You're agnostic." She smiled and held up the picture of the elderly woman. "This is your grandmother, the one who gave you the locket." The one who awaited his return.

"Miriam Quest. A kind and beautiful lady."

Dark skinned, gray haired, she wore a black dress, a lacy white collar. "And your father."

Cally examined the brooding features. Paul Michael shared none of the blunt facial traits. She raised her eyes, taking in his prominent cheek bones, fine skin, delicately defined brows. "No pictures of your mother?"

47

He sipped his coffee, eyes veiled. "Only an old address and the name Pennington." His inflection rendered the name foreign.

"Pennington?"

He nodded.

She handed back the pictures. "Your grandmother is lovely. Tell me about her."

"We will eat. I will tell you then," he promised.

"No," she said quickly. "Coffee will be fine."

Her stomach came to attention, rumbled painfully. She rose from the table, took her glass and the cat to gaze out a window. Behind her, Paul Michael opened the refrigerator, rattled utensils and what sounded like foil. Below, Ebony lay on her stomach at the edge of the field, staring up at the room, forlornly, Cally thought. Feeling guilty, jolted back to reality, she stepped back from view.

"Paul Michael, really. I can't eat."

Wordlessly, he prepared the table at adjoining corners, turned on a nearby fan, and produced a tray of food.

"I can't . . . but thank you," she said lamely.

He fixed the purple chair for her to sit again. "You are hungry, Cally. It will bring me much joy if you eat." He waited, his hands on the chair. "I know that is what you want—to eat *and* to bring me joy."

Their eyes held as she slipped into the chair and placed the napkin on her lap. The fan cooled her face, stirred her hair, almost soothed her.

"Jerked pork and chicken," he announced, taking her plate, filling it. "Pears. Mangos. Avocados from California. Eat, pretty Cally. Enjoy." He sat down.

"California. You said it." Her tone was accusatory.

He waited, nodding, fork and brows raised.

"Say Cally," she prompted.

"Cah-lee," he said carefully.

She felt caressed. "Call me whatever you like, as long as you call me on Tuesday nights."

He laughed softly. "Yeah, girl." He began to eat.

"Your *grand-mère*," she reminded, taking care with the inflection. "Tell me about her. About your family." She selected a piece of meat, and following his lead, shredded it with her fingers.

"My father was an English professor at the university in Kingston. He left me with *Grand-mère* and my aunties, to grow up in the country in St. Mary's parish. They were all I knew as a child."

"Did you go to the university and major in English? Like father, like son?"

"The son is nothing like the father." He smiled wryly. "The son hardly knew the father. When I double majored in art and music, he wanted to know me even less." His eyes stormed, then cleared.

She said, "One major could at least have been . . . finance, maybe? Or marketing. Art *and* music is more frivolous than my art degree. I wanted to paint portraits."

"You, too, love art. We have that in common."

She nodded. "Fathers are usually too practical to be art enthusiasts. What will you do to make a living in Jamaica?"

"Here, I must have three jobs to support my obsession for art. There, too, I am sure. My father would be big-time disappointed." He picked a breast off the platter, placed it on her plate, took a leg for himself. "Are your parents disappointed or proud of you, pretty Cally?"

"Highly disappointed. I squandered a generous trust fund before my twenty-fourth birthday. I'm a lowly laborer now."

He rolled his eyes and laughed aloud. "Woh-ho! You surprise me, baby girl."

At the sound of his laughter, a stifling weight lifted from her bruised soul. She could remember no one having laughed over the misused money before. "More was expected of me. My mother was an Englander."

He shrugged, shredding pork with his fork now. "In Jamaica everyone is dying to be an Englander."

"Englander Fine Furniture," she explained. "My great-great-grandfather started the business on his plantation near Augusta with slave labor."

Paul Michael's eyes quickened, seemed to deepen.

"I was expected to invest my portion wisely rather than spend it. Also, I had a scandalous first marriage. My father was a senator at the time, and my mother wanted an extravagant wedding with the

49

governor in attendance." She attempted a smile. "She's determined to get that wedding this second time around."

"With Hugh Masters, AIA" His eyes moved solemnly to her adorned ring finger, back to her face.

"Yes," she murmured.

"A slave driver grandfather and a politico father. In Jamaica, slave runners are hated and politicos are not always the best thing to be." Lowering his plate to the floor for Ziggy Marley, he crooned, "Poor Carolyna."

Her laughter rang in the big room, floating out a window. "You aren't impressed."

"I am impressed by your honesty." He was slow to move his eyes from her face. "I saved something for you from Reggae Ruby's last night. I want to watch you eat it."

"I couldn't possibly eat another bite."

He rose and retrieved his offering from beneath an inverted bowl on the counter. A worse-for-the-wear, cream-filled chocolate éclair.

Her stomach jolted with desire. "Oh my" she moaned. "I'm sinning."

"You are plenty skinny, little sister." He sat down again. His forearm adjoined hers on the table top, as he leaned to cut a bite with his fork, raised it invitingly.

Her mouth opened of its own will. Though the pastry was past its prime, the cream a bit flat, it tasted heavenly. She took the fork from him, speared another, larger bite, closed her eyes and swallowed. She opened her eyes to his delighted smile when he dabbed the corner of her mouth with a napkin.

His smile unlatched the door to her caged soul, releasing sensual pleasures too long denied. Scooping the remaining bit of pastry from the saucer with her fingers, she stuffed it in her mouth, sucked her fingertips, matching his hearty laughter.

"P.M.! Boy, you better git yourself to this door!"

The call pierced the room, vibrated in Cally's conscience. Her head jerked around and she met Ebony's stare through the rusty screen door. While the words were caustic, the tone held concern, or something close to fear. Paul Michael's chair scraped back. He smiled down at Cally before ambling to the door. She heard their hushed, urgent voices before the screen opened and Ebony slammed the soccer ball into the room, then hammered down the wooden steps.

"Awk! Ebony!" Pierre screeched. "*Entrez chérie*! Ebony! *Entrez*!"

Paul Michael flicked the ball up gently with his toe, catching it and balancing it on the top of his foot. Then he bounced it effortlessly from one foot to the other, the muscles in his thighs working frantically, appealingly.

Cally bolted from the chair. "I have to go."

His head jerked up, eyes narrowed.

"Thank you, Paul Michael—for feeding me. You're too kind, sir." She searched around anxiously for her bag, making a show of consulting her watch. "I'll see you on Wednesday."

"You are leaving because of Ebony?" His brows hiked slightly, and his blue eyes caressed her warm face.

"I'm due back on the island. When you call Tuesday night I'll have a long list of pickups." She moved past him to the door.

"Cally?"

She turned, wary and expectant. He had dropped the ball and picked up Ziggy Marley. Her gaze fastened on his long, slender fingers moving languorously in the tiger fur. Her belly rippled.

"Do you want your chair, girl?"

Her cheeks flushed, singed. "Of course." She waited by the door, disturbed that she had forgotten her reason for coming. She took the tiny chair from him, examined it, adopting an overdue business air. "It looks great. How much do I owe you?" She saw his disappointment. "I'd have to pay anyone else."

Eyes clouding, he stepped to the screen and onto the tiny landing, waiting silently for her to precede him down the stairs.

She got into the car, rolled down the window. His brown hands rested on the door. She fired the engine, overcome with reluctance to leave him, longing to stay, to go back upstairs.

"Until Wednesday." Her voice caught.

"Tuesday night, baby girl."

He backed away, leaving Cally with a yearning she could no longer deny and with no choice but to leave him.

51

<h1 style="text-align:center">Chapter 7</h1>

Ten miles out from the Sea Island causeway, traffic slowed to a crawl. A stop by the Renfro house, once she left Paul Michael, had kept Cally from beating the Saturday afternoon exodus from Savannah to the island.

Being on time for the impending dinner at the club with the Steinbergs would be difficult now. Not for the first time, she regretted having agreed to go. Complying with Hugh's wishes wreaked havoc with her schedules. Of course, if she hadn't stayed so long with Paul Michael . . . .

Dialing the phone by rote, her eyes strayed to the convertible in the next lane. Rock music blasted. A blonde girl bounced in rhythm with the pulsating beat. Had she ever been so young? She pushed in a Tory Amos cassette, then lowered the volume when Geneva's housekeeper answered the phone.

"Hi, Mikela. Do I have any messages?"

"Yore Mother called. Yore Daddy called. Schoffstalls say that jacket you ordered is in, come get it. And that Turner Cole done called."

Cally lurched, snapped the stereo off. "What did he want?"

"What do he *always* want?"

"What did he say? Tell me what Turner actually said, Mikela. Not what you think you heard. Every word you remember."

"It weren't that hard. He say he comin' over here straight away. 'Spect he be here real soon." Melodic door chimes charged the background. "'Spect that'll be him now."

"Mercy! What did you—where does he think I am?"

"He think you on yore way home, missy. And you is. He ain't comin' here to see me. He ain't very smart comin' to yore mama's house to get next to you, neither."

"Mikela, please be kind to him. He's having a bad time."

52

"Good." Mikela spoke with conviction.

The phone went dead. Cally turned the stereo back on and listened to the poetic lament of woman abused by man. She used the remaining forty-five minute drive to take herself once again through the Turner Cole event, from inception, into tangled involvement, to ongoing resolution.

Turner's first year at Sea Island Golf Club had been Cally's last privileged year at the renowned School of Arts in Winston-Salem. Turner was fresh from a golf scholarship at Arizona State University. His desert tan, crowned by red hair, caught her eye when she went into the golf shop at Christmas break, and again at Easter.

She drove home the following June, degree secured, champagne-colored Porsche crammed with tartan plaid clothing she would never wear again. She took her first golf lesson from Turner the following afternoon. The rest, including the clandestine courtship during her parents' summer absence, the elopement, the tumultuous marriage, squandered trust fund and disinheritance, were history.

When she finally left, three years into the marriage, returning home chastened and contrite, the will was reinstated. She relinquished her craving to be a portrait artist. Instead, she sold the Porsche and used the pitiful remainder of the Englander trust fund to attain an interior design degree from the prestigious Savannah College of Art and Design.

She wasn't sure her marriage and all the repercussions hadn't damaged her in some irreparable way. But she was sure that her determination to stay away from Turner and slip into wedded conformity with Hugh would not bring back her wayward sister, Lucinda, or the squandered trust fund. Days evolved, however, when her resolve went a long way toward erasing the accusation in Geneva's eyes and the guilt that hovered just within Cally's conscience.

Turning into the drive at the cottage, Cally parked behind a generic Chevrolet that could only be a rental.

Turner lounged by the pool with a beer. His lean upper torso and long, freckled legs extended from baggy swim trunks she recognized as the senator's. She approached with dread and joy, reading only elation in his expression. He bolted up, grasped her waist, and whirled her around. He was rock-hard familiar. He smelled of Safari cologne, cigarettes, and sweat.

Depositing her feet on the aggregate deck, he took her in his arms, the cast on his right wrist rough against her back. His brown eyes laughed at her. Suddenly, perversely, she was glad to see him. Never good at holding grudges, she'd maintained amiable relationships with male acquaintances since grade school. But she knew which ones were bad news. Turner fit that category.

"You feel good, babe. Skinny, but good."

"No one is skinnier than you, and I can't believe you actually came here. You were supposed to use the money I sent to go home." To Los Angeles, back to his father's public driving range. "I should be incensed."

"Should is the key word. I came here for you. You know how it is with me, babe." Pulling her onto the lounge, he leaned back and cradled her against his chest. "God, Carolyna, you *do* feel good," he moaned, his hand caressing her back.

She sat up, kicked off her shoes, folded her legs. Stealing a glance toward the house, she wondered from which window Mikela spied on them. "*How* is it with you, Tee? Lead me on."

"Men are like linoleum. Lay 'em as good as you did me and you can walk on 'em for life."

"That doesn't fly." Smiling was difficult. "I couldn't even do a good enough job to keep you in my bed."

"That's another thing I like about you, babe. Your incredible memory. It doesn't, however, take precedence over your real talents." He smiled, leaning to touch mouths, rapidly inserting and withdrawing his tongue.

Shuddering, she ran the back of her hand over her mouth.

"Whew! You're mildewed," he announced. "If Geneva gets a whiff of you you're back in finishing school. No fine Southern woman—"

"I work hard. I'm my sole support now."

"Yeah? Doing what? Loading trucks?"

"Unloading, actually."

In her mind, she pictured her days with Paul Michael, his guileless face and graceful carriage; Paul Michael, straining in concentration, body tensed in effort. His blue gaze always encouraged her as they toiled in unison, accomplishing physical feats she never dreamed she was capable of. Paul Michael had a way of seeking and obtaining her best.

Sobered, she made a move to rise, bending to retrieve her shoes. "This is a bad time to visit, Turner. I'm going out. I have to take a shower."

"Great timing. Me too. I won't hog the water or drop the soap. Hopefully."

Her smile erupted from deep reserve. "Amusing. But I'm now immune to your sexual innuendos, Tee." She slipped a denim hair band off, caught her hair, twisted it. "I've been deprogrammed at Erotica Rehab Central."

"Getting ready for Hugh, huh?"

Letting her hair fall, she slipped into one shoe. "I'm more interested in quality now than quantity. Hugh works for me."

He caught her wrist lightly. "Do that again . . . with the hair. I wake up nights remembering that, how your hair felt swinging against my chest. It was *really* long then."

Cally wished she hadn't boasted about deprogramming.

"How sweet." Easing out of his hold, she rose. "I have to take that shower. You can wait for me if you like, but I warn you, Mikela's not happy about this."

"Regarding the illustrious senior Sinclairs, you mean." He got off the lounge, drained the beer, then flipped the can, end over end, into the pristine pool. It bobbed for a moment, glubbed, and began sinking.

He laughed at her frown. "I've got Mommy and Daddy categorized now. I equate the senator with a shot out of the high rough and Geneva to an unplayable lie," he said.

"And we'll be fine if you keep that in mind."

Once Cally was dressed, they stood in the drive, Mikela eyeing them boldly from the open entry door. Locusts strummed late-for-dinner music. Moss hung oppressively in the live oaks that framed the golf course behind the cottage and lined the opposite side of the-cul-de-sac.

Turner lit a cigarette, released smoke in her face. Desire and memory overwhelmed her. She took the cigarette and dragged deeply, held the smoke for a moment, breathed out slowly.

"Mercy. That's good. It's been so long." She drew in more smoke along with Hugh's thin-lipped, disapproving image.

"Hugh really keeps you hooked to the plow, doesn't he?" Turner leaned against the fender of the white rental car and held her against him, his face buried in the hair at her neck. "I still love you, Cally," he whispered.

That never failed to work before. She was surprised he hadn't used it sooner.

"No, you don't, and you never did." She pulled away. Truth settled more peacefully on her mind than she could ever have believed.

Examining her lipstick residue on the cigarette, he smiled and stuck it in his mouth. "I still know your needs. They don't involve plowing . . . well, maybe they do."

"I'm going." She started toward the car. Five minutes late already and miring more deeply into complicated scum.

He fell in beside her, opened the door on the Volvo.

"It was wonderful seeing you," she said obligingly.

"Nice car. Fits the new image, I guess." He cocked a brow appealingly. "Does it?"

"Image isn't a consideration. It fits the profession."

"I'm going to try and get my old job back."

"They won't give it to you." She inserted the key. "You never should have gambled with the members." Somehow he had infiltrated their hallowed golf and gin rummy games. "You took everyone in the club for money and ego. What goes 'round comes 'round, Tee."

"Those old fogeys are probably ready for more action."

His red hair glistened in the evening sun and his face was luminously tan, still an intriguing combination. She had kept him prone for a weekend once, doling out intimacy and nourishment, trying to count every freckle. It suddenly seemed a very long time ago, and like a different Carolyna.

"They won't give you your job back, Turner. Just go home—if you have any of my money left. Tell your father all those things you told me . . . about the tour being his dream, not yours. Tell him how you'd be happy to live in L.A. and get a marketing degree. It isn't too late. And he's the one who needs to hear it. Not—"

"They'll give my job back if you ask them to."

She started the car.

"Ask them, Cally. Tell them I've seen the error of my ways. Ask the Old Pro as a special favor to you. Tell him I'm going to help you replenish the trust—"

"If he rehired you, it would only last until Mother and Daddy return for the winter season, just a few months. Not even that long if they get wind of it sooner."

"A few months is enough," he said quickly. "I'll get some paychecks under my belt and give my hand a chance to heal, then I'll get back on the winter tour. Will you ask for me, babe?"

"Will you leave me alone if I do? Not call me up in the middle of the night and drive me crazy?" Provoking her memory, awakening her regret. For the last few months, she'd been concerned about him and had served as his sounding board, his confidante. A signal existed. If she answered the phone, "Sinclair residence," he knew Hugh was there and was supposed to hang up. Sometimes he hung up, sometimes not. Either way, Cally was agitated, distracted from Hugh afterward. "You have to promise to leave me alone, Turner."

"That's a big price to pay."

She tried to shut the door, but he held on. He said, "It's going to happen again with us, babe. The job—or whether I call you or not—won't affect that. It's a done deal."

"Merciless son of a bitch," she said between tight lips. "I'm marrying Hugh Masters if it's the last thing I ever do."

He smiled. "That's a revealing statement. Must have been a Freudian slip. Will you ask Chester for me, Cally? I need that job. I want to stay here and be close to you."

"Get over it, Turner. Hugh is exactly what I want." She forced back the image of Paul Michael's face. "You—or anyone else—will not screw that up for me."

He only grinned, shut the car door. She reversed into the quiet street, certain she had failed to convince him or herself of her desire to be with Hugh. In the mirror, she saw Turner standing with his feet wide apart, as though balancing, in the center of the wide, flower-lined semi-circle drive. He was lighting another cigarette. Again she wrestled with Paul Michael's visceral image, as she urged herself to be grateful for the plow she pulled.

⤞⧯⤝

Attired in pin-striped finery and impatience, Hugh stood just inside the country club entrance. Cally stole a quick, light kiss, daring his aversion to public affection.

"You've been smoking."

Considering what she had just been through with Turner, the greeting jarred her. "I thought I'd taken care of that." She had sucked mints all the way to the club.

"Hardly. And masking it isn't the point." His face was grim, as she had imagined it would be.

"I slipped, Hugh. Even AA allows that."

He took her Ferragamo evening bag, looked in it. It contained lipstick and a tissue.

"Where is your license, and don't you have any money on you?" He frowned, his lips tightening.

"This reminds me of locker inspection in middle school." She sighed. "I don't need a license or money. I'm not going outside the security gate, and I'm with you."

"The Steinbergs are waiting inside. After dinner, we're going over to their island house to discuss the refurbishing plans." He pushed back his monogrammed shirt sleeve, consulting his Rolex. "Of course we're getting a late start now."

"I'll gobble my food to make up for lost time."

He looked appalled. "That isn't necessary."

"What is, Hugh? For me to win with you?"

Seizing her arm, he led her into the opulent dining room.

◦◦◦

"This house is charming," Cally assured Olivia Steinberg as they toured the premises. Hugh and Prentiss Steinberg had veered off to examine the more mundane aspects of refurbishing, such as outmoded plumbing and wiring.

Cally issued her confident technician smile. "It would lend itself nicely to rehabilitation. I only wish I had the time."

"Hugh keeps assuring us you're available."

"Once I move, commuting back to the island will be prohibitive. You and I could work on this house together in Savannah, since I'm there most of the time now. You live very near my present project. I could help you with fabrics and plan the furniture arrangement for you—if that would help."

She looked around the mismatched and dated room, taking in the deplorably heavy drapes blocking the golf course view. "You obviously have wonderful taste. You could do the rest yourself."

"I don't have time."

"Time is a precious commodity," Cally murmured.

"Hugh indicated there is no reason why you can't work on this project with him." Olivia's lips pursed, then tightened. Momentarily, she would be requesting reimbursement for dinner. Had she heard nothing Cally had said?

"How do you feel about *trompe l'oeil*?" Cally thought of the poignant mural in the Renfro guest room, envisioned the treatment in this room. Suddenly she realized she was caught in a tidal wave of Hugh's promises, slipping under, and facing the improbability of ever making it all come out even. Yet she wanted to.

Her voice seemed to come from a distance. "I'm doing a house in Columbia Square you might enjoy seeing, to give you some ideas you could work with on your own."

Framed photographs on a far wall caught her eye. She moved in that direction. The frames were old, and she speculated from the clothing that the images dated back to the sixties. "These are interesting. Would you want to keep them on this wall? You could reframe them to form a matched collage."

"Oh, heavens, yes. This display is the history of my husband's

59

career. We have friends all over the world. He was in the diplomatic corps, you know."

"Hmm." Cally removed a dusty, faded photograph of three couples, one black, two white, from the grouping. Hand-inscribed statistics marked the brown paper liner on the back: *Kingston, Jamaica, 1967. Stan and Valerie. Carl and Jeanette. Prentiss and Olivia.*

Olivia said, "We were posted at the American embassy in Jamaica in the sixties. Along with Stanley and Valerie. Troublesome times." She frowned. "We remained friends for years. Stan's dead now, of course." She took the photograph from Cally, placed it back on the wall. "You may use your discretion concerning framing, Carolyna."

"I'm not sure . . . I'll have to give this some thought." Cally listened to the men approaching, admitting to herself that her reluctance could cause Hugh to lose this project. "Why don't we go by the cottage for coffee."

"If I see the cottage again, I'll be upset if you don't take my job," Olivia warned. Then, "But I understand Hugh is having the contracts prepared."

⚜

The phone was ringing as Cally unlocked the cottage. Leaving Hugh to usher the Steinbergs into the main salon, she went into the study and closed the door.

"Sinclair residence."

A weighty pause. "How long is he staying, babe?"

"You're supposed to hang up."

"I wasn't even supposed to call. How long?"

"As long as it takes, Turner. Please hang up."

"I've got a room down on the beach. Cheap place, but you'd love it. Unlimited local calls, too. I've got all night."

The line went dead, his familiar voice, dreaded and revered, lingering in her ear. She left the phone off the hook.

She thought of Jessica Renfro's guest bedroom. No heavy coverings on the windows there, no dark paneling. A *trompe_l'oeil*

60

wall depicted a village scene designed to magnify depth with the rising sun each morning. Cally hadn't actually seen it at dawn yet, but the room was hers for the taking. Turner didn't have the phone number, but that wouldn't stop his pursuit for long.

A knot, staunch and sturdy as though formed from a stiff new rope, coiled in Cally's stomach.

Chapter 8

*O*n Tuesday, Cally stared out Dr. Ballentine's open window into the spreading, redolent pine. The branches bounced, alive with bird life. Normally the window was sealed tight against the heat, but a cool front had invaded the island sometime in the night. She wanted to believe it was a foreshadowing of fall, but it was only July. The cool was a respite, nothing more.

"How was your week, Cally?" Dr. Ballentine asked.

She chose a descriptive word, even though the doctor preferred to start with a feeling. "Revealing."

"How so?"

"Turner is here. I saw him."

"How do you feel about that?"

"I've decided Turner Cole is either skating on thin ice or he's it. After being away from him for awhile I can clearly see the difference between Turner and Hugh."

"And you like what you see." Then he added, "Today."

"I've always recognized Hugh's stability over Turner's recklessness. Now that I'm a grown woman, I appreciate that. I only wish Hugh was more accepting . . . more giving." She rose, strolled to the window, looked out, her arms wrapping her midsection.

"I thought of marriage as a destination. Now I'm beginning to question my tolerance for the journey. Barring a miracle, Hugh and I . . . our relationship is over." Saying it made it more real, though no less disturbing when she considered the consequences.

"Has something significant happened, Cally?"

Significant? Paul Michael's classic face swirled in her mind, his smile, his resonant voice calling her name. She attempted to focus on a relevant answer.

"To me, yes. Driving back from Savannah yesterday, a fan belt broke in my car. I sat on the highway for an hour, unable to muster the courage to call Hugh. I knew I was going to be late for our dinner date with the woman he's courting to head up his mayoral campaign. Finally I called a garage in Darien and they towed me in, but the belt had to come from Savannah. When I called Hugh to ask if he'd pick me up—it's only eighteen miles—he refused."

Face placid, the doctor asked, "Why?"

"He was breaking in a new yard man and needed time to shower and change before the dinner."

Dr. Ballentine nodded, rocked, hands steepled.

"I had a productive day. I felt satisfied . . . confident. It took Hugh only seconds to plunge me into despair." She relived the dizzying heat of the phone booth she had called from, saw the graffiti scratched into the side panels, like scars on a soul. "I can't see years and years of marriage in that vein."

"It's easier to get a marriage license than a driver's license, Cally." He paused. "It's much easier to *get* married than to *be* happily married."

"Hugh had a bad first marriage. Intolerable is the word he uses. He's told me he sometimes sees his wife's qualities in me. It frightens him, and he tightens the reins."

"That's a lot of garbage for you to wade through."

Inwardly, she smiled. Hugh had chosen this therapist, was paying him. The doctor's comment smacked of mutiny. "Mother is pressuring me unmercifully. I saw a picture of a wedding dress I didn't quite hate and she took the liberty of having Schoffstalls order it. Now she's insisting I go try it on. Some of her persistence involves Lucinda."

Having shared with him the story of her sister running off with the man who roofed Geneva's Savannah townhouse, Cally smiled wryly, rolling her eyes. "Mother is socially embarrassed. She sees *my* wedding as a way to compensate. She wants at least one of her daughters buried in conformity. I get caught up in guilt and try to go along with her. And I understand her insistence. In the beginning... when I met Hugh...I was so enthusiastic." She turned, saw the doctor waited. "Now I'm just trying to want the commitment I made."

"Very honest."

"I used to think of Hugh as having high expectations, being strong willed. I'm accepting the fact he's nothing more than domineering." She met the doctor's eyes. "His dominance makes me want to rebel."

Taking his affable nod as encouragement, she told him the story of the Steinbergs, of her insistence that Hugh not involve her. "He went ahead and had contracts drawn. It made me ill to sign my name on that contract."

"But you signed."

"Yes. When I met him I was the walking wounded. I wanted someone to take care of me. He thinks he's doing that by arranging my life, but actually he's exercising total control."

"These are hard times, Cally," Dr. Ballentine said kindly. "Women are told to crave and obtain independence when their nature calls for cherishing. Your spirit is at war."

She nodded, recognizing the turmoil he described. "Hugh is aiming for a higher echelon. He's determined to escape his middle class background. *I* am part of his decision."

"These are serious misgivings," Dr. Ballentine said.

"They've nagged at me for months. Now they're serious."

"And he's aware of your feelings?"

"I'm not sure. I've made every effort to tell him, to make him understand. Sometimes we speak different languages."

"Perhaps he would agree to come in. Often communication is much clearer with an arbitrator."

"I don't think so. If he came in he'd be admitting he could be partially to blame for our . . . impasse." She studied her ring finger, thinking of Paul Michael's blue eyes, how she sometimes felt his concern, his wisdom. "It's difficult to maintain control once you let your subject see you're fallible."

"That statement contains a lot of bitterness."

"I know."

"Bitterness can be a catalyst to irrevocable action. Something to consider if you still want this marriage. Ultimately, it's your choice."

"I'll ask him to come in."

⚜

Hugh was stunned. "Why does he want to talk to me? Your unstable tendencies and your past history are the reason for his services."

"Will you go? That's all I'm asking."

"No. There's no sense stirring up my first marriage when the object is burying your past."

"You have a past too, Hugh. I live with it constantly."

"My past doesn't affect our present or future. I see no reason to dredge it up. You're doing fine, sweetheart."

⚜

That night, Cally hovered with sketch pad and pens near the answering machine, monitoring calls. There were three. Hugh called, challenging her earlier decision to be alone and work on the upcoming Steinberg presentation.

"I'm coming over for a while," he announced.

"Don't, Hugh. I'm in my nightgown. I'm having a peanut butter sandwich, and I'm working. It isn't personal."

"I feel it is."

The way she'd felt in that phone booth in Darien. "I'm sorry if you do. The time I'll allot to the Steinbergs will have to come from somewhere. Tonight it's from you. Try to understand."

"I understand this is subtle manipulation."

"Actually, it isn't subtle at all. I'm simply taking care of a responsibility you forced on me. Good night, Hugh."

Turner called. She had only a faint urge to pick up. She listened. "Hey, babe. I got the job back. I waited until you had time to talk to Chester, but he said you hadn't. So, no sweat. I'm a big-name pro now that I've been on tour—a feather in Chester's cap. I saw Hugh this afternoon, coming in with his foursome. I'll bet his best wood is his pencil. He's un . . . friggin' . . . believable."

Her lips twitched. He could still make her laugh.

He went on. "He's old. He looks like he misplaced his Georgia corncob pipe. He's not your style, babe. I'll be in the pro shop when

65

you need stroking. Come by. I'll give you a lesson. Love you."

Near midnight, she curled on the sofa half dozing, watching a movie. The phone rang again. She shot up, hit the mute button on the remote control, and grabbed the phone with no hesitation.

She heard music and laughter. Her heart pounded, like high school, like college, like those first pulsating months when she was in love with Turner. She had no rationality or thought of restraint.

"Well, finally," she said.

He laughed softly. "Hey, girl. You were sleeping?"

"No. I was waiting for you to call." Breathlessly, she searched through remnants of work for the list. "This must be your double job night. Not a moment to spare."

"Very true. Are you ready, beautiful boss?"

Ready? Her mind ran a visionary gamut, finally seizing on the list in her hand. "The list is long."

"No problem. I can listen longer to your pretty voice."

"You have a knack, Paul Michael. Do you know that?"

"A knack? What is this knack word, girl?"

She laughed, pleased to finally best him in his extensive English repertoire. "A talent."

"Oh, yeah, girl. Very talented. I am an *artiste*."

"A talent for turning the most simple things into something fun and special. Something meaningful. Did you know that?"

"Life is very short, little sister. It is too short not to make every minute very good." He switched character. "Waste no minutes, then every t'ing going to be *awl* right. You know, girl?"

She no longer had to walk him through the list. He knew the vendors by name now, had taken time to familiarize himself with the better antique dealers and their locations. His growing knowledge had gone far beyond drayage into presenting her with astute room renderings and an impressive talent for choosing fabrics, mostly by feel. His apparent aptitude and interest in her trade was a continually pleasant surprise.

"That's a lot," she warned when she finished the list. "And some of the pieces are large. The store owners will help you load and I'll have someone lined up to help at destination. It may be late when we're finished."

"No problem. The longer to be with beautiful Cally."

She choked back a response, her throat aching.

"Good night, baby girl. Close your pretty Ziggy Marley eyes and dream only good dreams."

Cally held on to the receiver long after the line went silent. He was sweet; it was that uncomplicated. She reasoned his nature must have resulted from being reared by his grandmother and aunts. She liked to imagine they had given him an example of feminine gentleness that had melded into his masculine strength.

Paul Michael Quest was a rarity among men.

She woke near dawn with Paul Michael on her mind. Past the luxury of denial, she wanted only to understand what eluded her thus far, but the emotions were raw and undefined. One truth was inescapable: Paul Michael made her happy. He stirred her senses, aroused her longing for more than her life offered. His voice, his demeanor, being in a presence where life pulsated in a guileless, less demanding vein, mollified her.

In the sanctity of her childhood bed, she could admit their acquaintance was not naïve. In the beginning, she had tried to believe the association harmless, culturally stimulating only, their differences arresting. In truth, she had known from that first day on the dock, from the first time their eyes held, that there was nothing simple about the association.

Paul Michael was a fortress, a haven. There were times, such as these lucid moments before dawn, when she wanted to enter into him, go behind his impenetrable walls, and hide, stay until the chaos of her life ran butter-smooth. Instead, she had begun to function in anticipation of her one day a week with him.

Beyond that loomed the impossibility of ever knowing or having him fully, and with his expiring visa, the lurking certainty of soon not having him at all.

Chapter 9

$\mathscr{C}$ally haunted the window on Wednesday afternoon, ears straining for the erratic sound of the van engine. When the black, hand-painted box wheeled around the corner into Columbia Square, she hurried to the painter in the hall.

"Excuse me . . . Willie?"

He halted his brush in mid stroke, turned his sweaty black face toward her, his brows gathered in question.

"The delivery van is here." Willie had been there for weeks, watched the house taking shape, but she'd never had to ask for help before. "There are some very large pieces. Could I impose on you to help unload?"

He wavered for a moment, eyes downcast. Turning back to the wall, he raised his thin brush and stroked the wedding-cake ceiling molding. "I got's me a bad back."

Cally stepped through the carved door to the dining room. "Carl?" The paper hanger was older, reticent, white. She had come to appreciate his professional demeanor in the month he'd worked in the house. "Could you help unload an armoire from the van? And a divan?"

Paste swished onto paper, the sound permeating the grand but empty space. "You got insurance?"

"What?" The wrenching creak of the van door fell on her ear, then the rattly sound of its closing. She heard the clop of Paul Michael's Nikes on the walk.

"In case *I* get a bad back doing what I'm not suited for." Carl let the broad brush slide into the paste bucket, lifted the strip of paper, started up his ladder. "That's slave labor."

A warm flush moved along her neck, her face. "I'll be glad to pay you."

68

"Tell you what—" Halfway up the ladder, he twisted to look at her, eyes hard like an iced-over pond. "Why don't you and that big black buck handle it, like always."

Her stomach knotted at the sound of Paul Michael's clanking hair beads. His dark, slender form, uniformed in cut-offs and a clean, not-so-tattered Jamaica Jam tank, was haloed in the open door by the blistering sun. Cally's eyes took in his long sinewy body, the coppery hair, the bronzed countenance, the blue eyes that seemed to apologize to her for Carl's attitude.

She made herself see him through the eyes of Willie and Carl, see his smile as insolent, his gaze irreverent. Paul Michael Quest. Formidable to men, black or white, and forbidden to her.

He held out a bouquet of mismatched, wilted flowers. "From Reggae Ruby's."

Her heart twisted with the image of him gathering secondhand flowers the night before, saving them. She moved across the marble floor, past him onto the porch. Only then did she take the flowers from his hand. She pressed her face into the blossoms, their pungent scent and the feel of the workmen's' eyes moving her to ire and sorrow.

"I don't have a vase. They'll die," she said quietly.

"No problem." He shrugged. "There are many flowers every night."

She cut her gaze toward the men. "They won't help us."

He lapsed into jaunty Jamaican dialect. "Don' worry. Be happy. Every t'ing going to be *awl* right." Turning abruptly, he ran down the walk, across the square to where a truck, equally as shabby as the van, was drawing to the curb.

YANCY'S YARDS, she read from a rickety wooden slat as Paul Michael conversed animatedly with the driver climbing down from the truck. She turned, marched past her new adversaries toward the barren guest room in the shady far corner of the house.

"Mercy, Paul Michael. Are you really so happy?" she asked later as they stacked furniture in the room where they'd stored Jessica's desk the first day. Paul Michael had entertained her throughout the afternoon with Bob Marley lyrics and what he branded Ziggy Marley dance steps.

He raised creamy palms in protest. "Hey girl! Don't rock my boat." His upper arms ran to rigid muscle when he reached high to straighten and secure a delicate art nouveau night table at the top of the stack. "My soul is satisfied. Is ignorance not bliss?"

"It must have been. Once. But life isn't perfect. Not even yours."

He shrugged. "When I find my mother and go home to Jamaica, everything will be perfect."

Noting the momentary sorrow in his voice, she compared Hugh's ambitions, his wants, to Paul Michael's simple needs.

"And you are happy," he reminded. "You have a big ring and one big man, I am sure, to go with it." He turned, his smile gentle. "You have a fancy wedding coming soon. Going to make everybody big-time happy."

"We're talking about you."

"Oh, yeah. About me."

"Did you hear what they said . . . Willie and Carl?" Cally smarted, still, rancor getting confused with concern, even tangling into guilt by association. When he nodded, she said, "I'm sorry."

"Seven years not 'nough to wash speckle off guinea hen back."

"Translation?"

"Human nature never changes, little sister."

"It must have hurt . . . what they said."

He lowered his voice conspiratorially. "Does that fool, Willie, know I am pink? The joke is his ignorance."

She laughed, glancing over her shoulder toward the grating sound of a ladder being dragged into a new position.

"And," he added as he spread a soft pad over their treasure stash, "who works with the pretty girl at his side? Paul Michael Quest or those poor blind souls?"

She smiled, glancing at her watch to verify the late hour. "Is this your night to work at Ruby's? Should we hurry?"

"Only Jamaica Jam. Much later, though. Plenty of time." He sank onto the marble floor, his back against a furniture stack, legs stretched full length. Smiling, he patted the floor. "Rest, pretty

Cally. You work hard."

When she sat facing him, legs folded into a mock lotus position, he said, "Tonight when I should go to Ruby's—" He shrugged. "I braid Ebony's hair."

Craving, sudden and stunning, washed over Cally. "Really? Does she braid yours?"

He nodded, and she stifled the image, looked away, feigning interest in an unheard sound.

"Ebony is mad with me. So . . . tonight, I braid her hair."

"She's mad about you." Cally stared out the window.

"Angry with me. She thinks I cheat on her."

"Do you?"

He smiled softly. "Ebony is a mean woman. It is only a question of time for us."

"Do you fight with her?"

"Do fe do make guinea nigger come a' Jamaica."

His use of the word nigger surprised her. "Gracious. Two proverbs in one day."

His eyes narrowed. He leaned toward her and folded his legs into a position to match hers. "Fighting among themselves in Africa cause blacks to be hunted and sold into slavery," he quoted, then offered, "Fighting never gains anything. If I braid Ebony's hair, I have someone to braid mine. Peace."

Feeling like an intruder, she pushed the picture from her mind. "Commendable," she murmured, rising. "I'll check on Willie. They're supposed to finish that room today."

⚜

Once the last piece had been unloaded, stacked, covered, the house stood silent and empty except for Paul Michael and Cally. The workmen had long since gone.

"Do you believe Jessica Renfro would allow me to swim in her pool?" He smiled. "I have clean clothes in the van."

Cally considered the azure pool water, as yet untested, Jessica's warm voice and generous nature. Ebony's dark face, her sturdy form chasing the soccer ball, came to mind as Cally reasoned out Paul

71

Michael's desire to banish the soured sweat that covered each of them. He wanted to be clean for Ebony.

"No," she said at last. "Jessica wouldn't mind."

In the guest room bath, she locked the door, showered and donned her own clean clothing to drive back to the island.

The cellular phone rang in the outer room. She unlocked the door. When she answered, Hugh announced, "Carolyna, I saw the wedding dress today."

Her mind darted. "Where did you see it?" Even she hadn't seen the actual dress, only pictures.

"Geneva had Shoffstalls bring it out to the island. I went by the cottage to see it."

"That dress isn't—"

"Exactly. It's nothing like we talked about."

"Hugh, I—"

"The neck is too low. I'm afraid you'll look bony, sweetheart. You said you wanted something high necked and gathered across the front. This dress—"

"Mother had the dress sent out. I didn't." Something in Cally began to die.

"She told me you chose it from a picture. Maybe you need a wedding consultant to—"

She stabbed the power button on the little phone, then stood immobile, envisioning the look and feel of this room furnished and inhabited. By her.

A shrill ring pierced the quiet concept. Dropping the jangling instrument into the dark nook of her gaping bag, she folded her arms around her torso and stared out the window into the gathering darkness. The phone's persistent ring slashed at her resolve without severing it.

Paul Michael stood in the doorway, wet from the pool, barefoot, holding a clean shirt in his hands. When the phone quieted, he advanced into the room tentatively, his movements choreographed, dreamlike in her mind. Ringing resumed.

"Cally?" She read his peculiar mix of confusion and curiosity. "What is wrong, girl?"

A tremor rushed through her, wrought by his gentle concern. She

shook her head, faced the window, whispered, "Nothing."
He stood close. She sensed heat from his body, the chlorine smell in his hair. His hand on her shoulder turned her.

"Is it Hugh?"

She nodded, swallowed frantically, aching.

"What did he do, girl?" His tone, tolerant and placating, would have soothed a child. "What can make you so sad?"

She shrugged heavily, trying not to care. She struggled to find hope in her relationship with Hugh, attempted to view the complete picture, not this mere miserable segment.

"It's nothing, Paul Michael. You should go. Ebony's waiting."

"Don' worry, Carolyna. Every t'ing going to be all right."

"No. It isn't." Defeat tangled with remorse. "Things are just going to *be* . . . but they're never going to be right."

Her vision blurred as one hot tear slithered along her cheek, dropped, splattered—then another, and another. She gulped, sucked in a breath. The air trembled between them.

He whispered the words of a song she'd heard that day in his room. "No, woman, no cry." His strong fingers kneaded her shoulder, urging, consoling. "No, little sister don' shed no tears," he crooned softly, brushing the tears from her cheeks with a touch as light as a baby's kiss. "No. Woman, no cry."

Her defenses buckled beneath the avalanche of kindness. She seized his hand, pressed her lips into his palm.

He went rigid, planted his feet, tugged his hand.

She screamed inside, raging want demanding satisfaction. She stepped toward him. He stepped back. Holding fast to his hand, she drew it to her breasts, desire overriding logic at last. She wanted to know his gentle, harnessed power when the traces were down. She yearned to know the strength of his beautiful tri-colored hands, to yield beneath them, have them mold her into a vessel that could receive the tender hints behind his voiced concern.

Her yearning turned to need. She moved against him, arms firmly circling his hard waist, face pressed to his bare chest. And she felt gratified, as though she'd reached journey's end. He stood unyielding, arms stiff at his sides. His breath, rattly as a panicked animal's, stirred her hair. She raised her face to seek his mouth.

He held his head back, his eyes refusing, denying.

"Paul Michael—"

"We are friends, Cally. You don't want this, girl."

Holding fast to his hand, she sank onto the dusty plank floor, urging him to follow. He stood unyielding until he looked down into her face. In the last remnant of light his will faded, vanished. Her need raced through their joined hands, from her body into his. She tugged again and he joined her, his breath rushing out. Eyes searched and locked in the near darkness. Beyond the open window a child laughed shrilly, a dog barked, a car door thudded closed. In the troubled distance a siren wailed, and in Jessica Renfro's house tradition waned.

Cally allowed her fingertips to trace his face, feeding a hunger sustained from that first day on the dock. She grasped his hands, drew them to her face, and trembled beneath his exploration, eyes closed. She envisioned his mouth, sought it with her fingers. His lips swelled beneath her touch, parted, tasted. Her fingertips found his tongue, his teeth, lingered for a moment. Her groin quickened, throbbed. Withdrawing her hand, she pressed his moisture to her own lips.

He groaned, drawing her face to his, fingers so light at her temples she scarcely felt his touch. His mouth moved softly on hers, a whispered promise. He sought and yet not, offered, but denied, sucked her lips into him, released her. A bruised portion of her soul leapt to life, thrived again.

She lifted her dress in the falling darkness, holding his eyes, knowing what was in their depths, always having known. That memory, that knowledge, moved the dress up and over her head. She discarded it, unfastened her bra, let it fall.

The hot, humid night bathed her body as he ran his palms over her breasts, across her distended nipples, down her rib cage, pressing inward, lifting slightly. His hands rested on her hips, fingertips delving into the flesh of her buttocks. Their breaths merged and echoed in the darkness, collided in her chest. She released the button at his waist, started the zipper in invitation, then worked her underpants down, kicked them away.

Light from a lamp in the square fell across her body, lit his face, the stricken look in his eyes. For an instant she wavered, felt guilty, but she allowed her need to overcome reason.

She lay back, extended her hand. Aching, craving, she listened to him shed his clothing. He lay with her, took her in his arms, molding her against his rigid hardness, his own desire. Then, she felt him pull away gently. He turned his back, rummaged among his clothing in the darkness. She heard foil tear. Awed, grateful for his control and consideration, she waited quietly until he took her in his arms again.

She felt him give, his spine loosen as though he surrendered his mind and spirit, casting them out to take her in. His breath quickened against her face in a rhythm that echoed hers. His arms enveloped her, his hands gentle yet insistent, purposeful and greedy. She ran her palm across his hip, along his flank, up the silk plane of his back, pulled, sealed him to her, molded her breasts against him. His body was sinewy granite, his skin salty to her tongue. Her lips at the hollow of his throat sensed his pulse vibrating in pace with her own.

She drew his mouth to hers, seeking all she had feared she would never know. His kiss was deep, less gentle, implicit now. She answered, pledged, pleaded with her kiss. The gold locket nestled between her breasts when he covered her, tried to enter. His size and eagerness filled her. She heard an unfamiliar whimper, a soft feral cry, and found the sounds came from her. Grit and dust stung her shoulder blades, her back, her hips. When his hands went beneath her, cupped her buttocks, cushioned each thrusting impact, she found his mouth again, drowned in it, took him in and gave herself up to the forbidden truth of him. Her need culminated, imploded, flowed through her, held her suspended in infinite time . . . until she felt his body stiffen, then shudder.

He dropped his head, rested his cheek on her shoulder, and she felt him tremble, run languid. She sucked hot, sweat-and-chlorine-tasting air into her heaving chest, stroked his temples, his neck, his shoulders.

His withdrawal, his physical split from her, was sudden, jarring. She sat up, stunned, and stared at the broad back turned toward her. Silhouetted against the light from the window, his shoulders heaved in unison with her own ragged breathing.

"Are you . . . angry? Talk to me, Paul Michael." Strangely, she wanted to comfort, to reassure him. She touched her lips to his salty skin. "It's all right. It . . . just happened." For the first time she wholly understood the phrase.

"Do you remember the Chinese puzzle box, Cally?" His voice was unfamiliar. No merriment, no jaunty inflection, only precise, grieved honesty.

Silent, she nodded her head against his back.

"What I have done is to smash the box in my greed for treasure I have found but can never keep."

"I needed someone," she whispered. "You." And in that need she had taken and not weighed the consequences.

He found her hands, drew her arms around his waist and folded forward, into himself, into the deafening silence.

The ringing phone shocked them. Paul Michael thrust her arms away, rose, gathered his clothing, and left the room.

She lay back, imagining she could still trace the warmth of their bodies on the wooden floor as she listened to the pool water splash, slap furiously, then quiet. In her mind, she watched him dress and walk down the brick path to the curb. She heard the van door close, the motor grind to a start. Lying there on the hard, dirty floor, behind her closed eyes, once more she watched him drive away.

❦

The controversial wedding dress was the first thing Cally saw when she awoke on Thursday morning. It hung in all its detested splendor on the spindle of her cheval-mirror.

She closed her eyes quickly, feeling physically ill. She was clammy and weak in the aftermath of what had taken place the night before but resisted examining her feelings too deeply, those emotions wrapped around Paul Michael himself. What she felt, she assured herself, was remorse; she was engaged to be married and had seduced another man. Shame mingled with disbelief.

Behind closed lids, she relived Paul Michael's reluctance toward sexual intimacy—the stricken look on his face. If she had not been so wounded by Hugh's call . . . .

But blame belonged with her, not with Hugh, just as the decision whether or not to reveal her infidelity, could only be hers. Being with Paul Michael, indulging her latent desire, was of little consequence in the scheme of Paul Michael's life and hers. Soon, he would return to Jamaica; their lives would go on.

It was with this thought that realization dawned. She wasn't promiscuous, wanton, uncaring. She had seduced the man she loved. The man she would never have.

Chapter 10

"*Falling* in love, Cally, usually *is* spurred by strong sexual arousal and desire," Dr. Ballentine said as he peered over the steel rims of his half glasses and sucked on an unlit pipe. "Research suggests that arousal, at least in the beginning of a relationship, is affected by—"

"I never said I was in love with this man. It . . . just happened." The phrase sounded hollow. The doctor's assumption—all too correct—unnerved her. Denial was her only protection. "I'm not in love with him. You totally misunderstood."

His long scrutiny made her stomach clench. She considered going to look out the window but stood her ground, more denial for the doctor's sake, and her own.

"You're right, I'm sure," he said at last. I must have misunderstood. I was about to say: arousal is often affected by differences in people."

Her body jerked. She'd told him nothing about Paul Michael, leaving him a faceless, characterless nonentity. "Differences?"

"A theory exists that the greater the contrast between two individuals, the greater the arousal will be, especially in the beginning." He examined her carefully again. "Are you all right, Cally? You look pale."

She nodded, closed her eyes, envisioning Paul Michael's braids, the sapphire eyes in a brown face, his foreign air. Aching, she said, "I'm fine."

Dr. Ballentine concluded, "This theory is commonly referred to as nothing more exotic than 'opposites attract.'"

She nodded again, and he probed, "Do you plan to tell Hugh? This might help convince him to join you in therapy. Or end the possibility."

"I don't know. I'm trying to weigh the advantages against the damage telling him would entail." She had shared earlier the story of the wedding dress, Hugh's phone assault, her hurt. "I feel I'm on the edge of a cliff, and falling backward might be no better or worse than leaping forward."

"Then I would say you're very near a decision."

Cally ran out of plausible excuses and faced seeing Hugh on Saturday afternoon. In honor of a rare appearance by her father, she and Hugh formed a golf foursome with Geneva and the senator following Hugh's regular Saturday morning foursome.

Just as she had feared, Turner took advantage of the situation. As she stood at the back of the golf cart aligning her clubs in the bag, he left a student flailing away on the driving range to steal a moment with her.

"Un . . . friggin'—"

She held up a palm, glancing around for Geneva, or Hugh, or the senator. "Don't start, Turner."

"Hugh can't go double rounds, babe. At anything." He stood swinging a golf club lazily, barely clipping the grass at the edge of the cart path, following through, watching an imaginary ball. "He's old and out of shape. He'll croak. I hope."

She stifled a smile. "You are a gracious loser, sir. Does Mother know you're here? And Daddy?"

"Hell, yes." He grinned. "The senator fishtailed like the good democrat he is. Geneva is in there now threatening Chester's life for hiring me. You better pray he doesn't listen, babe. If I lose this job I'll have to move in with you, give you some more lessons maybe."

Spotting Hugh near the first tee, Cally got in the cart. She slipped the gear into place and spoke quietly over the bleating reverse signal. "Mother has given orders to shoot you on sight if you appear at the cottage."

He stepped in time to the slowly backing cart. "Guess who called me. Your baby sister."

She slammed on the brake. At the first tee, Hugh motioned to her to bring the cart. From the clubhouse veranda, Geneva's strident voice rang out. The senator, as usual, must be running late; there was no sign of him yet.

Cally gave Turner a grim look. "Why, for heaven's sake?"

"Lucy and I keep in touch. You know what Geneva always said about you girls."

"That Lucinda would follow me to hell." In this instance, Geneva was prophetic.

Lucinda had been a college freshman when Cally's and Turner's hormones merged. Cally knew Lucinda had experienced similar sensations regarding Turner. Because Cally deemed herself recovered now, she had believed Lucinda's fascination finished also.

"I don't see the advantage in your keeping up with Lucinda, Tee. She's most likely out of money now, too. You need to tap another, more lucrative source than the Sinclair sisters."

He laughed. "Well, actually you'd be surprised. She's been into some kind of post-hippie, screw-the-establishment frame of mind for the last few years. Seems like *her* trust fund's intact." He moved his gaze to where Geneva terminated her diatribe to the pro, Chester, and stomped down the clubhouse steps, glancing around wildly. "I'll see you, babe. Have a fun game. Do your teacher proud."

Mother and daughter whiffed the ball on the first tee.

⚜

When Cally stepped from Hugh's guest shower that evening, she found him waiting, perched on the end of the four-poster bed.

"Hugh . . . I didn't hear you come in. I'm running late, I know, but I decided to wash my hair."

She strained, hoping to hear some movement in the house below. Geneva and the senator had gone from the club to the cottage to shower and return for one of Hugh's legendary barbecue suppers. She thought of Paul Michael, the lurking emotional consequences of making love with him. Indecision hounded her.

"Have Mother and Daddy arrived?"

"What are you doing in here?" He indicated the guest room with his open palm. "You aren't still pouting over the dress?"

"I know you don't like clutter, and I always seem to travel with

80

so many trappings . . . ."

She pulled the wet rope of hair over her shoulder, twisted it. Her scalp cringed. Tucking the towel at her breast, she listened frantically for sounds below, not ready for confrontation. Not ready for Hugh. Consumed with guilt, she wondered how Turner had the stomach for infidelity.

"I'll get dressed and help you with dinner."

"What is it, Carolyna?"

He spoke tenderly, a bit out of character, feeling threatened, Cally supposed. Reaching, he drew her forward, eased her down on the bed beside him.

"Is it seeing Turner today? Or if it's the dress, maybe we could have some lace inserted in the neck. If you really like it, sweetheart?"

A familiar sensual sheen filled his gaze. Her gut clenched. "Mercy, no. I don't want the dress." Her stomach knotted with the thought of marching down the aisle in that hated dress, or any other. "I told you—"

"I know. We aren't going to talk about it anymore."

Easing her backward, he worked their bodies onto the bed, his hand going inside the towel, moving up her body to her breasts. She flinched, praying he wouldn't sense it. She had intended to talk to him after dinner, to tell him she—

The towel separated, and she lay bare beneath his eyes, beneath his touch. His hand moved across her stomach, over her hip, between her clenched thighs. Smiling tolerantly, he eased her legs apart, his touch tender but assertive, his eyes mossy, glazed now. He dipped his head, his thin lips seeking.

Her body betrayed her, forced a decision she was too weak to achieve. "Don't, Hugh." She turned her face away.

"Sweetheart, it was just a fight," he whispered huskily, lips hot against her ear. He turned her to face him.

She closed her eyes, rationalized, tried to yield, tried to forget. She needed to believe time was healing and could erase what she had done with Paul Michael. He would go and—

"I love you, Cally."

The declaration was like a familiar song she no longer favored, one that seemed to be on every station. She tried to want to make love with him, wash it all away in a fit of abandon. But she sensed the tremulous drag of guilt, like seaweed on a line, as chaotic feelings swirled in her inability to sort them.

"You're so beautiful, sweetheart." Hugh lowered his head to her breasts.

She bolted upright, off the bed, his ardor no match for her sudden strength. Scrambling, she seized the towel and shrouded herself hurriedly, determinedly.

"Beautiful, Hugh? Even though I'm not exactly busty and my chest bones are too prominent and my hair is too long?"

His face froze, a perfect blend of surprise and annoyance.

"Carolyna, you're being childish."

"I'm young. I have that right." The door chimes echoed in the upstairs foyer. "Your guests are here. I'll get dressed and watch you continue to mesmerize them."

He stood, reached for her. "Cally, stop this." The chimes insisted. He turned on his heel and stomped out of the room.

⚜

"I think it would be lovely if we sailed to Savannah tomorrow," Geneva announced at supper, her tone silky cool in the hot night. "Don't you, Wain?" In the flickering hurricane lamplight, she looked at the senator across the wrought iron table. "You haven't boarded *Wain's Whirl* all summer."

"These children probably have other plans," he replied, puffing an oversized, obsidian cigar. Cally caught his familiar, evasive tone.

"Sounds great," Hugh said, adding quickly, "Doesn't it, Cally? The yacht club is the place to be seen, considering Tybee Island's connection to the Olympic water games. Wain can show me how to trim the sails on that big beauty." He sat back, his tanned face glowing with satisfaction. "Good idea, Geneva. We'll start out early."

"I'm not going to the Savannah Yacht Club," Cally said.

"Why ever not?" Geneva asked.

"The Georgia Human Relations Commission has been looking

82

into claims that the club is biased against blacks." Cally felt Hugh's glare, caught the senator's relieved smile.

"Well," Geneva huffed, picking up her fork. "I don't see a problem there. Seeing as how none of us is black, I mean."

"I no longer frequent places that discriminate."

"Since when?" Hugh gave a soft, embarrassed laugh.

"Since I've been enlightened."

"Carolyna Joy Sinclair, are you testing me?" Geneva snapped.

It was easy to see that Geneva still smarted over Turner's reappearance, not quite believing Cally wasn't involved, and, considering the money she had sent him . . . .

"No, mother. I think I'm testing me." She placed her napkin on the table, abruptly visited with an ache not entirely physical, a longing to be in Paul Michael's presence.

Her chair grated on the flagstone, splintering the placid night. "I'm tired. I'm going up to bed. I would be glad to help with the dishes, but I'd probably get them all in the wrong place in the dishwasher."

"Sit down, Carolyna. This is a good time to discuss your participation in Hugh's mayoral campaign, while your father is here and—"

"Mercy, Mother. You don't need me for that. I'd make all the wrong suggestions." As Geneva rolled her eyes, Cally bent, kissed the top of the senator's bald head. He smelled of soap and cigars. "It was nice to see you, Daddy."

"I'll call you, sugar." He rolled the cigar between his thumb and forefinger, his own Ziggy Marley eyes studious in the candlelight. "I've been told you and I need to talk. About Hugh's bid and the wedding and other pertinent stuff on your mama's mind."

Cally looked to Geneva, then to Hugh. Their expressions could have been cloned. "Mercy, yes, Daddy. I think, once more, you got home just in time to try heading off a disaster. I'll look forward to your call." She knew it would never come.

She slept in the guest room, a cross-stitched DO NOT DISTURB plaque on the locked door.

"I have it all down, Mrs. Renfro. Hmm . . . ." Cally held the phone and surveyed Hugh's immaculate kitchen. No sign of last night's dinner with her parents, no indication life had ever infested the surroundings. "Opening the house with a yard party will be wonderful. I'm glad you thought of that. Especially if there are some last minute delays on the interior—although I don't anticipate any. I'll have the invitations printed and find some entertainment."

Hugh stood with his back to her, sipping coffee, staring out the white-framed French door into the Sunday morning downpour.

"No, you were right to call me here," Cally assured Jessica. "The time to discuss an idea is when it occurs to you. And . . . do you recall offering the house to me? I'm going to accept your generosity now. We're coming down to the wire on the finish, and with all the valuables accumulating in the house I'll feel more comfortable if I'm in residence. Fine. Thank you. I'll be moving in sometime this week. I'll have the phones turned on so you can call me there."

Cally listened to her client and watched Hugh's back go rigid, as though she'd driven a spike in his spine.

"Really? Sailing to Catalina from Santa Barbara sounds wonderful. No. It's raining here. I'll work, probably. I have a new project that I shouldn't have taken on. No! It definitely won't interfere with your house or party. You have my word."

Hugh turned, mouth tight.

"Good-bye. Have a wonderful trip to Catalina."

Cally took a paper towel from the Lucite holder on the counter and the Windex from beneath the sink and wiped the phone. Hugh stared, his eyes opaque moss, like scum on a pond bank.

Silently, she tossed the towel and replaced the glass cleaner. She took two of the Hostess Twinkies he stocked for his housekeeper, unwrapped one, devoured it, her gaze cast to the gleaming white oak kitchen floor. Unwrapping the second, she crossed to the coffee, filled a cup. She took Hugh's coveted raspberry jam from the refrigerator, removed the protective foil wrapper. Sitting at the cafe table near the rain-draped window, she slathered jam across the remaining pastry.

"Are you going to eat that?"

She ignored the question, took a bite, worked it, licked her lips. Carefully, she fitted the pastry into its plastic wrapper, laid it down, slipped his ring off her finger and placed it quietly in the center of the glass table top.

"My God, Carolyna." He crossed to the table, glared down at the ring, then her. "What are you doing?"

"I'm not sure if it's a postponement or a termination, Hugh. Only you can determine that." She finished the Twinkie.

Hugh seized the ring, clamped it in his palm. The ring was more than he could afford, wasn't paid for as yet. His insisting on a large stone was more of the new-money fallacy he struggled with.

"It *is* Turner, dammit," he said. "You've been seeing—"

She silenced him with a look.

He unclasped his fist, looked at the ring, then at the tiny white indentation that circled her ring finger. "You're angry that I wouldn't go to therapy with you."

"Not angry," she said quietly.

"Hurt."

"Yes. You told me—sitting at this table—if there were ever problems we'd see a therapist. I believed you."

"That was morning-after talk."

"No need for that anymore."

"I'll go with you, Cally. Maybe I can help you by being there."

"That's a misconception. Not a solution."

He pulled out a chair, sank into it, leaned forward, the ring resting in his upturned palm. "You think *I* need therapy."

"I can't be what you want, Hugh, because you want too much. I'm not going to try any more."

"Please take the ring back." He inched his hand forward.

"I won't wear it until—unless—things change between us."

He opened her hand, placed the ring there, sealed her fingers over it so tightly her nails cut into her palm. "My whole future depends on you, Cally. I can't lose you."

"You can. Try to believe that."

He seemed to remember. "I love you, sweetheart."

She stood and lifted the chair backward, careful not to scuff the floor. "I'm not so sure." She met his eyes. Thunder rumbled somewhere over St. Simons Sound.

She thought of the Renfro guest room. The barren, dusty floor, the undraped window overlooking the walled garden. In the mornings, the sun poured in, deepening the *trompe l'oeil* mural into an imaginary passage she sometimes felt she could take to eternal serenity.

"Sometimes I believe I'm just your path to prosperity and social acceptance, Hugh."

He stood, grimacing when his own chair scraped backward. "That's not true. I'll prove it to you."

"We'll see," she said softly, wondering if he ever could, if she even wanted that now. "I should go. I'll finish the Steinberg proposal today. At least it's not a good day for sailing. I don't have to feel guilty about that."

"Cally, about the Steinbergs—"

"You committed me to that. I won't let you down."

"I should have listened."

"I'll give you a clue," she said kindly. "It's not the Steinbergs." His anxious look almost touched her. "It's my never measuring up. It's always knowing no matter what I do, say, wear, or think, I will never please you. I wanted to love you, Hugh. I wanted to marry you because I thought we could have a decent, orderly life together—"

"We can! I swear we can, Carolyna."

"I want more than a decent orderly life now. So much more."

She went up the stairs to collect her belongings, for what she imagined would be the last, life-altering time.

Chapter 11

*E*arly Wednesday morning, Cally climbed the three flights of wooden stairs to Paul Michael's room. When the routine Tuesday-night call she had waited for, long past midnight, did not materialize, she had accepted the burden of bridging the gap between them.

The smell of coffee greeted her halfway up the stairs, and her empty stomach rumbled. Soft Reggae music and Pierre's cries drifted down to her. She stopped and gazed onto the vaporous and languid neighborhood, slightly breathless from the climb, unsure of her reason for being there.

"Awk! Hello. Awk! Pretty girl."

She climbed again, then stood at the door, peering in, waiting for her eyes to adjust from the sun's glare.

"Awk! *Entrez, chérie.* Awk! Pretty, pretty, girl!"

Paul Michael drank coffee at the kitchen table, long, brown legs stretched out, a towel circling his waist.

Their eyes met through the rusty screen.

"Come in, Cally," he said finally.

She opened the creaky door and stepped inside.

"Awk! *Entrez!* Pretty—"

Paul Michael's rubber-soled sandal sailing at the bird stopped the grating cry. Feathers ruffled, and the open perch swayed precariously. The oiled-onyx head darted beneath a lime, amber-lined wing.

Quiet settled on the room as Cally advanced to the table. Paul Michael drew his body upright in the chair, his bare feet shuffling against the worn wooden floor. She hung her bag on the corner spindle of the purple chair, sat down, and studied him, thinking how this stranger had once fed her pastry at this table. He appeared darker now, his braids longer, not so precise, his blue eyes, past a

87

deep-water hue, measurable in fathoms. Beneath his eye sockets the caramel skin seemed bruised as though he'd been ill or injured. Seeing the locket nestling against his bare chest, she relived the feel of it jangling against her breasts.

The air seemed to crackle when she lifted her gaze back to his. "Mercy," she said softly. "That can only be Blue Mountain coffee from high above the sapphire seas of Jamaica. I smelled it on the stairs. May I join you?"

He shrugged, his shoulders resembling boulders as they lifted and lowered. Heavy. Cumbersome.

"You've forgotten your perfect manners, I see," she admonished through a forced smile. She rose, found a cup and filled it, pulled the bracing aroma into her. "You didn't call last night."

When he didn't reply, she cradled the warm cup in her suddenly chilled hands, forcing a cajoling tone. "I live by your calls. Literally."

She waited, tried to read his riveting stare. Defiance? Not quite. "Not calling me was rude, Paul Michael. I have people expecting you this morning. There's furniture sitting on docks all over—"

He held a creamy, cinnamon-streaked palm aloft, his eyes narrowed with an unspoken message. His jaw was set. Resolve was clearly readable.

Cally sighed, sank into her chair. "Fine." The words were difficult to form. "I'll look for someone else."

His throat moved when he looked away. The thick lashes lowered for a moment onto his sharp cheek bones.

The chill from her hands moved into her mind. How empty Jessica's house would be without him. "I just never thought you would—is it because of what happened . . . ?"

The crudely rigged shower dripped into the ancient tub, shattering the silence. She waited for him to relent, but he offered nothing.

"Apparently you *want* me to find someone else."

"No problem," he said at last, his chin lifting slightly. His alien tone altered the familiar phrase. "You will easily find someone. You are very generous with your tips."

His words jolted her, scrambled like vermin in her mind. She sat wallowing in the hurt until she looked into his eyes and saw her pain mirrored there.

"I'm sorry. I never intended . . . ." Her hand went out, but he snatched his arm away. She was stunned. "You can't think I planned . . . what happened."

His knuckles whitened around his own cup. "I have been in Savannah long enough to know it was never supposed to happen."

In this moment of reality he spoke with a refined English accent. The contrast to his jaunty Jamaican dialect hit Cally sharply, and she wondered which was the ruse.

"We got too close." She leaned forward. He leaned away. "I was hurting. I needed comforting." She relived once again his kindness, his naked concern. "You could have . . . turned me away."

His mouth softened with the first sign of relenting. "I would have hurt you more."

"But not as much as now."

"What do you want from me, girl?" Although his words challenged, she felt he had touched her with the familiar form of address. "When I don't call you, it should be enough. What are you doing here now?"

"I don't know. I haven't let myself consider too closely." She studied the pattern on the cup. "I only know I hate dissonance—" She looked up. "Not getting along."

"I know the word dissonance." His lips curled down at the corners. "My father was the English professor. You remember? Dissonance is what I have with Ebony."

"Because of me."

"Because of you." His eyes and his voice softened. "What do you want from me, Cally?"

"I don't know."

"Well, think! You play with fire, girl."

"I didn't. You had the . . . foresight to take care of us, and I'm on the pill, if that's—" His incredulous looked stopped her rambling.

"It is more complicated than that, Cally. Your life is one big-time beautiful plan. Is there a place for me in this plan?"

"Paul Michael, we only—it just happened."

"Cockroach nebber in the right before fowl." He spoke quietly, without verve or dialect and translated without invitation. "The oppressor always justifies his oppression."

She absorbed the accusation. "I know you never intended—"

"Then you should take that knowledge and go. Now."

She shook her head. "I don't want to lose you." She examined and accepted the simple truth of the declaration. "That's all I know—today—now. You're good for me. I come alive when I'm with you. Your views are so different from any I've known. You make me laugh. You make me happy. We're friends. Is that wrong?"

He eased from the chair, crossed to a window, rewrapped the towel with his back to her. The muscles in his back rippled and ran taut, starting an ache deep in her groin. His shoulders curved inward as he leaned forward, bracing his palms on either side of the wide window. His head dropped, then Ziggy Marley rubbed against his leg, and he scooped the cat up, held him close to his chest and gazed out onto the rapidly aging day.

She looked at the tumbled bed, the circle of fans blowing the tie-dyed spread, the single pillow with the indentation of Paul Michael's head. Gripping the edge of her chair, she resisted the urge to lie there, luxuriate in his scent, rest in the residue of his sleep.

"We were friends." His tone was a quiet epitaph. "I will remember that when I return to Jamaica."

She questioned his back. "Return when?"

"My visa expires in a month."

Inwardly she cringed. She hadn't let herself measure his leaving in increments of time. She had lived only with the vague dread of his absence, until a week ago when she had realized the inevitability of his going.

"You don't have to go," she said tentatively, surprising herself. "You can get your visa extended."

He turned, measuring her. "Why would I do that, girl? I will go home and live my life. Find myself a woman and build a nest of pinks." His derision fell a little flat.

"You haven't found your mother. You don't want to give up. Stay. I'll help you."

His hand closed around the locket for a moment, adjusted it on the heavy chain.

"I should have helped you before," she said quickly. She had entertained a fear, unconscious before this moment, that he would attain his quest and return to his home, leave her.

"I have no more leads." He stared into the distance, sorrow and perplexity raw on his face. "It should have been easier to find her. It is an omen." Slender caramel fingers worked in Ziggy's loose fur as Paul Michael leaned back against the antiquated sink. "Do you believe in omens, Cally?"

She gazed into the yellowed mirror of the cat's eyes, studied the silent bird, watched art canvases sway in the cross breeze. Many of the paintings were of her now, dredged from his mind, not from her posing.

"If *you* believe in omens, stay with me," she heard herself say.

"Where would that lead? You are a white woman. I am a black man. I am poor. I cannot take care of you, girl. Here, I cannot even be seen on the street with you."

"Maybe if you cut your hair," she said senselessly. "Wore different clothes . . . we could . . . ." What?

He rolled his eyes, whites flaring. "Are you so innocent, Carolyna Sinclair, as to believe it is that simple?"

She sat contrite, staring out the window. She remembered the painter's face, his insolent resentment.

Paul Michael's voice emerged, shrouded in his own memory. "I watched my father grieve all of those years for a woman he did not have. I never want to be like him. For any woman. For any reason."

"It won't be like that, Paul Michael. If you stay, we'll go back to where we were . . . before that night. We'll be the best friends we can be. Nothing more." Regain the sweetness, the simplicity, the rare quality of improbability.

"You are marrying Hugh Wilson Masters." He spoke the name carefully, wrapping his beautifully carved lips around each syllable. "He is your savior. He will bring order to your life. These are your own words."

"Paul Michael—"

"What would Hugh Wilson Masters think of this friendship?"

She felt as though he'd inserted a screw in her and was turning it. "I'm not sure I'm marrying him. It doesn't seem so pressing now."

91

His eyes narrowed and darted to her bare finger.

"Hugh is . . . we're going to get counseling. I've postponed the wedding. For now at least."

"Because of what happened? It is your nice orderly life you are postponing. I want no part of that mistake."

He deposited Ziggy Marley in the battered sink. The cat leapt gracefully, raced across the floor, slithered beneath the bed covers. A similar spurt of energy propelled Paul Michael from his leaning position. Crossing to a table, he seized the Chinese puzzle box, twirled it like a basketball on the ends of his fingers. The lacquered, black and white diamond pattern whirled, faded to obscure gray.

"Please go now, Cally." He set the box down with a final thud. "It never happened. Go. Don't make it happen again."

"Me?"

Her incredulous tone brought him around. "Yes. *You.* We were friends. You could have left it that way."

"I know what you're trying to do." Suddenly she understood, but his attempt deepened her ache to put things right. "You're looking out for me and my needs. What you think I want. All I really want, at this moment, is to know we can be friends again."

"Friends?" He laughed bitterly. "After what you did, pretty Cally?"

A vision of Hugh and the returned wedding dress flashed in her mind, along with the worry of Lucinda's calls to Turner, the looming threat of her disillusioned parents if the wedding was canceled. The guilt Paul Michael thrust at her resembled too closely what she had driven away from when she left the island that morning, moving, the station wagon crammed to the ceiling.

"You wanted me," she said decidedly. "Why not admit that?"

Fire leapt in his eyes. "Take yourself back to the right side of town, little sister. Back to Hugh Masters—for the rest of your life. I pass on the small part of that life you offer me."

The screw he turned got dangerously tight. "You wanted me, Paul Michael. Just say it."

"I want many things in life. I do not take them all."

His words stung, acid in a festering wound. Her veneer of patience cracked. When she rose, her chair toppled, clattered against the floor. "You took *me*! You've been *taking* me since that first day on the Savannah dock. Slowly and surely."

She righted the chair, crammed it into place hard enough to make the table shake. "You just aren't man enough to admit it."

He caught up to her halfway down the stairs. She jerked her arm from his grasp. He moved one step beneath her, blocking her path.

"Get out of my way." She leveled her gaze on his, easily reading his regret, his dread. She saw acquiescence. Looking away, she wrapped herself in a cocoon, determined not to care.

"Forgive me, Cally. I meant not one word," he said urgently. "You were right. I only wanted to scare you away."

"Go to hell." She moved sideways, eyeing the Volvo.

He blocked her. "It was a speech, girl."

Her head jerked around, her chin lifting.

"A speech rehearsed for days, Cally, to scare you away. To save us both much heartache. And you believed it." He touched her cheek briefly but with infinite tenderness. "Come back upstairs. Every t'ing gonna be *awl* right. We will find a way. I promise."

She shook her head.

He tugged her down onto the steps, their hips and thighs touching. He slipped his arms about her waist, pulled her against him, held her. Her mind stopped whirling, accepted his earlier wisdom in chasing her away, insight he now seemed to spurn. Rocking her gently, he pressed his lips to the top of her head and waited.

An old black woman stopped in the street to eye them. Her gaze proved every bit as venomous as that of Cally's painter or paper hanger. The white dog from her first day at this saddened house left his puddle-bath at the corner of the yard, then inched lazily up the steps. He licked Paul Michael's knee, then Cally's. Paul Michael's hand found the animal's bony head, caressed it with a tenderness that made Cally want to weep.

"Come back upstairs," he whispered. "Show me you forgive me. I will feed you. Give you coffee." His smile tantalized. "Anything you need or desire, my beautiful friend."

"No," she said at last, gathering her will. "I have to find someone to pick up the pieces from the stores—and to help me. I'm moving into the Renfro's guest room today."

He sat back. "*Awl right!*"

"You like that, I see." She folded her arms rather than give in to the urge to move against him again.

"And you can change your phone number. No more bad calls from Hugh Masters. No more will you let him hurt you, Cally. He will learn to treat you good, and when I am gone I will know you are all right. Know—"

"Every t'ing going to be all right." She smiled painfully.

He nodded soberly. "I will get your things from the shops, pretty girl. Just like before. And I will help you move into Jessica Renfro's splendid house. You only have to tell me you forgive me for the things I said."

"I want to come with you."

His brows lifted in questioning surprise.

"To the stores. In the van," she said.

"Why? How is that the way it was before?"

"Before we made love, you mean. Two friends made love, Paul Michael." She raised a hand, traced his cheek. Catching the locket, she gave a little tug that made his head move, the beads jangle softly. "It won't happen again."

"I will meet you at Jessica Renfro's," he said quietly, his eyes drifting to the ramshackle van, then back to her. "A princess deserves a better carriage."

"Let me come with you. A month is not long. Let's not waste it. I have a lot of Jamaican proverbs to learn."

"And I must cut my hair and wear different clothes."

She laughed. "Forget that. Please. I don't want you to be like my other friends. Opposites attract." Her throat ached. "That's an old American proverb."

Understanding filled his eyes. "Opposites attract." His full lips curved around the words as though tasting them. "It is the same in any country, baby girl."

Their eyes held before she stood and looked down at him. "I'll wait in the van."

"You are sure, Cally?" He gazed up the stairs.

She looked with longing at the door of his room. But going back into that coveted haven with him at this moment would devalue Hugh's willingness to see Dr. Ballentine. A moment's indulgence with Paul Michael, no matter how precious, could deprive her of future knowledge that she had given the possibility of reconciling with Hugh every chance. If she walked away from the engagement—the marriage—then she wanted the slate unmuddied by guilt.

"I'm sure," she whispered. "I'll wait."

The slate would be muddied only by her love for Paul Michael.

Chapter 12

Cally lay in Jessica's rosewood guest bed that first night, bone weary but gratified, to a point. In the walled garden outside the open window, white mulberry trees stirred in the gentle midsummer breeze. Her eyes traced their shadow dance on the mural wall opposite the bed. Soothed, she allowed her mind to resurrect the slumbering day, along with the nagging suspicion of its significance in her life.

She had waited in the van for Paul Michael that morning, there at the curb of the saddened house. And as she waited, she considered their reprieve, thinking of Ebony, of Hugh. She tried to believe that to share the month left with Paul Michael would not damage his relationship with the girl any more than the threat of his inevitable departure was surely doing. A future for Ebony and Paul Michael was not in Cally's control.

She attempted to reason the remaining month as the trial period she and Hugh needed to test the validity of their own relationship, to explore the possibility of salvaging their pending marriage. She would use the time to condition herself to letting Paul Michael go.

Jessica's guest room was the first step toward attaining an independence she had never experienced. She hoped this liberation would enable her to consider her life from a better vantage. In re-evaluating her own desires and needs, she would realign the guilt of past decisions, guilt that could color a present decision unfavorably. Perhaps her new independence would allow her to see a way in which she and Paul Michael—

The cellular phone nesting beside her pillow jangled. She pressed the phone to her ear, knowing.

He didn't wait for her greeting. "Hey, girl. Congratulations. You are sleeping in your grand new bed."

"I'm too tired to sleep." She heard dishes rattle, raised voices, and pictured him at Reggae Ruby's, though she'd never seen the restaurant. "Shouldn't you be frying mangoes or stealing pastries or flowers . . . or something, instead of calling me?"

"Are you scared there in that big house?" The familiar concern in his voice touched her. "Is that why you cannot sleep?"

"No. I'm happy. I want to stay awake and enjoy it."

"Yeah, girl. Happy is a good thing to be." He muffled the phone, spoke in monotones, then addressed her again. "I am going now to Jamaica Jam. You have the number. I will be only minutes away. If you need me."

Needing him was indeed an issue. "Thank you, Paul Michael. Thank you for caring."

A brief, poignant silence. Then, "I care, pretty Cally."

"I know you do." Gathering strength, resolution, she said, "Good night."

She leaned against the carved headboard, drew her legs up, and cradled the phone between her knees and breasts. She resumed her reverie, recall punctuated now by a phone-inspired image: Paul Michael's anxious face, his concerned tone. Once more, she cast her mind back to the past morning.

They had driven to the first antique shop and had entered the place together. The elderly owner referred to Paul Michael, with a disdainful smirk, as Cally's "darkie." She ached for Paul Michael. For herself.

At the second stop, she said, "I'll wait."

Paul Michael gave an understanding nod.

Between stops, they talked.

"Tell me about your mother," she urged. "Are you sure you've made every effort to find her?"

His hand stole to his chest, fingered the small mound beneath his tee shirt, moved back to the wheel.

"What address do you have? Where did you get it?"

"Kensington Avenue. My *grand-mère* had a picture my mother gave to her. A picture of a once fine house that needed paint. She told *Grand-mère* she lived there before coming to Jamaica. The address was on the back." He shrugged. "When I came to Savannah, I went there first. The fine house is gone."

97

"Gone? You mean torn down?"

He shrugged. "Gone. Now, it is a shrine to Sylvester Stallone and Jean Claude VanDamme."

"A video store?"

When he nodded, she prompted, "You checked the census? Directories? All the available leads? No Penningtons?"

He nodded again, his face grim.

"I . . . can I ask you something?"

"Anything, Cally Sinclair."

"Why, after all this time . . . when she hasn't contacted you . . . why do you want to find her?"

"To answer the question in my head: why did my mother not want me. When I know that, I will go on with my life."

He stared straight ahead, searching his heart, she knew, not his head.

"I'll help you, Paul Michael. I'll think of something."

He smiled, blue eyes crinkling at the corners.

❦

When lunch convened at McDonalds, she asked for extra catsup for her large order of fries. Lips pursed around her straw, she reclined against the van door, pushing Hugh's disapproval from her thoughts. Paul Michael sat sideways, one leg drawn into the seat, his slender knee bouncing to the faint reggae sound issuing from the dash.

"I need a favor," Cally said. "Will you do it?"

"Woh-ho." He laughed. "Should I know this favor first?"

"Jessica Renfro and I are having a party. In two weeks—"

"You want me to fry mangoes. No problem, little sister. And I wash dishes perfectly."

"Cooks are a dime a dozen. This is a garden party. I'll decorate the yard like Jamaica. I need you to keep me authentic." When he nodded, his face alight with interest, she added, "I want you to provide the entertainment."

"Awl *right*!" He slapped a big palm against his bare knee, the sound bouncing off the van walls. "The Jamaica Jammers are

98

discovered at last. Big-time contract. Big-time, ugly long dreadlocks! We will be rich."

She kept a straight face. "You've done private parties before?"

Shrugging elaborately, he said, "No problem. Bull horn nebber too heavy for him head."

She pulled on her straw, eyeing him from beneath her lashes. "I'll just wait here to be enlightened."

"It means we always see ourselves in a favorable light," he said, a smile in his voice. "Jamaica Jammers will not let you down, little sister."

"I'll come to Jamaica Jam to check you out first, you know."

"It would be my pleasure."

Later, at Jessica's house, they had unloaded, then, at last, assembled the guest room. Carrying the heavy headboard, they stood in the double doorway, even Paul Michael swamped by its breadth and height. His blue eyes lowered and memory played across his face.

Now, the newly stained and varnished floor glistened. A midnight-blue Chinese carpet left only a foot of space around the edges of the magnificent room, mocking the grit that had pierced her backside when they made love just a week ago.

Slowly, Paul Michael looked at her. "Pretty," he said softly. "Very pretty."

Her throat warmed. "Over there." She nodded to the faux-marbled wall and backed in that direction, forcing him to follow. They lined the piece up, positioning it in the allotted wall space.

A Renegade tutu lamp was the last piece to go in place. Cally had cradled it in old sheets on the front seat of the car until at last she placed it on the night stand before the window. She sank to her knees, finding the wall plug, bathing the room in a nest of honey-hued light. "I love this room. I'm going to be happy here."

"So pretty." His voice came reverently from behind her. "This room is like you. Very nice, baby girl."

"Thank you." Rising, she joined him in the doorway to survey their accomplishments, their sweaty scents melding, contrasting the ambiance.

The house was Jessica's, but the room was Carolyna. She had

brought every personal item she could carry from the cottage. Her prized Porthault sheets clothed Jessica's luxurious feather mattress. Mounds of battenburg pillows completed the ensemble. Her clothing filled one corner of the mammoth closet. Books stood in the intricately carved shelves, framed family photographs scattered among them. Sketch pads, markers, designer magazines covered the campaign desk that occupied the window space opposite the bed. Atlanta Design Mart shopping bags, bulging with fabric samples designated for the Steinbergs, crowded the floor beneath the desk.

"I have supper—and champagne," she announced. "A celebration. Can you stay . . . if we hurry?"

"I can stay." His eyes narrowed with emphasis. "I never do windows and I never hurry. You know, girl?"

She laughed. "I'll remember, boy."

They brought a wicker basket filled with food from the kitchen. She arranged the cache on a yellowed lace cloth spread on the carpet. Paul Michael pilfered a sketch pad from the desk and drew quietly as she poured Dom Perignon into Erté flutes that matched Hugh's. She had borrowed the glasses from the cottage.

Paul Michael's pencil moved with feathery grace on the paper. His blue eyes lifted for a moment, lowered back to the paper. "Is this feast for me, girl?"

"For me, actually." She smiled. "I could only hope when I packed all of this that you'd be here, too."

She settled against the corner of the armoire, folded her legs beneath her, and raised her glass, recalling how much she'd hoped, how much she'd wanted him. He leaned across the sketch pad to click his glass to hers.

"To your new home."

She met his eyes. "To lasting friendship."

He tore the sheet from the pad, presented the sketch. "It is pretty Cally."

"This is wonderful." He had captured her wistfulness, the slight edge of trepidation, the excitement coloring this move. "I'll hang it over there." She pointed to a space across the room. "I'll see this first when I wake up every morning."

"Very fine. Congratulations to a liberated woman."

"Amen. Let's eat."

They stood on the porch in the gathering twilight and listened to a choir of cicadas beginning the evening's lunatic hymn. A welcome breeze bathed their sweaty bodies. Beyond Paul Michael's shoulder, the black van loomed at the curb, and the house gaped dishearteningly empty behind Cally. Paul Michael took her hands, raised them to his face, but she felt only his warm breath before he released her. Folding her arms across her breasts, she tucked her hands against her rib cage, savoring his touch as he walked slowly down the newly refurbished brick walk.

His backward glance as he rounded the van's corner mirrored her hunger.

As she lay in Jessica's bed, one clear conclusion sifted out of her quandary. Whatever existed between Paul Michael Quest and Carolyna Joy Sinclair transcended color and culture. It was pure and precious, rare as any jewel treasured by the highest dynasty. If they nurtured the gift tenderly enough, they could assure holding the memory forever.

A phone rang in a distant part of the house. She pulled herself from the feathery bed and moved down the hall in the dark toward the one phone that had been installed thus far on the new Renfro line. On the kitchen counter, outlined in the light from a street lamp, the phone menaced her. She lifted the receiver on the eighth ring.

Hugh's voice assaulted her ear. "Carolyna? Is that you? Cally? Answer me, if you're there."

"I'm here." She leaned against the counter and relinquished her serenity bit by precious bit. Light from the window fell across her cotton gown, her bare feet. She reached for one of the Erté flutes on the counter, twirled it in her fingers. Putting it to her lips for a moment, she wondered if it was the one she'd used . . . or Paul Michael's. "It's late, Hugh. Is something wrong?"

"Yes, sweetheart. Something is wrong." He spoke with heavy patience. "You're living in a strange house and I'm—"

"There's nothing strange about this house."

"Strange to me." He sighed heavily. "But I don't want to debate the topic over the phone."

"My sentiments exactly. What *do* you want?" She blotted her sweaty forehead with a napkin from the wicker basket, assuring herself she detected Paul Michael's distinctive scent in the fabric folds. "I have to get back in bed. I'm freezing—catching my death of cold standing here." Sweat drenched her body.

"Nice joke." His laugh sounded dutiful. "Does that old relic not even have air conditioning?"

"It will have. By the time Jessica moves in, in two weeks, it will be perfect." To her the house was perfect now. "If there's nothing specific, Hugh, I'm tired."

"I've made an appointment with Dr. Ballentine for tomorrow."

Her hairline tingled with surprise and irritation at his assuming she'd be available. "Tomorrow's impossible." In truth, she couldn't recall.

"When then, sweetheart? I don't want this to escalate."

"This?"

"This estrangement."

"Is that what it is?"

"It is to me. Cancel whatever you have going, Cally. This is important."

"And what I have going pales in comparison." Rancor sharpened her voice. "Your failure to see what you're doing has a distinct bearing on this little estrangement, Hugh."

"Can we talk about that in the doctor's office?"

"What time tomorrow?"

"The appointment's at two. I'll come to Savannah for you. We'll have lunch at Cafe Allegra when we get back to the island. After we see the doctor, I'll take you back to the city. There's a water color showing at the Telfair Academy I think you'd like. Then dinner at Elizabeth's on 37th."

Ironic. Two weeks ago he wouldn't even drive to Darien when she was stranded. The marked change staggered her. "That sounds wonderful, but I have plans for the morning. I can make the two o'clock appointment. Barely."

He was quiet for a moment. "You'll stay for dinner, then."

"No. I have plans here for dinner. Good night, Hugh."

Using both hands to cram the receiver back into its cradle, she braced against it as though holding down the lid on a bulging garbage can. She stood for a moment, realizing that neither her feelings nor her actions were those of a woman trying to salvage an estrangement.

She returned to bed but had barely fallen asleep when her cellular phone jarred her awake.

"Hello." Her voice hung groggily in the now cool night. She nestled into the feathers, into the sheets.

"Carolyna Joy Sinclair!"

Cally shot upright. "Mer-cee, Mother! It's the middle of the night."

"Not in Alaska," said Geneva, and Cally remembered that the senator, under protest, had agreed to an Alaskan excursion.

Geneva said, "What is this Mikela tells me about you moving out of the cottage today? Lock, stock, and barrel, I might add. You took a television and my good crystal and china. Have you lost your mind, Carolyna?"

"I'm not absolutely certain, Mother. Maybe."

"What? What? I didn't hear that."

"No, Mother. My mind is safely intact." Her heart was extremely fragmented. "I borrowed the television from my room and some glasses and plates. You have plenty of trappings left."

"Young lady—where in tarnation are you anyway?"

"At the Renfro house. I'll be staying here for a while."

"You prefer that stranger's house to your own mother's?"

"Jessica Renfro is no stranger. We've become very close—"

"Well, I am just shattered."

"You shouldn't be. My moving has no slight attached to it. This is just something I have to work out."

"With Hugh, I presume."

"Concerning Hugh, Mother. Whether or not it's to be *with* him remains to be seen." Cally smoothed back the hair from her forehead, enjoying the breeze on her face and the truthfulness of the answer she'd given.

"Well this is typically rude of you. Just stealing away in the middle of the night, gratitude be damned. That's so like you, Carolyna."

"*Au contraire.* I'm very grateful to you for giving me a roof over my head and furnishing me a maid who detests me. I was just in the throes of dashing off a change of address and pouring out my gratitude."

"In the middle of the night?"

"Priorities are everything. I learned that from you."

"Well," Geneva huffed. "At least I know it has nothing to do with that Turner Cole."

"How do you know that?"

"Because, Carolyna, your baby sister is back on the island and she has taken your place in that red-headed scoundrel's bed. Not in his heart, most assuredly, as he apparently has none."

"When? How do you know that?" Cally tried to get a read on her feelings. Shock? Jealousy? Envy? No. Dread covered her emotions precisely.

"I will have that interloping parasite fired before the sun goes down tomorrow," Geneva vowed. "I'm holding you accountable for this, Carolyna. While you are fraternizing with the likes of that California trash you seem to hold such an affinity for, you are jeopardizing a perfectly good marriage—and your inheritance, I might add—while you let your family go to hell in a hand basket."

The phone went dead. Something settled heavily in the pit of Cally's stomach. This was Geneva's first mention of disinheritance in a while, but she probably believed it had been influential in ending Cally's marriage and was worth using again.

Cally was visited by a flashing image of Turner and Lucinda clasped together, a vision her intellect bolted to erase. Was it envy or hate that caused Lucinda to persist in duplicating Cally's past blunders? The flattery she had experienced through the years, based on Lucinda's mimicry, turned to murky panic.

Tomorrow, when I go to the island, I'll talk to Lucinda, reason with her . . . .

She would call Geneva and plead with her not to get Turner fired. Lucinda's trust fund would go up in the smoke of pressure and insecurity much more rapidly if Turner wasn't allowed to remain under Chester's wing . . . .

A wave of longing swept over her, strong enough to make her curl in upon herself, draw her legs to her chest. Her eyes sought the lighted clock face on the marble-topped commode by the bed. Paul Michael would be home now, back in that sacred room, his lengthy frame reposed, peaceful. She closed her eyes to hear the rusty screen door creaking, Pierre announcing her. Paul Michael welcoming her.

She relinquished that image and wept into the night, assured only of more lonely nights to come.

$$\mathcal{C}hapter\ 13$$

$\mathscr{C}$ally managed to move her appointment with Olivia Steinberg up an hour the following morning. She stood at the door of the elegantly revived mansion on Victory Drive at exactly nine, juggling bags of fabric, her sketches, and DayTimer. A butler of considerable years ushered her into the foyer and left her to study her surroundings, a pastime Cally did not mind since it might help her to avoid surprises in the weeks to come.

She perched on a citrus silk camel-back settee and let her eyes linger on a pair of 17th century temple jars banking closed double doors. There was no similarity between this elegant house and the island home she and Hugh would revamp, and yet they shared the same owner—

"Good morning, Carolyna."

She rose as Olivia approached. "Good morning, Mrs. Steinberg. I appreciate your changing our appointment. I'll try not to make a habit of that, however."

"You must call me Olivia, dear."

"Thank you. Did you know your door is a cooling board?"

Olivia frowned. "Excuse me?"

"Your door is no ordinary door, Olivia. It's referred to as a cooling board. They were once used for laying out corpses and preparing them for burial. It's a typical feature of old houses like this one."

"Gracious, how interesting." Olivia eyed her appraisingly. "I didn't know. We inherited this house from my husband's family. What wonderful cocktail conversation!"

Cocktail conversation? This was history unveiled, Cally thought, disappointed in this client Hugh had forced on her. Olivia had no design expertise and very little taste, as her house on the island had proclaimed. She appeared to have an abundance of funds, however.

"The arrangement you have with Jessica Renfro would suit me just fine, Carolyna, dear," Olivia concluded their first meeting, her steel-gray eyes skimming over the sketches and fabric samples before her. "Would that be satisfactory to you? I have no specific requirements other than superior quality and impeccable taste. Yours."

A ripple of excitement akin to drawing the winning gin rummy card ran up Cally's spine. "In the trade we refer to my arrangement with the Renfros as *carte blanche*. Your confidence in me is a designer's ultimate aim."

She packed the sketches away. "Actually, I'm able to work very well from the personality profile you and your husband filled out." When she stood, Olivia rose as well. Cally shouldered her bag. "Could I show you the Renfro house sometime?"

"That would be nice. Whenever it's convenient."

Apparently, Hugh had not yet informed the Steinbergs that Cally resided there now, a major convenience. "The Renfros are having an open house in two weeks. They've told me to invite my friends and clients. Should I send you an invitation?"

Olivia's hesitance hung gravely in the staid air. "Oh . . . well. I'm not certain. Hugh led us to believe they . . . ."

"Hugh has never met the Renfros and he's no proper judge, being from Chicago. Please come."

"Well, I suppose so, dear." Olivia's smile spread thinly. "You've completed the house then? You were worried, as I recall, that our project might be too much for you." She began walking toward the door where the butler hovered.

"I'll be working hard in the next two weeks, but I'll get your fabric on order and line up tradesmen." Cally stood in the open door, caught in a blast of oppressive heat. "There are a few loose ends," she said. "Little details. I have to find a doll for Jessica's antique doll chair. It's the focal point of her bedroom."

"What sort of doll?" Interest sparked the gray eyes.

"An antique. A Jumeau." Cally considered. "I *would* take a Steiner, I suppose. Or a Casimir Bru. I should have started to look sooner."

"I have a friend who's a collector. She was in the diplomatic

107

service for years. She has dolls from everywhere. Should I ask her?"

"Are they for sale? Would she part with one? I'd really like a Jumeau." She thought of standing outside Paul Michael's house in her blue dress, watching him drench himself with a water hose. He had called her a Jumeau doll.

"I'll ask her and call you, dear. You'd better run along. You did say you have a bothersome day."

Bothersome. The word rang highly apropos.

⚜

Five minutes before noon, Cally slid into the chair at Curly Cue's Hair and Nail Salon, clutching a bulging McDonalds bag and a profusely sweating Coke. She waved a ragged-edged tear-out from a vintage *People Magazine.* "I know I didn't allow you enough time for this, Yolonda, but can you make me look like Barbra Streisand?"

Yolonda dug in the bag for a French fry and munched. "With your nose," she mused, "not in your lifetime, sweetie."

"The hair. Just all her wild curls. What do you think? What does this entail?"

"Two hours and eighty-five dollars." Yolonda reached for another fry. "Are you game? It's a great way to save time. Just wash and wear it. Goes well with an active love life."

When Cally returned from donning a lavender smock, Yolonda eyed her critically. "Are you putting on weight, sweetie? I thought so last month, but . . . ."

"Probably," Cally murmured as she slipped back into the chair, peered at what was left of the bag's contents. "I've rediscovered food. I'm enjoying it totally."

⚜

"The doctor will be a few minutes late."

Hugh didn't utter a sound until Dr. Ballentine's receptionist left him and Cally alone in the inner office.

"My God, Carolyna. Your hair—"

"Don't start, Hugh." She held up a palm, remembering her

108

mirrored image. Wild curls—just as she'd requested—touched her shoulders. Allowed to air dry, they bounced, gleamed. Perfect.

"No," he said quickly. "I like it. I really do."

She almost laughed. He'd recovered with the haste of Adam, who'd just been caught in the original sin and given a reprieve. Dressed in a stiff white shirt and a well-pressed wheat-colored suit mirroring his tan and flaxen hair, he made her realize, suddenly, if character had colors, his would be dun. The safety of that had lured her . . . once.

"How have you been?" he asked, leveling those mossy eyes on her, running them down her body to judge for himself.

"It's only been four days."

"It seems longer," he offered. "Doesn't it, sweetheart?"

"I've been very busy. The time goes quickly."

"Carolyna, I—"

The door opened. She felt like genuflecting.

"Well, here we all are." Dr. Ballentine took his seat behind the desk, shuffled files, opened one. "Shall we get started? Who wants to shoot first?"

At the end of an hour of moderate to heated exchange, Hugh's main thrust was Cally's failure to live up to her potential. Hers hinged on his lack of feeling and acceptance. She was given a "ladies first" opportunity to summarize.

She crossed to the window, braced a shoulder against the gleaming white frame. "I come from a long line of women who marry well and keep their mouths shut, accepting the benefits and the drawbacks, whichever way the chips fall. My mother refers to the custom, as, 'making your bed and lying in it.'"

From the corner of her eye, she saw Hugh nod. Her spine went ramrod stiff. She spoke around her heart pounding in her throat. "I don't really see a need to do that in this day and time."

"As opposed to what?" Hugh crossed his legs and his arms.

"This is *my* summary," she said quietly.

"As opposed to what, Carolyna?" Dr. Ballentine invited.

"To taking care of myself," she said without hesitation, even though plagued by Geneva's recent threat of disinheritance. "Women didn't always have that option. I do. I can support myself.

Vote. Purchase property. Hugh doesn't want children. On my own, I can have a love affair with a sperm bank and have a baby to raise with my own principles—not compromise mine for someone else's. I'm free. I propose to stay that way unless someone can prove to me the benefits of a different arrangement."

"Son of a bitch." Hugh rose noisily and paced to the far wall, studied a badly framed Currier and Ives print. He addressed the art. "Since when? When we got engaged, you wanted a traditional, conventional, conformity-laden, establishment-sanctioned marriage—a direct quote." His struggle for control surfaced in his tone, the rigid set of his shoulders. "At what point did you change your mind?"

"When I realized I was engaged to a control freak." He turned and glared at her, and she said, "Couples with traditional views don't tend to divorce, Hugh, and just coming through a hell of a divorce I was definitely interested in that possibility. But since then I've realized traditionalism—in marriage or otherwise—doesn't guarantee happiness. I don't think I'm cut from a subservient mold. In fact, I know I'm not."

"No one is asking you—"

"No?" She laughed, too bitterly. "Good sex when *you* deem the conditions are perfect? Size six black dresses on my five foot nine frame—God forbid I should ever show an ounce of flesh. Work where you tell me, for whomever you deem suitable? I tend to conform and then pout, Hugh."

She folded her arms, hugged her waist. "Where is this all leading? We'll occupy the same house, share rooms, breathe the same stilted air, have periodic sex, but live the lives of quiet desperation that Thoreau wrote about? I don't think so. I won't settle for that. There *is* more." She'd had a taste and now hungered.

"You read too much, Cally," he murmured, his bluster gone. He appeared to sink into himself. "This is real life."

Into the ensuing quiet Dr. Ballentine said, "Hugh's turn. Would you like to give us your summary?"

Hugh jammed his hands in his pockets and plopped into a stiff, garnet-colored leather chair. "I want a marriage that's a cut above the atrocity of my first. Cally could be everything I need if she'd

110

relinquish that streak of rebellion and would just do what I ask of her." He fell silent as though examining his declaration, then said, "I'm older and more experienced. I can steer us around the pitfalls."

"I want to experience my own pitfalls." She slipped into the chair, next to him. "I want acceptance, not judgment."

A Grecian mantle clock ticked, inordinately loud, suddenly.

"My turn." The doctor closed the file. "What we have here is an impasse. It's not unusual. In fact, it's common and plays a very big part in the traditionalist relationships Carolyna pinpointed, those where people suffer in silence." He leaned back, rocked placidly in his high-backed chair. "In a normal intimate relationship there's an unspoken exchange which goes like this: I'll give you what you want if you'll give me what I want. But if I feel you're not meeting my needs, I may respond in kind by refusing to meet your needs and withholding what I know you want from me." He paused and then asked, "Does this hit a nerve with either of you?"

In the laden silence he continued, "Unfortunately there are no winners in this battle, but there is a way out of the trap. It's doing what we are so resistant to do: Giving the other person what they most want. From where I sit it would appear, Hugh, that you need to give Carolyna enough freedom to cause her to nestle in your offered protection. That's an opportunity for the two of you to break into a brand-new level of intimacy." He rocked forward, his forearms planted on the desk. "Practice that and we'll talk next week."

He looked at his watch, a signal that the session was over.

Standing beside the Volvo station wagon in the shade of a big cedar, Hugh drew Cally into his arms. "You're gaining weight." When she stiffened involuntarily, he said quickly. "It feels good."

She relaxed a little, and he murmured intimately against her ear, "Don't go back to Savannah."

"I have no choice, Hugh." She straightened in his arms, met his gaze. "I no longer live on the island."

"Come home with me. Katharine is still in Chicago and—"

111

"And you wouldn't ask me if she were here." She stepped back, fished for her keys. "She's twelve years old. Children are wise now. If we had married, she would have been a part of our lives. Would you have hidden me from her, or the fact that we had sex?"

The frown line in his brow deepened to a furrow. "You're talking in past tense, Carolyna. Are you aware of that? Is that the way it is? You've decided?"

"No." She unlocked the car door, lowered her body into the stifling interior. "But if you persist in trying to control me, Hugh, you've decided." She pulled the door closed, lowered the window. "I'm glad you came today, but I have to go. I'll see you next week."

⚜

She found Lucinda on the club driving range, flailing away at a trail of assembled white balls. She squared her slender shoulders and wiggled her rear methodically before each swing.

Memory rushed over Cally with hurricane force.

"Keep your chin on the ball and your right elbow in," she called quietly as she approached from the rear.

Lucinda whirled, her eyes wary. "Hey."

"Hey." Cally took her in her arms and held her. "Welcome home. You look—" Lucinda appeared a bit rag-tag. "Familial." Cally's lips dragged on her smile.

"Thanks. I guess." Lucinda leaned on the golf club. "I suppose Mother called you. I guess you heard she's having a command performance dinner on Sunday to welcome me home."

"Loud and clear. I'll be there."

Lucinda's glance darted to the opposite end of the range where Turner was involved in a lesson. "Are you mad at me?"

"About Turner?" Cally's glance followed, then returned to her sister's anxious face. "That's over, Lucy." She sank to the thick grass, tucked her legs in, acknowledging inner turmoil, mockery in the verdant serenity. "I am concerned, though."

She caught Lucinda's hand, urged her down next to her. "There's an end to imitation being the sincerest form of flattery. I went through hell with Turner Cole. Are you just going to wade blindly

112

in behind me?"

Lucinda smiled placidly. "Don't you remember how I used to go through those care packages Mother gave the maids—"

"And take out my discards and wear them, even though you could have anything new you wanted."

"I wanted the world to see it looked better on me."

Cally laughed, that particular puzzle solved at last. "Mother is going to get him fired. I begged the number from Mikela and finally reached her. I talked like hell, but she's unrelenting."

Lucinda shrugged. "We don't care. Turner's hand is better. He's ready to go back on tour. He wants me to go with him."

"You and the money." Their eyes locked.

"Don't you think he could like me for me, Cally?"

"That's what I thought about me. I'm smarter now."

"He loved you." Determination filled Lucinda's eyes. "He'll love me, too."

"Physically, yes. He'll love you ragged, Lucy. But he'll blow the money anyway. Then you'll feel like a fool and be out, grinding away for the rest of your life, like me. I made the mistake. You don't have to."

"I like making my own mistakes."

Cally rolled her eyes, grimaced.

"What?" Lucinda grinned. "What, Cally?"

"We're definitely cut from the same mold. Just promise me you'll think before going on tour. You'll hate it, but it's like drugs. It's hard to break away once you're out there."

"Are you saying you hated it?"

Cally nodded, remembering. "After a while, I did."

"Well, as I said . . . I want to find out for myself." Lucinda fell momentarily quiet. "I'd go anywhere with Turner."

With the aim of an automaton, Cally's head turned. Turner's graceful form headed toward them. He stopped to swing a club, following through, watching the imaginary ball soar, roll, drop into the hole. He took off his visor, preened for the crowd.

Cally got to her feet.

"Don't tell me you didn't feel the same way about him." Lucinda gazed up, squinting in the sun. Her dark eyes and hair were

Geneva's, her face, their father's. "I won't believe you."

"Then I won't bother to tell you," Cally said resignedly. Leaning downward, she kissed the top of her sister's head. "Take care, Lucy. Just don't get pregnant."

"I won't," she promised. "I'll let you lead the way."

Turner, driving the senator's golf cart, intercepted Cally in the parking lot. "Hey, babe."

He got out of the cart, ruffled her hair, and his smile rippled brilliantly in his tanned face. "I like the feel of that. You're gorgeous."

She stepped out of reach, not out of range. "Turner, go easy with Lucy."

"I wanted *you*." His eyes bored into hers. "You know that, don't you?"

"Between events, as I recall. Please don't do that to her."

"There's one way to make sure of that." He arched one auburn brow. "Say the word and we're out of here. You and me. What God joined together, let no man—"

"Go to hell. Just don't take my sister with you."

"That's a done deal, babe." His drawl mocked. "Unless you change your mind."

"I'm broke," she reminded him.

He shrugged. "Remember what I told you on the number five tee that morning all those years ago. It's not the money with you, babe. It's love."

She did not want to remember. "Don't take Lucinda on the tour. She's too vulnerable."

"Hey! That's up to you and Geneva. You're calling the shots."

Lucinda joined him in the parking lot as Cally drove away. When she saw Turner's arm go around her sister's waist, she scrambled for the number Mikela had given her and dialed Geneva's hotel again, prepared to beg her not to have Turner fired. Or to bargain, should Geneva so desire.

Chapter 14

*J*amaica Jam failed to meet Cally's standards but was a cut above her apprehensive imaginings. To any Savannahnians who held an affinity for Saturday night fare, the night club straddled the fence between respectable and disreputable. A jaunty black valet who greeted Cally at the curb lent an air festive enough to offset the darkened side-alley and ramshackle storefronts across the dim and narrow street.

She stood for a moment watching the direction of her departing car as two more parties, white and attractively groomed, arrived. They alighted at the curb and abandoned their cars confidently, motors running. A black couple approached on foot, arm-in-arm, out of the dark alley. Neon lights proclaimed REGGAE LIVE TONIGHT, painting the skin on Cally's bare arms and hands pink, blue, then green in turn.

Music beckoned from inside. The metal building pulsated with life. After observing her keys hung on a nearby pegboard, Cally entered a narrow door banked by two matched and discernibly fake palm trees.

Inside, she let her eyes adjust to the darkness. The room, while not large, accommodated a multitude of bodies. She was struck by an illusory line dividing the crowd into sections of blacks and whites. No "gray" area existed. Glowing cigarette tips penetrated a curtain of smoke as dense as morning fog. Spandex leggings, moiré crop tops, dangling earrings, and no tables for one, showed her that she was odd one out.

She made her way around the back of the room, hoisted onto a stool at the crowded bar, ordered a rum special advertised on a hand-lettered sign, then turned to observe the raised bandstand. Her eyes immediately sought out Paul Michael.

Cloaked in a striped knee-length tunic, he appeared more African than Jamaican. She reminded herself Africa was his origin. The garment hung straight from his shoulders, a waist-deep slit exposing the gold locket nestled against the tightly curled hair on his chest. The trinket caught the stage light with his every movement. He wore jeans, faded to sky-blue and ending in frayed bottoms just above his sandaled feet. His hair, newly braided and adorned with tiny gold bands, also new, appeared shorter, glowing like warm copper.

Cally forced her eyes away, seeking her drink, but almost immediately watched him again.

Paul Michael played the steel drums expertly, from what her limited knowledge allowed her to judge. He stood at the rear of the group of six, a faint smile on his classic face, his blue eyes fixed. His rangy body moved in a rhythm joined to and yet apart from the collective music of the group. Halfway through her drink, she knew that her hunch had been good. The Jamaica Jammers played songs apparently cloned from the idolized and idealized Bob Marley. They were wonderful. She had the perfect entertainment for Jessica's party.

When a final song before an announced break began, she placed money on the bar and slipped from the stool. She paused at the edge of the room for one last look and felt the hot, moist pressure of a hand on her arm. Wheeling, she stared into Ebony's dusky and somber face.

"Ebony . . . I didn't know you were here."

"I believe that. What *you* doin' here girl?" Her tone was accusatory.

"I came to see Paul Michael—to hear him play." Cally tried to pull her arm away. Ebony's hand clamped shut, circling her wrist. "The same as you."

Ebony scoffed. "Not the same as me. I got a right here. He done got him a day job, workin' for you. Nuthin' else. What you doin' sniffin round him at night?"

"Paul Michael and I are friends." Senseless guilt nagged when Ebony sneered, her eyes challenging. "I've hired the band to play for a party. I wanted to hear—"

"Well ain't that the honky way? You done got your cart before your horse, I'd say. If you hired him, it's too late to test him out. You bought yoself a party—good or bad."

Cally saw the logic and the futility of argument. "Of course you're right." She smiled, tried to free herself again. "I'm going. Please tell him—"

"You ain't goin' yet. We ain't finished." Positioning her stout body between Cally and the narrow entry, Ebony raised her voice. "You got a lesson to learn."

Heads swiveled. Audible above the music, chairs scraped the wooden floor. Helpless, Cally glanced toward the stage. Blinded by the stage lights, Paul Michael and other members of the band peered narrow-eyed into the crowd. Cally attempted to step around Ebony, but the girl's strong hands caught her forearms, pushed her back.

"Don't do that," Cally said softly, cheeks flaming.

Ebony shoved harder. Cally's thigh collided with a table. It skidded, a chair teetered backward, rattled on the floor. People stood, gawked, interest in the stage dead.

"What you got there?" Ebony's hand shot up, roughing up Cally's curls. "You got you a 'fro, girl? You think P.M. gonna like that?"

Cally raised her forearm, struck her, knocking her away. Quicker than breath, Ebony's hand shot out again, raked Cally's cheek. Fire bolted from her hairline to her chin.

The music stopped, instruments clattering on the stage. Dead quiet fell over the room. Cally heard running footsteps, the slap of sandals against the wooden floor. Just as Paul Michael reached them, she grabbed Ebony's shoulders and, with all her might, turned her, shoved her into his reaching arms. Paul Michael's and Ebony's bodies collided, staggered, fell against a nearby table. Glass crashed, shattered, dispersing the curious nearby.

Cally ran from the building, grabbed her keys from the crude valet board, and raced along the narrow dark street until she spotted the Volvo. She drove off, her last sight in the rear view mirror of Paul Michael running behind the car, sandals in his hand, the tunic flying. Even through the raised window, above the car engine, she heard his shout, commanding her to stop.

She drove with no aim, no destiny, like a ship without a compass, adrift in a squall of emotion. She brushed at tears of humiliation and cringed at the raw fire burning on her cheek. Memory of Ebony's contempt brought a shudder. Cally had invited her wrath by ignoring the girl's link to Paul Michael. No more immune than Cally to his foreignness, his exotic nature, Ebony had sensed a threat. Recalling her own feelings at seeing Paul Michael on stage, the distinctive erotic stirring, Cally embraced Ebony's reasoning. But for Ebony, there was a hint of a future with Paul Michael—a possibility that did not exist for Cally.

She relived the image of Paul Michael's desperate look when she'd shoved Ebony at him, of him chasing the car, his shout. Giving in to hopelessness, she considered how easy it would be to head the car toward the island. How right it would feel to pull in the drive at Sinclair Cottage, or even to park by the honeysuckle hedge in Hugh's back drive. He would welcome her, but the welcome wouldn't last. Scrutiny would follow. She squelched that image, too, continuing to drive aimlessly.

Recognizing the fringe of a familiar neighborhood, she turned down Derene Street for a few blocks and then onto Reynolds toward the aging Colonial home of her childhood, no longer a part of the Sinclair estate.

Pulling to the curb before the house, she doused her lights and left the engine running. This community had not fared as well as Lafayette Square, where her parents lived now. The houses suffered neglect, the lawns lay unkept. Her eyes sought the front corner window of the room Lucinda and she had shared, then shifted to the opposite corner, to her parents' old room.

The years in the house had been settled, secure, until James Wainwright Sinclair embraced a political career. Geneva had endorsed his ambitions by leaving her adolescent daughters in the care of nannies to join him on the campaign trail. It was not a period Cally liked to recall. But she could remember, with great clarity, the advent of politics in her life. Her parents' absence created an uneasiness, a vague sense of deprivation that nothing, to this day, had put to rest. But when Geneva and the senator were home, stress caused once-mundane disagreements to explode into shabby hostility, resentment, and blame.

Once the senator was elected, Geneva had refused to move to Washington, citing the change of schools as her reason, but then purchased the cottage on the island, changed her daughters' schools after all, and began a new round of frequent and famous parties. Only the senator was missing from the picture.

And since Geneva had attended an exclusive private school, she followed suit and sent Lucinda and Cally away to school, limiting their family time to once-a-month weekends at home. Their brother, Jim, was installed in the prestigious Georgia Military Academy. Like a child of divorce, Cally considered her exile a retribution for not measuring up to her parents' desires. By running away repeatedly, she managed to raise enough hell to get Geneva's attention, sometimes enough even to get the senator home from Washington. The pattern had held through Turner Cole, whom she'd used to further demonstrate her contrived rebellion.

Giving the old house one last, long look, Cally started the Volvo and headed for Columbia Square, the comfort of the Renfro house.

Paul Michael's van was parked in front of the house. Her car lights illuminated his form when she turned into the side drive. As she got out of the car, he rose from the front steps, met her on the walk leading to the porch. A forgotten light spilled out of the undraped dining room, caught his bare feet and a tee shirt that replaced the tunic.

He reached out. She stopped cold.

"Don't touch me." She stepped back.

He advanced slowly.

"Stay there, Paul Michael."

The light revealed his troubled face. "You are blaming me, girl? For what Ebony did?"

She dug fiercely in her bag, produced a folded bill of lading and made a show of thrusting it at him. "The neighbors. You can bet they heard the van, and they're watching us now." She forced the paper into his hand. "There's no reason for you to be here—"

He waved the paper. "Not this reason. That is for sure."

"Pretend! For God's sake, just pretend." Hovering tears began to roll. "People are vicious!"

"Cally, girl . . . ." His soft inflection caressed her name. "Whom do we fool with this piece of paper in the middle of the night?"

She turned her back to the street, just enough to surreptitiously cover her face with her hands. Her shoulders shook uncontrollably.

"Come inside, baby girl. Let me wash your face." When she shook off his touch, he whispered, "I will show you how sorry I am for what Ebony did."

She shook her head.

"Then come sit on the steps," he coaxed.

She gauged the soft porch light. "No. They'll see us. They'll call Jessica and tell her I'm carrying on in her house. She'll be angry— I can't move out of here now." Near hysteria assailed her, deepened his frown. "I have no place to go."

Expelling a breath, he planted his feet and folded his arms, the paper dangling from the tips of his long fingers. "Go inside and wash your face. I will wait here."

"No. You have to leave." She wanted so badly to be held.

"Nothing between here and Hades can make me do that, girl."

"Leave and call me." At least she could talk to him then.

He measured her silently. "I will take the van around the corner. If they heard it come, they will hear it leave. Go inside. Turn off these lights. I will walk back, and we will talk. It is my best offer, Carolyna Sinclair."

Striding to the van, he made an issue of folding the paper, cramming it in his jeans.

She went inside and doused the lights. The noise of the van engine accompanied her to the guest room shower, where she scrubbed away the reminders of her encounter with Ebony. As she slipped into a robe, ran a comb through her wet, kinky hair, applied ointment to her raw cheek, she avoided meeting her eyes in the mirror. She did not want to see what must be clearly visible there.

Paul Michael was waiting on the porch steps again. As she slipped through the door, he held out his hand, drew her to sit two steps below him, then snuggled her between his long legs. And, at last, she found the comfort she craved.

"Pretty, pretty Cally," he crooned gently, one finger tilting her face, examining her in the dark. He pressed his lips just above the scratch, whispering, "Bad Ebony." One of his large warm hands gently stroked her hair, the other, her throat.

"I shouldn't have gone there alone," she said finally. "But, I wanted to see, to satisfy my curiosity. I never considered—I didn't know she would be angry. Mercy! Fighting is so cheap. Brawling like two cats." She quaked, repulsed.

"Ebony has feelings. She is vulnerable. She wants to look big-time tough, but inside she can hurt. She knows the feeling between you and me and would have it for herself."

"Then she wants what I can't even identify."

"Peace, Cally. Caring."

She waited for him to say the word she wanted to say, but could not. When he didn't, she was disappointed. And relieved.

"Ebony hates me."

"She does. She is afraid. She has reason to be."

She lifted her head to search his face in the moonlight. "You sleep with her."

His hand stilled at her throat.

"Of course you do. Why wouldn't you?"

"No. I haven't and I will not. I want only to be her friend, to help her. It is Ebony who wants more." He kissed her brow, pressed her face against his chest, murmured against the top of her head, "I am not every man you know, girl. I am choosey with whom I make love."

He moved down a step, drawing her closer. One hand slipped inside the collar of her robe, down her back, caressed her waist, moved up her rib cage, his fingertips brushing her breast.

She felt his heart race beneath the thin cotton shirt, heard his breath deepen, the rhythm ragged. His erection formed against her midriff and his desire seeped from his body into hers. She felt like sobbing again, longed to stretch out, heathen-like, on the new lawn, lie with him, take his strength and comfort into her, finding absolution and creating havoc.

Pushing his hand away, she wrapped the robe across her chest. "You should go."

He released his breath slowly. "You are sure, Cally?"

She had never been less sure, or acted more opposite her feelings. "Yes."

She rose, stepped backward, urged him to follow. At the hedge that separated the Renfro yard from the neighbors, she paused and eased them into the shadows. Mosquitos buzzed around them. He slapped his arm. She did the same.

"I want you to know I'm not sleeping with Hugh. I haven't since you and I . . . were together."

"What does that mean, baby girl? To you and to me?"

"I don't know, exactly. I only know it's significant."

"*I* know." She heard the smile in his voice. "It is big-time significant and I am big-time happy."

She began to quake, and he drew her into the shelter of his arms. "What is it, Cally?"

She waited until she trusted her voice not to reveal her thoughts. Indecision regarding Hugh was being annihilated by no more than Paul Michael's gentleness and concern. She had never known she craved sensitivity so avidly until she witnessed it.

"I'm sorry," she whispered. "I can take anything but tenderness." Torn, she asked, "When will I see you again?"

"When you close your eyes, I will meet you there."

She caught his hand, touched his fingers to her closed eyes.

He laughed softly. "Tomorrow is Sunday. No work. It will rain. You will come to my house and see how beautiful the rain is there. I will feed you. I will make up for Ebony. I will make you happy. Will you come?"

"I . . . can't."

"I will braid your hair." He paused. "I will give you a bath. I will make love to you." When she laughed nervously, he inflected humor in his voice. "I will do anything to make you happy. Will you come?"

She looked away, across the square, her eyes straining through the moss-laden trees, into the trouble-laden future. "We said we'd be just friends."

"I want to be your friend and your lover, Cally. I will be there. I will wait for you."

⁂

From the guest room bed, her eyes traced an illusory path through the mural on the opposite wall, made visible by the waning moonlight. A call she'd had from Olivia Steinberg earlier in the day filtered through her mind.

"I spoke with Valerie, dear," Olivia had announced.

"Valerie? I'm afraid I don't—"

"Valerie Michelson. My friend who collects dolls."

"The dolls . . . yes." Suddenly she remembered a photograph in the Steinberg's island house that first night. The date, 1967, the place, Jamaica, had tweaked her interest. Three couples, mixed races and cultures, friends from a past diplomatic assignment. One of the women had been named Valerie, her husband, Stan, "dead for years," Olivia had explained. "You've spoken with her?"

"She's going away for a few days but would be glad to show you the dolls when she returns."

"That's very nice of you. Did she have a Jumeau?"

A small silence ensued. "I forgot to ask."

"It doesn't matter. I'm sure there will be something wonderful. Thank you so much, Olivia."

Cally had gone to a doll shop a few days before, seen a Jumeau, held it. Not for sale, it was available to covet only. Its thick almond-shaped blue eyes were mesmerizing. Tiny pink hands were so perfectly wrought, Cally imagined them capable of grasping. The face, the expression, intrigued her: curious, innocent and introspective. One finely painted brow slightly different from the other, rendered the doll even more realistic.

Paul Michael's words had repeated in Cally's head, caressed her again. "You are a Jumeau doll." She had been tempted to beg the shop owner for the doll.

Now, lying in the dark, the effect of Ebony's venom, the cheapness of the episode, shamed her still. She longed for the pure and simple beauty of the doll, envisioning her as a bit of order in chaos. She turned away from the mural and closed her eyes. A gentle rain began to fall and fulfill a part of Paul Michael's promise of tomorrow, a promise she coveted, yet of which she feared the consequences.

Chapter 15

$\mathcal{P}$ierre Parrot announced Cally when she arrived early the next morning. "Awk! Pretty Cah-lee. Pretty, pretty Cah-lee."

She had hoped to catch Paul Michael sleeping, but he was awake, with coffee made. Expectant.

She smiled. "Pierre's dialogue has improved."

"We have worked hard on it, girl. No rest for the weary."

"Some say, 'for the wicked.'"

"But who can say who is wicked?" Paul Michael kissed her warmly but with reserve. Then, without comment, he pressed his lips to the scabbed-over scratch on her cheek.

"I have Blue Mountain Coffee," he announced. "Much sugar and much cream." At the makeshift counter, he slathered a croissant with butter and jam and passed it to her on a paper napkin. "Eat, pretty Cally. Give me the pleasure of watching."

She ate, hunger and anticipation tangling her mind, then rinsed her hands at the sink and turned back to face him. He handed her a watering can, his smile and eyes mischievous.

"We will start here, girl." He took her hand, approached a flourishing fern near the window. Current ran from his fingers to hers.

"What about my braids?"

"Good things—"

"Are worth waiting for. Where did you learn all your American proverbs?"

He raised his brows. "An inheritance, maybe?"

She thought of his mysterious mother, then remembered Ebony and wished she hadn't asked.

They watered plants—some, not all—in deference to a varied weekly schedule he outlined verbally as they toiled. While trusting her to sprinkle food atop the watery habitat of Diana and Major

James Hewitt, Paul Michael dished out food for Ziggy Marley. Then he placed berries and minced vegetables in a metal bowl attached to Pierre's perch.

Chores done, he wordlessly positioned Cally before the sink mirror on a low stool placed atop the purple chair. After training two whirring fans on her, he began to braid her hair, his hands working rhythmically.

Pierre Parrot continued to go wild, his repetitive dogma piercing the backdrop of gentle midmorning rain. "Cah-lee! Cah-lee! Awk!"

Paul Michael smiled apologetically. "That bird is big-time happy. Like me, pretty girl. But he will take a nap soon."

Their eyes locked in the cloudy and cracked mirror and her lips formed a smile. She sipped coffee, her hands working Ziggy Marley's tiger pelt as Paul Michael's slender fingers moved with graceful purpose in her hair. Braiding. Sectioning. Braiding. Within two hours, nearly half her locks hung in intricate plaited splendor.

Periodically, his fingertips stole along the side of her neck, a move that set his blue eyes to gleam beautifully and caused her spine, the hairs on her arms, to tingle responsively. The caresses progressed to the hollow of her throat, set her pulse to pound, and his eyes to darken.

With half a head to go, his gentle forays lowered. His fingers dipped inside the loose neck of her cotton dress, running across the swell of her breasts, his eyes imparting a message that tapped her groin and her yearning.

His fingers slowed from braiding, then stopped. Watching her in the glass, he unfastened the buttons on her dress down to the waist, then loosened the front hook of her bra. Cupping her breasts, he leaned to press his mouth to the top of her head.

"Pretty, pretty Cally," he murmured. His thumb and forefinger kneaded her nipples. "Sweet. So firm. So warm."

Her cheeks flamed as she thought of the returned wedding dress, Hugh's complaints about her small bust and prominent chest bones. A worn cliché wafted through her head. *Beauty lies in the eye of the beholder.* She swiveled on her perch to look up at him, smile encouragingly.

He knelt before her, and Ziggy Marley stiffened, bolted from her lap. Palms at her temples, Paul Michael drew her face to his. His mouth sucked hers gently, drew her in, released her. Lowering his face, he kissed her breasts, bathed her nipples with his tongue. She arched invitingly, but, surprising her, he bounded back to his position behind her, retrieved a half completed braid and smiled into the mirror.

She laughed, the sound ragged. "There's more to braiding hair than one might suspect."

"Oh, yeah, girl. So much more."

She willed herself to be patient, to enjoy. "And it takes a long time."

"Yeah, girl. It takes hours. Good things—"

"Are worth waiting for." Her anticipation rippled, flowed.

"This time, good things come to those who wait." He smiled, a masterpiece of foreshadowing. "You will see."

When one tiny section of hair remained, he stopped again and kissed her. Her whimper evoked his pleased laugh and seemed to propel him to the huge porcelain bathtub where he opened the corroded brass spigot. Water trickled weakly, but steam was clearly visible.

Paul Michael moved to a hidden switch beneath the floor mattress and turned on the collection of electric fans. In their wake, the edge of a sheet flapped gently. He returned, braiding quickly, with evident purpose now, as the sound of the filling tub blended with continuing rain.

With the last silver band fastened to the last braid, he surveyed her image, his eyes glinting in satisfaction. He helped her down from the chair to work the dress off her shoulders, strip the bra away, dropping it on the floor. When he held her, the rough-soldered locket was cool, bulky and hard, sealed in the warmth of their melding skin.

"Bath time," he whispered, the tip of his tongue bathing her ear.

Anxiety akin to that of losing her virginity all those years ago, ran through her as he guided her to jars of dried herbs lining the window sill. "Choose the ones you want, Cally. For your bath. It is a Jamaican ritual."

She shook her head, unaccustomed to the feel of the braids

jangling softly. "I don't know which ones. You choose."

He turned her hands palm up, placed them together to form a receptacle, before opening one jar, then another. He filled her cupped palms, then helped her transfer the treasure to a small cloth pouch with a drawstring. He broke off sprigs of fresh herbs from the plants in the window, then led her to the tub, dropped in the sprigs. She moved instinctively, releasing the sealed pouch beneath the spigot. It swirled wildly before the deepening pool sucked it under.

"In Jamaica, when a young girl is to marry or to become the mistress of an influential man, she is turned over to the old women for . . . preparation."

His eyes deepened to oily blue, reflecting desire that made her quake. He unbuttoned the skirt of her dress. "For days the young girls are told of the mysteries of love."

The dress fell around her ankles. She moved against him, circled his waist, her face turned up. Waiting. His hands massaged the small of her back, pressed her against his hardening arousal. Yet again, he began to speak.

"These girls are told women have the happiest duty of any creature on earth and they must perform it well. Their one purpose is to bring love and comfort to man. They are told that is all men want from women. Love and softness and peace."

Protest formed, but before she could speak, he said, "I believe, Carolyna Sinclair, you and I were put on this earth to bring love and softness and peace to one another."

She smiled, soothed, relieved, assured.

He eased her panties down, his eyes resting briefly on the long, jagged scar on her inner thigh. He kissed her navel, buried his face at the juncture of her thighs, causing her to sway, cling to him, before he rose and turned off the water. Ziggy Marley brushed her bare legs, trailed to Paul Michael. Rain curtained the windows.

Paul Michael scooped her up, stood her in the deep tub. The near scorching water swirled about her legs. His hands on her shoulders eased her down to her knees. The water was white hot, searing, then the pain eased.

"Get in with me." Her voice sounded foreign, without strength, almost plaintive.

He knelt beside the tub, cupped his hand and dribbled water over her shoulder. "It is not tradition, baby girl."

Tradition. The word ricocheted, echoed. She pushed it away, sank against the high back of the tub, his hand pillowing her head. Her skin felt scorched yet soothed.

His voice was scarcely above a whisper. "The girl is given a bath of hot herbs. A balm bath. Only the old women know the secret of which herbs to use to steep a virgin for marriage and remove everything mental, spiritual, and physical that could work against happy mating. When the virgin leaves the bath—"

"Paul Michael—"

"Quiet, Cally." He cupped a breast, then the other, moved his hand over her body beneath the water, between her thighs, then down her knee to her ankle. He retraced his path.

Hot vapors saturated her face, ran down in tear-like droplets, melded into the water that swirled around her throat. Lethargy arrested her body, but not her ability to reason.

"I'm no virgin," she protested softly. "This bath—"

"In my heart you are a virgin, Cally. More beautiful and pure than you know. Today—not that night in Jessica Renfro's house—you are my bride."

His words filling her heart and mind, she closed her eyes, lay submerged, basking in the purifying water.

"Come, Cally."

The gurgling drain shattered the quiet, brought her face around, her eyes back to his. He rose, helped her to her feet, but not from the tub. Satisfied to take his lead, she stood in the faint undertow as the water rushed toward the drain, flushing away any maladies she might have possessed.

Paul Michael turned on the shower, adjusting the stream away from her precious braids, then stripped off his jogging shorts. His desire pulsated without restraint. When he joined her in the tub, drawing her against him, her breath caught, her groin coiled, released, flowed wet and anxious.

He soaped her, worked the slick lather over her body, his hands gliding in evident joy. She took the soap, holding his eyes with hers, running her hands over his body now, issuing an invitation he could not decline. He turned their bodies in a circle beneath the cleansing water, then silenced the flow.

Moving down her wet body, he suckled her breasts, explored the hard plane of her diaphragm, his tongue caressing the indentation of her navel. Her hands stole to his face, fingertips seeking his mouth, attesting his tenderness. He sank to his knees, buried his face in her soft mound, nuzzled the hollows of her thighs, his mouth warm, moist.

She moaned, closed her eyes, drew him in. His hands grasped her buttocks, sealing her to him tightly. He tasted her, his tongue unhurriedly exploring her hot, wet cleavage. She swayed, and he lifted his face, eyes dark and cloudy with desire.

"So sweet. Taste you, Cally. So good."

He helped her from the tub, drew her to the mattress, lowered her. The fans whirled, reached out to possess her, their cool fingers racing along her wet skin, creating a sensation she had imagined and craved. She was faint yet empowered by longing. His skin, silky like hot oil, glided beneath her hands. Just as she remembered, his body was granite hard, sinew and muscle, yet it fitted pliantly within the undulations of her own. He was big, gorged, as she had dreaded, coveted. Her want coursed upward, wet and grasping. She whimpered, knees raised, feet planted, lifting to meet him, to accommodate him.

She looped her legs around his back, locking him in. His satisfaction rushed up in a soft moan, and she met his anxious gaze with a smile as the tide pulled her under, plunged her into the drowning pool. She convulsed spasmodically, then shuddered, quieted, restored and sated.

Tears rushed, spilled over as though she'd walked into a sudden and fierce wind, not sadness, but a cleansing that emptied her soul of yearning. She hadn't let herself cry out. Her jubilation was inside, whole, beautiful and complete.

She read agreement in his eyes. His powerful body concentrated its strength, one last thrust into his own spasm. Abandonment moved in waves across his face. He lowered his head, pressed his mouth into her neck and murmured her name as she stroked his back.

He didn't withdraw as he had that night at Jessica's. Rather, he kissed her mouth, her breasts, her mouth again and again, remaining inside her, sustaining oneness, thrusting gently, lying still, thrusting again. Eventually, he eased them onto their sides and allowed gradual withdrawal.

His hand stole to the scar on her inner thigh, his fingers caressing, soothing.

"When I was a little girl," she whispered into his ear, "I climbed a barbed wire fence in search of stolen delight . . . an apple. Big and golden." Then, as now, she had rebelled against logic, against the knowledge that some things were not meant to be attained. Rebellion had scarred her for life.

He whispered, "If I had been there . . . ."

"I know." She smiled, ran a fingertip around his full lips, explored the miniscule gap between his upper teeth. "You would have reached it for me."

"I love you, Carolyna Sinclair."

She wondered if he felt her heart lurch.

"I must not love you, baby girl. I don't want to—"

She pressed her finger to his mouth. "I don't want you to."

He moved his head. "I *do*, girl." His smile contained little mirth. He raised on his elbow, stared down at her. "I loved you the first day I saw you on that dock. You tried to look so tough, baby sister. A little girl, playing dress up with a fancy briefcase. You had a fancy card with your name spelled all wrong." Dipping his head he kissed her, swallowed her rebuttal. "Later . . . when I knew you and saw how hard you work, how hard you try . . . I wanted to help you. I wanted to take care of you."

"I felt it. You stole my heart, Paul Michael."

"I wanted to make love to you, girl, that very first day."

She had always known, without full comprehension. She wondered, now, how earnest her endeavor had been to turn his desire, and hers, into the friendship she touted so adamantly. Her brief success had met with complications that night in Jessica's barren guest room, and vanished today.

"I will go back to Jamaica to stay. You know, girl?"

She nodded. Her throat clogged, pained, when he voiced her

130

nearly constant thought. Turning on her back, she fixed her eyes on Ziggy Marley sitting beneath Pierre's perch. The tiger tail swished an anxious rhythm as he gazed at the bird longingly. Cally pulled herself up. Paul Michael's brown hand came to rest on her naked thigh, casting her into turmoil.

"It hurts, Cally, to know I will leave you."

"It hurts me."

"But that is better?" One perfect brow arched. "Is this what I feel you thinking, baby girl?"

She shook her head, still surprised by the jangle. She swallowed. "I don't think it's better, Paul Michael. But, I know it is. I'm trying not to think about it at all. I want all we can have, now. I want you to want that, too. Maybe you could—" She clamped her lips against mentioning the visa extension again.

"There is no maybe in this world, girl." He lowered her gently, moved to cover her. "We choose our own destinies."

❧

She showered again while he went down to the station wagon and returned with the change of clothing she'd brought. He watched as she applied makeup at his murky sink mirror and attempted to regale him with her predictions of the dinner scheduled at Geneva's that night. Her brother, Jim, would be there from Ashville, with his family, responding to Geneva's commanded homage to Lucinda's return. Cally laughed, painting pomp and circumstance, past sibling feuds, the pitiable relationship between Geneva and the senator.

She failed to bring the light back to his sapphire eyes.

"Will Hugh Wilson Masters be there, girl?"

"I'm very much afraid he will be."

Paul Michael folded his muscular arms across his chest, his chin rising slightly, a muscle pumping in the side of his face.

"It doesn't matter, Paul Michael. There's nothing left between Hugh and me." Replacing her cosmetics in the silk case, she studied her reflection, the braids. She turned to him. "Especially after today. You may have marked me for life."

"And when I go home, girl, will that mark go with me, then?"

131

She moved into his arms. "I'm very much afraid it won't."

⚜

Cally considered the situation as she drove the few blocks from Paul Michael's ramshackle house to her parent's town house in Lafayette Square.

In the beginning, sharing with him had been like pouring leftover coffee into an open drain. He had been receptive, in a wide-eyed, soft-smile kind of way, to the splash and gurgle of her revealing the nuances of her life, her work and aspirations. He absorbed her offerings willingly, eagerly. He never asked uncomfortable questions and almost never reminded her of things she'd said, never used them to persuade or influence her. He had been the essence of acceptance and empathy.

"The Evangelical Free Church came to the island when I was thirteen," he had told her. "I learned, girl, that I am only responsible for myself. Not to pass judgment. The only perfect man ever to walk the earth was Jesus. To try to be perfect or expect it from anyone else is a big-time waste of energy."

His philosophy had, both, exhilarated and soothed her.

Mostly, he had responded to her by sharing his aspirations and views, nuances of his own life in Jamaica, colorful stories that passed the hours of enjoyable drudgery in Jessica's house.

Having sex with him that first time had altered the innocence of their relationship. Making love with him today, on his terms, his profession of love, would alter the original relationship beyond restoration. Making love with him, hearing him say he loved her, enriched her life. Their coupling, powerful, spiritual in quality, touched her beyond anything she had known. His sensitivity was heady, addictive. But it was not enough to build a lifetime relationship on, if even the remote possibility of permanence in their union existed.

And it didn't. He would go; she would grieve, as she grieved now. This wasn't new knowledge. He had loved her from the first fated moment. She now loved him, too. But, in the end, an ill-fated love like theirs could lead to nothing but heartache.

132

Chapter 16

*C*ally clinked cocktail glasses with her sister-in-law, Prudence, and glanced around Geneva's garden. After the rain the atmosphere could only be defined as "sweltering." In short order, perspiration ran between Cally's breasts and circled her waist. Her family looked equally uncomfortable.

In spite of the invariable neglect resulting from Geneva's summer travels, flora and fauna flourished. The space loomed pungent and ripe, teeming with red-tip photinia, coleus, and confederate jasmine. Pink trumpet vine, invasive in Savannah, had commandeered the rear wall and wormed its way into the nymph fountain in the corner. Moss hung oppressively from the massive water oak next door.

She accepted a second brandy milk punch from Hocum, Geneva's butler-chauffeur-gardener since the days prior to the senator's political career. "Where's Mother?"

"Oh, I 'spect she be in the kitchen redoin' everthing I done done. She be out drec'ly."

Cally squirmed under her sister-in-law's scrutiny of the braids but met Pru's gaze boldly. "What do you think?"

"I'm not sure what to think." Pru wore a headband.

"Take a chance. It's not a multiple choice question." Cally made her smile congenial and a little self-deprecating. "Braids haven't caught on in Asheville, I assume?"

"Not where I've been spending my time."

"You're still sacrificing your family for the Junior League, then?" Cally made sure her tone was tolerantly teasing.

Pru searched around for rescue, settled on one of Cally's three nephews. "Reggie, don't pull up Grandmama's dieffenbachia." Another frantic eye search. "Jim, could you do something with the boys?"

"It's years too late, Muff." Jim and Turner were sequestered in a far corner of the yard, Turner executing the perfect drive with a choked down garden hoe Hocum had brought him. "I wash my hands of the whole thing."

Lucinda's alert laugh peeled across the courtyard from where she was engaged in conversation with the senator. She was not a great admirer of their sister-in-law.

"Excuse me, Carolyna." Pru stalked off, sloshing white punch. Seizing her son's arm, she marched him to a heavy wrought-iron bench.

Cally watched the verbal lashing, then Jim's golf swing with the hoe. Voices drew her attention to the kitchen door, where Geneva descended the back steps with Hugh, their arms interlocked. Geneva's toe caught an uneven brick, and she stumbled a little, her eyes fixed on Cally's hair. Cally squelched the urge to touch her braids, to verify she had actually let Paul Michael practice his expertise on her. She conjured a smile.

"Hello, mother. This is lovely." Her hand indicated the garden, the terrace with a table for eight, and a triple place setting at a smaller table. The soft patina of Geneva's second-best silver, inherited from her grandmother, complemented hunt-club patterned china and pristine white linen. On the large table, a perfectly sculpted and scaled floral arrangement added the proper aura of dignity.

"The garden will be bearable—perfect—once the sun drops behind Flannery's house," Cally said.

"Carolyna, don't be snide. It's almost the end of summer. I've hardly been able to enjoy the garden. Indulge me."

She did, with a smile. "Hello, Hugh."

"Hi, sweetheart."

His eyes riveted on her hair, the contrition in his tone, his smile, his manner, were for Geneva. He embraced Cally's shoulders, kissed her temple. Beads jangled predictably, no more than a whisper on the soft evening, a scream to Cally.

"You look . . . cool." He observed her bare shoulders and her sandals.

"Fortunate for me." Glancing at her watch, she blotted her forehead with a cocktail napkin. "You're never late, Hugh. We're a few brandies ahead of you."

"He broke down on the road," Geneva explained. "No harm done. Dinner kept nicely."

"Hmm. I didn't think a BMW was allowed to malfunction, especially on Sunday. Where?"

His expression told her before he spoke. "Darien."

Stifling a smile, she nodded. "Not the best place to be stranded."

"I'll leave you two." Geneva was off in a flash. Cally wondered if Geneva had heard Hugh's rendition of his failure to come to her aid in Darien.

Once Geneva was out of earshot, Hugh lost no time. "My God, Carolyna." Eyeing her hair, he looked like he'd just taken a swig of spoiled milk. "Have you lost your mind?"

Annoyance pricked. "Just my heart. If I'd lost my mind, too, I assure you, wild horses couldn't have dragged me here."

"I have no idea what the hell you're talking about." His thin mouth tightened. "Ever, anymore."

"I'd be the first to agree." Across the yard, Reggie and his brothers sought territory other than the dieffenbachia to plunder. "Mother shouldn't have thrown us together this way. It's uncomfortable for me. I have to be here, for Lucinda. *You* could have declined."

"Hardly. I want to marry you. Dinner with my future family doesn't fall into the 'to be declined' category."

A wave of nostalgia swamped her. She couldn't lose the feeling that she had married Paul Michael, just hours before, in that antiquated tub, in that unconventional ceremony.

"If we were married, Hugh, would you have called me when you broke down in Darien this afternoon?"

"Of course." He recovered, too late. "I mean—if it wouldn't have been an inconvenience for you."

"Even if it was, I would have come for you."

"Hell, Carolyna. I never figured you for holding a grudge."

"Then try to think of it as rationalization, getting my priorities in order, as you advised." She thought of the sweltering phone booth from which she'd placed the call, the leering truckers. In her side vision, Geneva mounted the steps again. "You'd better check to see if Mother needs you."

"Because you don't need me? Sweetheart—"

"Hugh, this is what you're paying Dr. Ballentine for. It isn't fair to subject the rest of the family to our differences. In the South we're still attuned to etiquette." She looked around, weighed the possibilities. "I should practice my manners now and say hello to my brother."

As Cally approached Jim, Lucinda separated herself from the senator in deference to his ringing cellular phone. The three Sinclair siblings stood united on the same ground for the first time in years. Cally hugged Jim, pecked his cheek, then bestowed the same greeting on her sister.

"How many phone calls has Daddy had?" Cally threw out the question in general.

Jim's answer was a crooked smile.

"This is the fourth one," Lucinda admitted. "Mother is ballistic, in a refined way. Not much has changed, has it?"

"Nothing has changed," Cally assured her. "Except they spend even less time together now. How are you, Jim?"

"Fine, Carolyna. *You* look—" The smile he'd inherited from the senator surfaced. "Exotic."

"Where can *I* get that done, Cally?" Lucinda demanded.

Warning bells pierced Cally's mind. She thought of Paul Michael, and a sensation wafted through her that mimicked jealousy. "You can't, Lucy. The mold was broken after me."

"That's mysterious."

Jim hadn't lost his ability to pick up on Cally's disquiet. "Braids aren't you, Lucy. Anyway, there's something to be said for individualism. If you copy Carolyna, she loses hers and you never find yours."

"Very profound. But don't you mean, if I copy Carolyna again?" Lucinda smiled at her brother over her milk punch. "What do you think of Turner?"

"The same thing I thought of him the first go-round. He has an awesome swing. Not much depth beyond that." Jim's eyes drifted to where Turner was giving little Jim a putting lesson with one of Geneva's silver knives and a plum pilfered from a tree in the garden.

"Maybe you could just sign your trust fund over to him, Lucy. Then we could forego all the grief Geneva is going to dish out on your road to that eventual point."

"It's wonderful to see you, Jim."

Cally caught defiance intertwined with the hurt as Lucinda turned on her heel and walked away.

"It's probably gone already," Jim murmured, draining his glass, signaling Hocum. "Scotch," he called loudly across the courtyard, then turned back to Cally. "The trust fund I mean." When she nodded, her cheeks going warm, he warned, "I'm getting damned tired of working my ass off in that furniture factory to keep this family's bank account balanced, what with the drain you and Lucy have—"

"Nice to see you, Jim." She followed Lucinda for a change.

There were no place cards. It seemed to Cally there was a lot of jockeying for position. Geneva, not one to fawn over the grandchildren, banished them to the small table and then, following tradition, she and Wain took the end chairs at the main table. Pru and Jim showed no predilection for sitting next to each other. Turner quickly chose the chair across from Cally. Lucinda sidled in beside her, a conspiratorial sibling smile lighting her pretty face. Hugh doggedly took his seat beside Turner. Never having seen them together, much less side by side, their contrasting physical makeup, coloring, and mannerisms surprised Cally. Hugh paled in comparison to Turner.

Geneva did a commendable job of pretending Turner was not at the table. The senator, all amiability, inquired about the current big-money winners on the PGA tour, his graciousness firing Turner's determination to fit in. Hugh and Jim discussed period architecture. The women, for the most part, ate in silence.

Mid meal, in the throes of discussing the perils of a strong right-hand grip with Jim, Turner's foot found Cally's ankle. She looked up, meeting his heated brown stare, before she eased her foot away. He smiled and continued talking to Jim.

Cally scowled, putting down her fork, when he slouched in his chair, straining to caress her calf, then her knee, with his foot.

"Turner. Sit up," Lucinda barked.

He gave her a perfected innocent-and-mildly-hurt look. Cally was torn between laughter and anger.

"We aren't eating in the motel in front of the television," Lucinda scolded. "This is a test. You're failing it. Again."

When he withdrew his foot, Cally decided the situation was more pathetic than amusing or irritating and thought of the haven of Jessica's house, almost furnished now, almost done. Then she envisioned Paul Michael's room, heard the rain on the windows, the fog horns in the distance, Pierre's ebullient cries. Ziggy Marley's silky pelt came back to her, the mattress on the floor, the sheets so clean and fresh.

Letting herself think of Paul Michael at last, she acknowledged the longing ache she'd brought with her to this house. She tried to imagine him in either of the chairs across from her, tried to think what topic her politically gracious father might offer him for discussion. She came up void, her ache deepening. Paul Michael would never be welcomed here.

At last, Geneva invited them into the house for coffee and dessert. The senator used a side entrance to his study, phone to his ear. Turner excused himself and strolled toward the corner of the yard where the gardening tools were kept. Cally lingered at the table, talking to Hocum, then followed Turner. Kudzu vines had taken over the old brick shed, once a wash house, green tendrils winding and twisting intricately, the way Paul Michael had invaded her life and seized her heart.

Turner leaned against the shed smoking a cigarette. His red hair shot sparks into the last sunlight, his lithe body issuing an old familiar invitation. His smile showed satisfaction as he watched her approach.

"Un . . . frigging . . . believable," she said softly. She took a draw from the offered cigarette, another, handed it back to him. "What was the idea of the under-the-table choreography?"

He shrugged. "I like to keep in touch."

She laughed then, powerless. "I can't believe you're here—that you had the nerve to come."

"The balls to come." He offered the cigarette again, dropped it when she declined, crushed it.

"Mother hates you. Daddy, too. He's just phonier."

He shrugged. "All that dislike is a challenge all right. Lucinda wouldn't come without me, though. I couldn't let her disappoint Geneva."

"You're impossible."

"You're gorgeous." He reached, bounced her braids in one cupped hand. "Cool."

The braids swayed, jangled. She felt a little ill.

"There's a story here." Getting no response, he said, "I know you're on the severe outs with Hugh. I was concerned about your celibacy." His eyes taunted. "I see that was wasted."

Her brows rose, her chin lifting voluntarily.

"You've got the smell of semen all over you," he said. "Hell, you're still a little breathless. Your throat's still glowing. You give a whole new meaning to the term, "red neck.""

"Turner—"

"Been there, done that, Carolyna. I remember how your skin got all flushed and stayed that way for hours. Who is it?"

"Let's go inside. We can't risk the wrath of the gods any longer."

"I wish it were me giving you that afterglow. That's the only reason I came back to the island." When she turned her back, tried to leave, he caught her hand, dropped it with her warning look. "I still love you, babe. I know we can make a go of it this time—"

"I have no money. Accept that."

"Get some self-esteem, babe. Screw the money."

"And what do we do about Lucinda?"

"She'll be all over Hugh before we get your station wagon packed."

"Damn you, Turner." Her eyes smarted. "If you hurt her—don't do this to her." Useless. She was the only one who could stop it, and she was unwilling to pay the price. "Never mind. Take her. Tomorrow. Just get the hell out of here and get it over with. The sooner she goes, the sooner she'll come back and start a life."

"Like you've done?"

"Exactly like I've done."

Cally found Geneva in the kitchen giving Hocum instructions about the leftover food—what to take home, what to leave. The doling out commanded the gravity of cutting the Hope diamond.

"Mother, I'm going. I have paperwork to do."

Geneva assumed her adversarial posture. "You should have done that earlier today, dear. This is a family gathering and I'd like it to last for a while. It only lasts as long as the first one to leave. Let's not have that be you, Carolyna."

"Mercy, Mother. I can't be responsible for family unity."

"It's bad enough with Wain on the phone all evening and now holed up in that study talking to God knows who, planning God knows what. The height of rudeness. At least you—"

"Mother, he's been on the phone all my life. How would my not leaving, now, change that?"

"I want you to spend some time with Hugh. I understand you've been avoiding him. How do you ever expect to get this worked out if you continue to do that, dear?"

"To be truthful, I don't expect to *get this worked out*."

"Well, Hugh does. You could meet him halfway."

"Every time I tried that in the past, he walked backward, or sideways, or whatever it took to wring extra effort out of me." Cally paused. "I don't want to be put through my paces anymore, Mother. Or only through paces that will be self-orchestrated."

"Thanksgiving has obviously been sacrificed for childish squabbling."

"What?" Cally said dumbly, lost for the moment.

"I want a Christmas wedding, Carolyna Joy. White and hunter green with crimson cummerbunds and sashes. I want no arguments."

Cally wished her hair wasn't braided, wished she could twist it until her scalp bled. She wiped her perspiring palms, heard Hugh's and Lucinda's laughter in the parlor. "*You* want?"

Geneva nodded firmly, cutting her eyes to the butler's pantry where Hocum banged an oversized metal coffee pot and pretended not to listen. She looked back to Cally. "What is that on your cheek? That wound?"

140

Cally's hand flew up, dropped. All the humidity in the garden had done away with her Estée Lauder camouflage.

"You look like you've been brawling in some alley. And those braids! You resemble a Rastafarian refugee."

Geneva was perceptive. Disturbingly so.

"I'm not at all comfortable with what's going on here, Carolyna. Whatever *is* going on. When you moved into that woman's house you seemed to lose all sanity." Geneva eyed her, measured, deduced, "I know you. You have your father's genes. You're a bitch in heat. Who is following the scent?"

Not even trying to hide her pain, Cally asked, "Is this tough love, Mother?"

"This is survival, Carolyna. Yours. Someday you'll thank me."

"And will I treat my own daughter like this someday? If I do, Mother, will it be for her survival, or mine?"

"Here is all I have to say on the subject, young lady."

Cally braced herself.

"You will be thirty years old in eighteen months. Too old to act irresponsibly—the way you are acting now." Geneva cocked her dark head, her gray eyes hard, flat. "Maybe you aren't acting, dear. Maybe you *are* simply immature and irresponsible . . . too much so to be trusted with the next installment of your inheritance that's due then."

Cally fought down panic. "Mother, I'm counting on that money to start my own design firm. I'm not immature, and I'm not irresponsible. I know my mind and know what's best for me. It isn't Hugh. It's independence."

"I'm not so sure, dear. I'm really concerned. It's totally in my hands, you know. I may see fit to move the date back . . . say ten years or so." She studied Cally, waited for the effect. "Of course if you were married to Hugh, I wouldn't worry. He has a strong head for finances."

"*I* have a strong head for finances. I live on a shoe string. I have since the day I left Turner and came home, all in order to put back the money he and I spent."

"That's another thing—"

"You can't hold me responsible for what Lucy's doing. I've tried

141

to warn her."

"I can, and I do. If you get your inheritance when you're thirty and waste it on another scoundrel, she'll follow right in your footsteps two years later. I can't risk that, Carolyna. I won't."

Heavy silence fell between them.

"Now you go on into the parlor and settle down. Hugh will need a ride back to the island, but he won't be ready to leave this early."

"I'm not going back to the island." Their eyes locked, then Cally looked away. "I'll stay, mother, but I'll ask Lucy and Turner to take him back."

❦

Hugh walked Cally to her car while Turner and Lucinda waited at the curb in her new Lexus coupe. Turner sat behind the wheel, his foot massaging the gas pedal just enough to be evident in the quiet dignity of Lafayette Square.

Hugh caught Cally's arm to draw her into the alcove of a high wall and a hedge. His eyes widened. "My God. You have a muscle. Are you working out?"

She eyed him coolly. "I developed that carting around all the Steinbergs' renderings and samples."

Scarlet mottled his cheeks. "We have an appointment with Dr. Ballentine Wednesday afternoon. Can you make it, Carolyna?"

"Yes."

"I'd like you to stay on the island that night. With me. There's a party at the beach club. A fund raiser."

She shook her head. "I have to stay at Jessica's. I'm responsible until she gets home in a week."

He might as well not have heard. "It's a benefit staged by the marine life advocates, sweetheart. Five hundred dollars a plate."

"I don't have five hundred dollars to spare."

"My treat. It will be a good investment in our future. Lots of the better people have sent their RSVP's—a crowd we should be part of. I'm counting on you."

"I'm sorry, Hugh. I'll see you at Dr. Ballentine's on Wednesday afternoon."

142

She drove straight to the house with the saddened colors. The lights were out in the attic room. The van was absent from the curb. She should have stayed with Paul Michael, right there in that room, beneath that fan, beneath him, full of serenity, full of him. That was blatantly evident now.

She fought an urge to drive to Reggae Ruby's, then remembered it was closed on Sunday night, as was Jamaica Jam. Geneva's "bitch" label echoed in Cally's head. Overcome with sudden loneliness, she realized she was well on her way to sacrificing everything stable in her life for Paul Michael Quest.

Chapter 17

*C*ally pulled up to the Sea Island Golf Club gate on Wednesday morning. "I'm meeting a delivery service here this morning to pick up something from my mother's cottage. I called ahead to clear him. Has he arrived yet?"

"Mornin', Ms. Sinclair. How y'all?" The guard's eyes fastened to her braids, his stare rude, dubious. "If you talkin' 'bout that male Whoopi Goldberg drivin' the van from hell—yes, ma'am. He went through ten minutes ago."

The comments irritated and saddened her.

Paul Michael's van was parked at the curb in front of Sinclair Cottage. Seeing the unconventional vehicle shocked her conscience, even though she expected it to be there. When she parked, she heard strains of reggae. The metal van body rocked gently as she approached the driver's side.

Paul Michael saw her, jumped out, dressed for the occasion. Jeans. A tank top with no commercial lettering. Painfully new Nikes.

"Pretty Cally. Bright, but soft. You are a flower, like those in your mama's beautiful yard." He looked toward the brilliant flowers banking the circular drive, back to her again.

Memory of being with him on Sunday jolted her senses. The past two days seemed wasted, empty. She wanted to hug him but knew it was impossible, here.

"Do you want to move the van into the driveway?" she asked.

"It leaks ugly black oil. It would be a shame to spoil such a nice driveway." He moved to the back of the van and extracted the furniture dolly he always carried.

"With an attitude like that, you have a future in this business."

He stopped, gave her a startled look. She thought she saw color rise in his cheeks. She said, "Clients would appreciate your courtesy and consideration. You're kind, Paul Michael. There aren't enough kind people."

When he nodded, she moved toward the driveway. He followed, pushing the dolly.

"We'll get the chest Mother wants. You have the refinisher's address, the one I gave you on the phone?"

He nodded again, patting his jeans pocket.

When she unlocked the back door, frigid air rushed out at them. The house was quiet. The inordinately loud hum of the double-wide refrigerator, the only sound in the empty kitchen, affirmed Mikela's day off.

Paul Michael lingered on the flagstone stoop.

"Come in." Her whisper was unnecessary. She held the door wide, passed him an encouraging look.

Muscles worked appealingly in the backs of his arms as he moved the dolly up the steps and carefully through the door. The large room was smaller, friendlier suddenly. The aroma of his bay-rum cologne, the one she'd seen near his sink mirror, had begun to mingle with sweat after the ride in the hot van.

He looked around, his feet rooted to the brick floor. "Nice." He looked self-conscious. Uncomfortable.

"I have to get something from the study. Come with me." When he shook his head, she said, "All right, wait here. Then we'll go upstairs for the chest."

In the senator's study, she worked the lock on the wall safe. She removed her personal papers and a small black velvet box and returned to Paul Michael, still anchored to the same spot. His arms hugged his rib cage as if he was cold.

She placed the files on the counter, crossed to the cushioned bench in the sunny bay window. "Come over here. I have something for you, Paul Michael."

He approached slowly, almost reluctantly, but his warmth counteracted the overzealous cooling system when he sat facing her, folding one leg onto the seat. She opened the little box, held it out to him. A small blue, gold-mounted earring glimmered in the sun.

"Sapphire . . . my birthstone. It's an antique." Remembering her father presenting the set to her on her eighteenth birthday, Cally took a folded piece of paper from the bottom of the box, unfolded it gently, and read, "One of the hardest, most durable of gems, revered for thousands of years. It's rumored that the Ten Commandments were written on a sapphire tablet."

Still Paul Michael did not speak. "It matches your eyes, Paul Michael. It's strong, the way you are for me." She offered the box. "It's for you."

The clanking beads were as gentle as his smile when he shook his head, his eyes on the box, then seeking hers.

She caught his hand, deposited the single earring in his palm and reached to extract a gold stud from his ear. She replaced gold with sapphire and sat back, comparing blue to blue, the nagging urge she'd had since meeting him, finally satisfied.

She nodded. "It's wonderful. Will you wear it?"

"Oh, yeah, girl," he said softly. "I will. But where is the other one?"

She caught his face between her hands, drew him close, her body jolted by the contact. Against his mouth she said, "Don't be greedy."

His kiss was guarded but his hands stole up her rib cage to caress her breasts. She sat back, raised one side of her braided hair and exposed the sapphire's mate.

"Awl . . . *right!*" His smile rivaled the blinding sun that poured through the window.

She stood, pulling him up. "Come upstairs." When he turned toward the abandoned dolly, she said, "Leave that for now."

They climbed the back stairs to the second level and went down a long, darkened corridor, past several bedrooms. His hand in hers conveyed his unease. She knew he was intimidated by the house, almost reluctant to accompany her, by the heaviness of his arm and the hesitance in his normally bouncy step. She stopped, opened a door, drew him inside.

"This was my room. From the time I was ten." She pushed thoughts of boarding school and extended summer camps to the back of her mind.

The furniture was mostly Chippendale with curved cabriolet legs and claw-and-ball feet. Cally had come to appreciate the furniture only when she began to study design. As a child she had coveted white wicker, a trend favored among her peers.

Turner's eagerness to make love to her in the rope bed beneath a ceiling canopy of rock posters, invaded her memory. He had laughed appreciatively when she explained that the cliché about 'sleeping tight' had come from the ability to tighten the ropes on these antique beds to form a firmer support. Turner was never privileged to make use of the bed again. Hugh's lingering presence in the room loomed fresh and strident, however.

Cally released Paul Michael's hand, and he began to move about, the way she had explored his room that first visit. When he stroked the smooth mahogany surface of an armoire, a powerful craving flooded her with desire. It drove her to undo the top button of her shirt. And the next . . . .

Her action caught his eye; he turned, and she saw instant perception, even if not agreement. She kept her eyes on his as she released the button at her waist, lowered the zipper, stepped out of her slacks. His expression ran the gamut between caution and want as she threw back the covers purposefully. His movements were automated when he joined her, took her in his arms, insinuating his body between her and the bed.

"We will get the chest and go, girl. Back to my house." When she shook her head, seeking his mouth, he reasoned, "It will not take long. Good things are worth waiting for. Remember, Cally?"

She caught his tank top, worked it from his jeans, pushed it up and nuzzled the hair on his chest, ringed his nipples with her tongue. "I want to make love with you. In this bed," she whispered against his mouth.

Rigidity drained from his stance, manifested in his lower body, and she witnessed the sensation of coming home. As though the leader in a dance team, she turned them again, removed her underclothing. She petitioned him with her eyes as she climbed onto the high bed and between cold sheets.

He lay beside her, bodies aligned, his big hands pressing her against him and asked, "Why, Cally?"

She shook her head. She ran her tongue over his mouth, invaded the corner, caressed his teeth, exploring the little gap with the tip of her tongue. The ragged sound of their mingled breaths permeated the stillness. Overcome by desire, curiosity and hesitance seemingly left him as he drew her beneath him, parted her legs with one sure hand and complied with her wishes.

⚜

When she lay in his arms, quiet, satiated, he ran his flattened palm along the rumpled bedding, then up her backside, his brow furrowed. "Why this bed, girl?"

His voice, his touch, the caring in the question touched her, cast her into dread of his leaving and her imminent grief. She had been ticking off the days left to them, counting down to inevitability.

"To make a memory. Someday . . . when I leave Jessica's . . . wherever I go, this bed will go with me. For the rest of my life, I want to remember the way I feel at this moment." Her throat tightened. "Tell me you understand that, Paul Michael."

"Oh, yeah, baby girl. I understand." He kissed the top of her head. "No need for memory, though. You can come with me, to Jamaica."

She shook her head, smiled, swallowed furiously.

"This bed can go, too—to make more big-time memories while we build a nest of pinks. Everything would be fine," he coaxed, showing his delight at the thought with childlike openness. He caught a single rolling tear from her cheek with his tongue. "Now you tell me you understand."

Turning, she fitted her body to his, spoon fashion, until his groin hugged her buttocks. She looped his arm around her, pressed his palm against her breasts and lay in silence as a perfect wave of momentary contentment crested, washed over her.

Propped on his elbow, he peered down at her. "Jamaica is not the end of the world, girl."

"It's another world. Yours, not mine."

"We can make it ours. You will be a queen there, a big day when you register on the census as white. And a big day every time a new pink created by our love registers as white."

She fell silent. The emphasis he allotted color troubled her. Realization nagged. Her being white was as triumphant for him as

148

his being black was problematic for her. How much had her rebellious nature contributed to her desire to have him in this bed? Sudden futility and a sadness she longed to conceal overwhelmed her. She pulled out of his arms, settled against the hard cold wood of the headboard, and tucked the sheet across her breasts.

He sat up, his body bronzed by sun from the window, his eyes rivaling the sheen of the sapphire stone. "Cally? What is it?"

"My parents were in Jamaica in the seventies . . . Kingston. They weren't treated well."

His smile teased, yet didn't. "Black people in Jamaica are not into bowing and scraping."

"It was more than that." Geneva had admitted to actually being frightened in that tense atmosphere and told stories of rude treatment, confrontations between vendors and armed guards on the beach.

"Oh, yeah. There were big political differences then. Everyone is sorry now." Paul Michael shrugged, mimicked a popular television commercial. "Come back to Jamaica."

"I read a book."

"Awl *right*! This book tells you Jamaica is beautiful? Jamaica is friendly. No more trouble with politicos. Peace ever after." He was only half teasing; beneath the banter, she sensed seriousness. "Tell me I am right about this book, girl."

"Yes. All of that. But . . . more."

"What is this more? You should only judge this book by its cover."

Her smile erupted of its own volition.

"Cutacoo on man back no yerry what kim massa yerry."

"Paul Michael . . . ." She ran a fingertip across his brow, down his cheek, across his lips, aching at a previously untouched depth.

He caught her hand, held it. "The basket on a man's back does not hear what he hears." His eyes narrowed as he strove to be understood and believed. "You want to know about Jamaica, I tell you, girl. Promise me you will only look at the pictures in your book."

He watched her as she twined a finger in a loose thread in the quilted spread, gazed out the window. She had seen women with

149

beautiful café-au-lait children, the mothers wearing vague, harried expressions on their faces. She remembered how her stomach had lurched with curiosity and judgment just before she'd turned her head away. It was an innate action driven by muscles that lived apart from her heart or mind. Now she tried to imagine herself in the place of those women she'd seen.

"Talk to me, baby girl," he prompted quietly, his warm hand coming to rest where the sheet covered her thigh. "Give me your thoughts. I will give you my arguments."

"It's a book from the humanities section of the library, written by a Jamaican woman. She claims there's a very strong gender classification. Man is considered, by both genders, as superior."

"Jamaica has its share of poor fools, Cally. I would not deny that."

The chameleonic ease with which he slipped from jargon to perfectly honed, persuasive King's English, still intrigued her. His ability to be two different people disturbed her.

She asked, "And is it true even the female intelligence is questioned? That any attempt toward discussion outside of bed and babies is pitied, not only by the superior male, but even by her female peers?" She quoted almost directly from the book, feminist concern, rebellion, and disappointment of her discovery clouding her tone.

He kneaded her thigh, then caressed it. "That, too, is a class distinction. Women of good family—mulatto women of any family—are treated with respect. You are white, Cally. You would be a queen. Any man in Jamaica would fall silent to hear your opinion on any subject. I would, most of all."

"And education," she continued as though she hadn't heard, not as though she didn't care. "Women aren't given the same opportunity as men, according to this author." She met his eyes. "I couldn't bear that, Paul Michael. To have a daughter who—"

"A mulatto girl child would never be denied an education. You have to trust what I tell you, Cally. I care about you. Do you even know the woman who wrote this book?"

"The book states polygamy is rampant. A way of life. It's not uncommon for men to have multiple families, as many as they want, all living in poverty. Can you tell me that isn't true?"

"I can only tell you I am happy that you would even read this book, that you would consider going with me. I cannot begin to tell you, however, how happy." His smile was tender, candid. "The way I love you, Carolyna Joy Sinclair, do you think I could ever want another woman?"

"Paul Michael . . . ." She looked away, but the image of his face, the hope, the tenderness, pulled her back like a magnet. "I never said I was considering—I know only one thing. I have to be secure in myself, know I can stand on my own, or I will never feel secure with anyone else. That's the only kind of relationship I can ever be a part of."

Geneva's theory of marrying well and suffering in silence nagged at her. Past, misguided attempts to conform to Hugh's imposed standards invaded her mind with vivid clarity. "I'm beginning to realize one person can never base his or her contentment on another."

"Don't make no little thing big, little sister." His lapse into Jamaican cadence was a kind of protection, she suspected. He smiled appealingly, the tiny gap drawing her eye. "Come to Jamaica with me. Be a queen. Mine. You know, girl?"

She couldn't give the answer he wanted. Slow, deathlike atrocities were committed within relationships that began with the claim of love, even without the added difficulty of one partner having to embrace an alien soil. Suddenly chilled, she slipped under the covers, turned to him, moved by the gravity of his going and the inevitability of the grief to come.

They made love in the silent solace of their souls, tenderly and grasping, unhurriedly and urgently, without the blessing or the burden of promise.

Hugh and Cally sat side by side in tense silence as Philip Ballentine put the finishing touches on a phone call. After watching the van chug away from the cottage, Paul Michael's juices still warm in her body, she had headed directly to the scheduled

151

appointment. Now her spirit traveled with Paul Michael along the road to Savannah. She put her hand in her pocket, fingered the engagement ring Hugh had talked her out of returning the day she'd moved to Savannah and drew a fortifying breath.

Dr. Ballentine pressed the intercom. "Linda, hold my calls please." He turned his attention to Hugh and Cally. "Well?"

"I've made a decision," said Cally.

Hugh's head jerked around, surprise and hope in his eyes. Her hand quaked when she extracted the ring from her pocket.

Hugh kept his hands on the chair arms. His knuckles turned white. She knew he waited to see if she would slip the ring onto her finger. She held it out to him.

"I'm sorry, Hugh."

He shot up, a rigid jack-in-the-box. His jaw clenched as his eyes turned stony. "Come outside. I want to talk to you."

She shook her head. "That's why we're here. I purposely waited to give you this in Dr. Ballentine's presence to avoid—there's nothing else to talk about, Hugh."

He looked incredulous.

The doctor settled against the back of his chair. He stuck his pipe into his mouth, patted his breast pocket, then bit down hard on the cold instrument.

Cally began her carefully considered statement. "The time for blame and bargaining is gone. I care for you, Hugh. I don't want to hurt you. I will, if I marry you. I would be unhappy, always questioning my decision. You'd feel it and that would eat into your confidence. We'd both suffer."

"You're involved with someone else."

She tensed painfully. "Why do you say that?"

"There are signs. You're a very sensual woman, Carolyna. I've been there. Remember?" He looked at her hair, then his eyes fastened on the single blue stone in her ear. The other ear held a gold hoop. "Lately you can't be bothered. Who's this someone else?"

"I'm involved with myself, Hugh. Finally."

He looked to the doctor, who had become a mannequin. "Say something. What am I paying you for?"

Dr. Ballentine looked bland.

152

Cally felt close to tears. Hugh's typical handling of defeat assured her she had made the right decision. "We're an excellent design team, Hugh. You're one of the most gifted architects I know. We have people clamoring for us. I know how important that is to you. There's no reason that can't continue." She placed the ring on the edge of the desk. The big stone glinted, mocked.

"What about Geneva?" asked Hugh.

"What *about* Mother?" She rose, shouldered her bulging bag.

"Does she know about this?"

"I'll let you tell her. She's somewhere between Vail and Shangri-la. If I were you, I'd pick my moment. Timing is everything with Mother."

His mouth turned grim.

"I have to go." She faced the desk. "Thank you, Dr. Ballentine. You've been very helpful."

"Will I see you again?"

"At the moment I don't think so." She offered him a self-deprecating smile. "I won't throw away your number, however."

"I'll walk you to the car," said Hugh.

"No." She spoke firmly, apology and closure in her smile.

⚜

Cally drove past St. Simons's King and Prince Hotel to East Beach, where she had spent so many childhood days. The last rays of sun kissed her neck and shoulders through the open roof. Leaving her shoes in the car, she descended a dune, the water summoning.

Gulls circled, struggled against the wind. The sand, a thin sugar coating above the crust of the tide, echoed the spray off the whitecaps, stinging against her bare legs and feet. Beyond the waves, the water was a deep, inexhaustible blue. It spoke to her of uncomplicated childhood days spent on this very ground, promised future days of serenity and clarity. A sense of relief, then healing, settled on her.

She sank onto the sand, lay back in its residual warmth. Paul Michael had denied the infeasibility of their union, and in voicing his love for her, allowed a dream to form. He saw them conquering the world, having it all. If they were to bond, their dreams must be the same, with their relationship at the center.

Growing up in Savannah and on the island had left her with memories and places she longed to share with him. Common things. Strolling River Street and Factors Walk, having him do her portrait there, not caring if people sensed their closeness. Picnicking in Forsyth Park. Wetting their feet in the spouting mouth of the griffin in front of the old cotton exchange. Dinner at the Shrimp Factory. Tybee Island Beach . . . .

Her one attempt to be with him, the day they'd gone in the van to collect Jessica's antiques, had proven that what Savannah lovers took for granted, she and Paul Michael could never share. His asking her to return to Jamaica with him was an emotional bid; asking him to stay with her would throw them into futile limbo. Their future had been decided and cast in tradition centuries ago. Their only choice was to adhere to what had gone before and trust time to heal them.

Cally closed her eyes and bid the ocean breeze to soothe her. She thought of Paul Michael and the fans and all the rapidly passing days.

Chapter 18

Two nights later, Cally celebrated the freedom from guilt—concerning her engagement to Hugh—by going to Paul Michael's room unannounced. She hadn't seen him since their tryst at the cottage, and she hoped he'd return to the attic room between his shift at Ruby's and Jamaica Jam. When she heard the distinctive van engine, she moved to the screen door.

He had seen her car at the curb and climbed the steep steps two at a time. Yet when he entered, his demeanor failed to match his eagerness. He seemed to regard her in a new light, his gaze wary, guarded, measuring. He took her in his arms at last, held her silently, rocking her a little.

"How long do we have?" The anticipation she'd nursed turned tentative, tempered by a difference in him she sensed but failed to comprehend.

"Enough time," he whispered against her mouth. "We need no rehearsal."

He led her to the bed on the floor where they undressed hurriedly and threw back the garish spread, eyes searching, then pulling away. When she lay down, he knelt between her legs and gripped behind her knees, lifted her to him, his manner and touch purposeful. She was wet and he entered her. Their coupling was over in moments, but the urgency lingered in his touch, in his tone.

"Sleep with me tonight, Cally. Be here when I come back from Jamaica Jam. Be here when I wake up tomorrow. Will you do that, girl?"

"I have to stay at Jessica's. It's an agreement we have. You know that, Paul Michael."

She felt his disappointment, and, she thought, resentment. "Then wait until I come home. Will you?"

She didn't wait. She stole from his hot, dark room almost the minute she heard the van turn the corner, the ragged edge of her desire only partially smoothed.

Cally and Paul Michael angled a Hepplewhite table, an excellent find from Scrooge and Marley, through the library door. The room was cool. The new air-conditioning system altered the milieu of the house. Shutters tilted against the sun at some windows while at others sheers muted the glare. The air was dry, pristine. Cally felt a nostalgic stirring for the past when windows and doors had been flung wide to allow a breeze to waft through, humid, tinged with sea air.

Talk had been scarce since Paul Michael's arrival near noon. Knowing the furniture designated for this room, he had sat on the floor, his face grim, and wordlessly sketched a rendering that awed and pleased her. She consulted the sketch now and motioned with her head toward the medallion-back sofa in the center of the room. He backed in that direction.

"Paul Michael?"

"Yeah, girl?" He raised his head, adjusted his hold on the table, backed slowly in order for her to match his step.

She half whispered. "Is something wrong? Are you . . . angry? Hurt? About the night I didn't stay with you, maybe?"

He stopped, searched her face, then backed again, denying her access to his eyes. She followed his lead as he bent his knees to lower the table to the floor in front of the sofa. He adjusted it, lined it up, inch by inch until satisfied.

She looked around the elegant room, the burgundy walls, the tasseled, thick velvet draperies banking the windows. Pride in her work surfaced, and she couldn't squelch a triumphant smile.

Paul Michael traced a finger across her lips, none of her own pleasure in his gesture. When voices erupted outside the library door, he withdrew his hand quickly, as though the voices had eyes.

She began again. "About that night . . . I knew if you came back I would never leave. I *wanted* to be with you, but—"

"What is it you can do for this grand house, girl, should

someone evil decide to take what they want and leave their mark in return? You have the fine new alarm now. What is it for, Cally, if not to use?"

His petulance was new and disturbing. She pulled her braids together at the nape of her neck, scrunched them, let them drop. "When Jessica and I agreed that I would stay here, my end of the bargain was to be responsible for the house and its contents. You are one of the most responsible people I know. I'm sure you understand my wanting to keep my end of the bargain."

She was met with uncustomary silence. He feigned concentration as he employed the tip of a screwdriver to stuff an unsightly electrical cord into the crack between the baseboard and the floor. She smiled, touched by his conscientious pride.

She crossed to a round marble-topped table, dragged it into place near the end of the sofa. From its resting place in the corner of a Victorian wing chair, she retrieved a lamp she'd converted from a Tang dynasty horse sculpture. She concentrated on securing the shade, draped a silk damask cloth over the table, and placed the lamp in the center as she tried to understand what had changed between them.

She had sensed a distance in him the past few days, felt him watching her, his look measuring, almost suspicious, the way it had been that night in his room. He was less patient, less concerned for her feelings, more goal oriented, almost grasping. She had credited his actions to the dwindling days, his imminent departure magnifying the tension for each of them. To relinquish his spontaneity, his kind smile, the jaunty demeanor she loved, grieved her.

He stood at the window now, gazing out as though trapped. She sensed that the new elegance and heaviness of the house reminded him, as it did her, their job here was ending. She resisted the urge to go to him, circle his waist, soothe him, draw his warmth and strength into her. Rather, she addressed his strong, broad back.

"Paul Michael, when I'm thirty—" No. If she burdened him, he would be intuitive enough to feel responsible for her inheritance when he was only a catalyst, not the problem. "This is a small town. Not so much in circumference as in attitude. My business future

157

could depend on my reputation with Jessica Renfro. She'll be home in two days—"

He turned, his eyes naked with feeling. Crossing the floor in two steps, he lifted her effortlessly onto the Hepplewhite table. His hands clutched her knees, parted her legs, and he moved between them. He held her fiercely, no longer caring about the voices outside the door.

Still concerned for propriety, she whispered against his ear, "I know. Everything is changing too quickly."

All was escalating out of their control, rendering time no longer theirs to spend luxuriously. The house, once their bond, was full of people, full of tangible demands. And now Jessica's arrival would bring it all crashing to a halt. Cally lifted her face for his kiss, then broke away, easing down from the table.

"We knew we wouldn't have this house forever, Paul Michael. No matter how much we didn't want to believe, we knew."

"I saw Hugh Masters."

She suddenly understood his disquiet. "When? Where?"

"In Darien, when I was on the island."

Her scalp tightened. Now his new behavior bore a name. "Let's finish in here and go outside," she said softly. "Where we can talk."

Paul Michael split the sides of a huge corrugated carton with a box knife, pulled back the carton flaps, and dug protective bubble wrap from around a white wrought-iron chaise. The locket swayed gently against his chest. Perspiration ran down his face, his neck, inside his T-shirt. He swiped his brow with a forearm. Cally did the same.

In her peripheral view, a black maid, one of the Merry Maid crew, eyed them scornfully while she cleaned a kitchen window. Affecting purpose and efficiency, Cally gathered the plastic wrap Paul Michael discarded and added it to an accumulating pile. She hastened to help him lift his burden from the deep carton, then tilted the front end upward, rolled the chaise to an earlier designated spot on the terrace.

"All right," she said softly, returning to his side, watching him deftly split a cushion carton. "I didn't want to talk in the house. Tell me about seeing Hugh last week."

His full lips tightened in a hard, thin line, creating tiny mirthless dimples on each side of his mouth. The box knife ripped through the carton. She had never seen him angry before. Anger directed at whom? In Darien, he'd said. She had been with Hugh at the doctor's office that day until mid-afternoon.

Then she remembered Hugh's broken-down car. "Were you at the BMW dealership?"

He gave her a kind of wild, incredulous look, his irises flaring. "At a garage beside the highway. As I left your mother's house, I saw a car—yes, a fine BMW—with the initials AIA. I followed him to some office, then to that garage."

"How did you know it was Hugh?" She caught the corners of the cushion, extracted it while Paul Michael held on to the carton.

"What else could AIA mean, girl? And everyone between there and Hades knew. Wasn't he screaming, waving his arms, crying out his name? As though that fine name and that architect's degree might take away that big scratch on his fine car."

"The garage had towed his car?"

"I see you already know this story, girl."

She shook her head quickly. "No. I only know—from seeing him at my mother's that Sunday—that he broke down in Darien. The garage must have towed his car to the dealership the next day. He must have gone for it on Wednesday and found it scratched. He went back to the garage and blamed—" Her lips toyed with a smile Paul Michael couldn't appreciate. "A Texaco station, by any chance?"

"You know this story," he said quietly. "You got it straight from the fine mouth of Hugh Masters."

"Hugh has told me nothing, Paul Michael, other than his car breaking down on the way to Mother's dinner."

The grim set of his mouth eased somewhat.

She fitted the cushion to the chaise, returned to his side. "Did he say something to you? Something that bothered you? Do you think he knew who you —" Her heart raced suddenly.

He worked silently, split another carton, dug plastic. The air crackled with his unrest and her curiosity.

"Are you going to tell me?"

"What could he know? He only looked, baby girl. At the van. At me, as he flashed his credit card, and I counted pennies to pay for my gas. That look said every little thing."

The look was honed. She'd been the recipient too many times. But no more. She nodded, brushed Paul Michael's hand when she reached for the plastic. He glanced at her, his eyes grim. She smiled assuringly.

"He didn't know who I am. To him I am no one. Did he never stop to think that van—" He motioned to the street. "This hair—" He shook his head side to side. "These clothes . . . could be the tools of my trades, just as his fancy rulers and pencils are the tools of his?"

"No. He never did. And he'd never care."

He swiped sweat, ripped another carton wordlessly.

"Paul Michael, look at me."

He looked, his eyes and mouth softening slightly.

"Would it have mattered how he looked at you if you hadn't known he was Hugh?"

"I would not have let it matter."

"I can tell you why he was angry—angry beyond what was called for."

"Because he is a hard man. How do you believe that makes me feel, Cally?" He stopped working, clicked the knife inside its case, dropped it into an open carton. He folded his arms, sank onto his haunches against the trunk of a shade tree, as though the strength had gone out of him. "He is very well named, this Hugh Masters. If you do not come to Jamaica with me, he will be *your* master. When I close my eyes, how do you think—"

"That's not true. That's why he was so angry. The fury he raised over the scratch on the car was his way of dealing with the fact that I gave his ring back that same day."

His blue eyes brightened, quickened. "Awl right."

Although his reply was too quiet to hold much conviction, its familiarity comforted her. She gathered her braids up, held them, enjoyed the breeze on her neck. "When you and I left the cottage on

Wednesday, I knew there was no way I could ever marry Hugh Masters. He's not worth your thoughts, Paul Michael. Tell me you believe that. Don't give him the satisfaction of spoiling the time we have left."

"There is no reason for you not to come with me now."

"Hugh wasn't the reason before."

"Only for a while, girl. I want to show you *Grand-mère*, and you to her."

She drew a breath, released it, tried to smile. His lack of guile, coupled with his focused eagerness, caused an ache so deep, so wrenching, it staggered her. She searched for deferment. No. A gentle closure. "I have the Steinberg house to do. I can't leave it. Not for months."

"And then you will come." He held her gaze with his.

She retrieved the knife, passed it to him, then caught the arms of a wrought iron chair in the carton, waited for him to help. "Let's finish this so we can go inside and hang pictures in the cool. This house is having a party in five days. We have to get her dressed."

"I love you, Cally." His cultured voice caressed her.

"Even so, we still have to hang pictures." She smiled, swallowing the lump in her throat. "And we have to reserve time for you to re-braid my hair."

"And give you a bath."

In the waning throes of early evening, Cally trailed a realtor through an empty town house on Taylor Street. Fragile light rested in the deep window wells, draped gently across the mellow oak floors.

"Are these the original floors?" Cally's tone was as hushed as the light. She stooped, drew an index finger over a wooden nail.

"Absolutely. This level is considered to be a raised basement."

They stood in the breakfast nook. A filigree grilled window overlooked the sidewalk and Taylor Street beyond. The woman began walking. Cally followed, their heels echoing through the structure.

"I believe you mentioned you'd be wanting a design studio," the realtor said. "There's a large room on the north with perfect light, if you enlarge the windows."

"What about the zoning? I'd want to operate my design business from the premises. Would that be a problem?"

"Oh, no." She opened the door to the described space.

Cally crossed straight to the window that would have to do for a time. Track lighting could supply—she squelched enthusiasm, returned to imagination and hope.

"This was a servants' quarters originally. There's a service entrance off the alley, should you have need of deliveries, and a large walk-in pantry that should suffice as a supply room. The central stairway coming down from the entry would allow you to use the summer dining room as a lovely reception area for clients. Of course, the formal dining room is on the main floor."

She joined Cally at the north window. "Lovely neighborhood. Some of the best families still live here, the parents at least. Elevators have been installed in some of the houses. When you described your needs—it's perfect for you."

Cally nodded. "When will it go on the auction block?"

"Soon, if a buyer doesn't materialize. It needs paint and wall covering. New fixtures. A lot of people can't visualize . . . ."

Cally could, too easily. "May I see the upper floors?"

"Of course. They're lovely. The parlor is large, with two fireplaces. Bedrooms are on the third floor. A nice breeze, perfect for sleeping."

"Is this neighborhood integrated?"

"Not overly, although all neighborhoods are now, dear. Do you have children?"

"No. I'm . . . alone.

"Come along upstairs. You'll fall in love."

⚜

Cally sat in the Volvo at the curb, holding in her hand the realtor's card and a promotion sheet that featured a photograph of the house. She studied the payment and tax schedule, noted the house was underpriced, comparatively. A death, the realtor had said. There were relatives in the Northwest who detested humidity.

Then Cally allowed herself to look at the house again. Like so many others built around 1800, it was built vertically for coolness and to escape early Savannah dust. Its narrow front crowded the sidewalk, facade reaching for the sky. The side stoop was Georgia marble with a spiraling iron staircase ascending to the weathered original front door. Long ago, the door and shutters had been painted *haint* blue to keep Savannah's legendary ghosts away.

A soft light inadvertently left burning spilled from the second floor, the parlor, she remembered. If she were ever fortunate enough to have a house like this—this house—she would leave a light burning to splash over the little second-story porch and stream down the marble steps to constantly welcome her home. A home that would never know Paul Michael's loving presence.

Chapter 19

*O*n Sunday afternoon, Jessica Renfro and her husband Alain, cocktails in hand, followed Cally through the rooms of their refurbished house. The long phone association with Jessica had left Cally feeling close to her, almost as though family had returned home.

Finally meeting Alain, Cally now understood why Jessica's voice maintained a breathless quality. Alain was at least twenty years younger, in his forties, and apparently enjoyed prime physical condition.

In French, Alain meant handsome. Jessica's Alain would have been handsome in any language, and for all appearances, he was devoted to Jessica. He trained his brilliant smile on her, his eyes adoring, his voice reverent. The Renfros' Los Angeles origin nagged Cally. She suppressed suspicion of Alain's acting ability.

"Carolyna, this is fabulous—I suppose." Jessica's sated smile negated the qualifying edge of her compliment. "Victorian antiques aren't my forté, but they seem to have gone into place well."

"They aren't all Victorian, darling," Alain scolded mildly, winning Cally's appreciation. His accent was perfect, just foreign enough to warrant riveting on his words. "Carolyna has achieved the proper balance, just as a nineteenth-century family would have done. Your house is authentically restored, *chérie*."

Cally sipped her cocktail, a perfect martini Alain had mixed. She adjusted a gilt-framed oil over Jessica's bed, crossed to the child's rocker sitting empty before the tea table that fronted the serpentine sofa. She picked up the rocker, remembering how Paul Michael had dangled it from his long fingers the day they'd eaten chicken on the front porch. An erotic stirring in her lower body evolved to longing.

"I have a source to get a Jumeau doll for this chair. I'm sorry I couldn't—"

"Ah, Jumeau," Alain exclaimed. "Yes. Jumeau is you, Jess." He turned his slate eyes to Cally. "She must have it."

Cally relinquished the chair, turned away smiling. In her mind's eye, she compared the Jumeau doll she'd seen and Jessica's bleached, buxom figure. "If there's anything you don't like, Jessica . . . everything is here on approval. I'll have no problem exchanging for what you'd prefer."

"No, darling. Everything is wonderful, at first glance. Why don't we just live with it for a few days—you are still living here, Carolyna?" She arched a carefully penciled brow. "It appears you're ingrained in the downstairs guest room."

Cally's throat warmed, the sensation moving onto her cheeks. "I'm afraid I haven't made other arrangements. I've been concentrating on the house."

"That was the agreement. Stay as long as you like, darling. Alain will have someone to talk to, on his level."

Her smile, that of a sixty-year-old coquette, produced what Cally imagined to be the desired effect. Alain caught Jessica in a bear hug, whispered something in her ear. With a wry smile that made Cally feel like an interloper, Jessica passed him her empty glass and collected Cally's scarcely touched drink. He went out of the room, his smile conspiratorial.

"No one told you Alain was younger?" Jessica asked.

Cally's eyes darted back to Jessica. She smiled, shook her head. "No, but he's—"

"Lovely," Jessica provided, her raucous laughter instantly putting Cally at ease.

She laughed, too. "He's nice, and he's devoted to you."

"That's sweet, darling. But, I've seen devotion. That's how I got all the money he's actually so fond of. His monetary affinity works for us. Thank God I have it—the money."

Envying Jessica's honesty, Cally's curiosity rather than sympathy, surfaced. "Does he want to live here in Savannah?"

"Actually, he wants to build a house on Sea Island. Live there. Boats. Tennis. Golf. All the trappings of a kept man."

Cally's spirits lifted even as her mind ran an anxious gamut, taking mental inventory of anything in this house Jessica might not approve of and be too nice to admit. Were there any contingencies that would prevent Jessica from hiring her again?

"Does that interest you, Carolyna? A little Renfro extravaganza on the island? We could start toying with design plans once we have all these loose ends tied up."

The town house Cally had viewed on Taylor Street vibrated in her mind. For the bank loan, she needed a firm projection of future design projects, one of which Jessica offered her now.

Jessica sought Cally's eyes, her own perceptive. "I understand society is not quite so discerning down there."

"I'd love to do something for you on Sea Island."

"And society?"

"Everyone on the island stems from Savannah roots, Jessica. Well, not everyone, but Southern proprieties being what they are . . . ."

"Do I hear a hint of discontent?"

Cally's shrug was in her voice. "At times I question all the pomp and circumstance. If I hadn't been born to it . . . I took it for granted for so long. I should have questioned attitudes sooner."

Jessica eyed her shrewdly. "Traditional attitudes, you mean?"

Cally nodded. "Why would you leave Los Angeles and come here?" She had always wondered. The few sips of gin had given her liberty to inquire. "And why would Alain . . . ?"

"I ran out of sequined dresses, and Alain got too old for casting couches." Her facetious smile edged into truth. "We made a trip down here a couple of years ago. And the rest is history. Victorian mostly." She smiled again, glanced around. "Do you suppose I can buy Alain Lamartine and Jessica Renfro social acceptance with this house?"

Concern nagged. "Lamartine. You aren't married?"

"Of course we are. I've had five husbands, dear. After the second, changing my name was too time-consuming. We'll just refer to him as Renfro. We'll say his mother was French," she said decisively. "Can I, Carolyna? Buy my way in with this house?"

"Why would you want to?"

"A challenge, more or less. And to make Alain happy. He misses all that royalty crap in Europe. Can I?"

"I'm afraid not. Unless this square is named for one of your ancestors." The vague sense of pity she'd held for Jessica from the start was alive and well. Cally thought of how she'd coerced Olivia Steinberg to say she'd attend Jessica's housewarming party. And Geneva.

Alain returned with fresh drinks, passed them out as Jessica addressed him in French. With an amiable smile, he disappeared into his mammoth walk-in closet, drink in hand. Clothing had arrived by van carrier a week before. The following day, a butler-type individual had appeared, unpacked, and hung the clothing, filled the vanity with male accouterments. The butler had remained ostentatiously in residence.

Jessica took a seat on the brocade fainting couch before the window, curled her gold-lamé-sheathed legs beneath her and patted the provided space. Cally sat down, crossed her legs primly, balanced the new martini on her knee. The sapphire stud, in an added hole in her left ear now, had drawn Jessica's eye. Self-consciously, Cally straightened her back.

As usual, Jessica's manner was forthright. "I tried to think I was imagining this, Carolyna, but you strike me as glum."

"Oh?" She straightened her back a little more, took a sip, felt her parched throat burn. "I'm sorry."

"That you're glum?"

"That it's evident. I don't want to spoil your homecoming."

Jessica smiled, patted Cally's knee. "Is there something I should know? Such as the Renoir in the library is a fake?"

There was, of course, no Renoir. Cally's lips twitched. "I think I'm just tired."

"As in pregnant?"

"No!" All kinds of horrendous visions flashed in her mind.

Jessica laughed outright. "You are being *exposed* to conception, aren't you, dear? If not, that could account for the pallor—in your mood, not your makeup. You're lovely, as always."

Cally heard herself say, "I've broken my engagement." To Jessica's surprised look, she offered, "It's . . . complicated."

"Did your moving into this house result in the complication?" Jessica waited while Cally squirmed. "I see. A complication caused you to move. A kind of which came first, the chicken or the egg, situation."

"It all just evolved."

She'd told Paul Michael on Jessica's floor that it *just happened*, believing it only for the seconds needed to form the words. Sometimes, on sleepless nights, she believed the situation to be fate and coveted knowing all of the divine plan. In the next breath she would assure herself divinity was not a factor.

"My whole life is in upheaval. Transition, I suppose." Geneva's threats of disinheritance loomed in her mind. "It isn't affecting my work. Please don't think that. Actually the opposite is true. My work affects—" Remembering Paul Michael's perplexed, gently insistent face, she caught her breath.

She looked into Jessica's kind eyes, carefully placed her drink on a small granite-topped table, and hid her face in her palms. Her shoulders shook, and tears slid past her hands, staining her linen skirt. Jessica's hand patted her knee. Muffled footsteps made Cally raise her head to see Alain offering her a cool, wet cloth.

"I'm so sorry," Cally whispered, dabbing at her eyes, not wanting to mar the new linen hand towel with mascara. "Please forgive me. I ruined everything."

"Like what," Jessica said.

"Your homecoming."

The backs of Jessica's slightly gnarled fingers caressed Cally's cheek, brushed her sapphire adorned ear. "Oh, I don't think so." She unfolded her legs, rose, and looked down at Cally. "For once I don't feel I'm conversing with a business card. I'm relieved to know Ms. Carolyna Sinclair Design isn't a wind-up doll." She smiled. "Drink that martini, dear. I promise you, things can only get better."

She turned to Alain, offered him her hand, drew him to his feet. "Darling, if I slip you my Master Card, would you like to take two ravenous, ravishing women to dinner?"

"It would be my pleasure, *bien-aimée*." He offered Cally his arm, extended his hand to Jessica, palm up, awaiting the card.

Jessica threw back her head, laughing heartily.

On the morning of the party, Paul Michael smiled at Cally from the opposite end of his big bathtub.

"Awk! Pretty Cah-lee. *Chérie! Chérie!* Awk! Awk!"

Rolling his eyes, Paul Michael found the soap and heaved it across the room, artfully missing Pierre. The perch rocked, the bird crammed his head deeply into the feeding bowl, then murmured, "Awk." He clucked softly, sadly, making Cally laugh.

"He is happy you woke up in my arms this morning, girl."

"I share his happiness. Boy."

She stretched her leg out, caressed his dark chest with her foot. His hands encased her ankle, lifted her foot. He sucked her toes, gently, his eyes holding hers, then darted his tongue along her sole. She jerked back, laughing. He straightened her leg, caressed the long scar inside her thigh, his smile loving. Her heart surged. Hugh had hated the scar, talked of cosmetic surgery, frowned critically when she wore tennis clothes.

"Party day," she said quietly, coiling and pinning her hair on top of her head. Paul Michael had spent hours, two nights before, gently removing the first set of braids. "Are you ready? Are you going to braid the Jamaica Jammers' hair and bathe them too?"

"Only you, baby girl."

"You *are* ready for the party, though?" Butterflies swarmed in her stomach. "You can come early . . . help me set up? The way we planned."

"Every little t'ing going to be *awl* right."

"You've been wonderful, Paul Michael. I couldn't have done this—"

"Ain't no big-time t'ing, little sister." His voice softened. "I love you, Cally. I am happy when I help you."

Cast back to that first day on the dock, she cupped her hand and studied the rivulets of water she dribbled across her shoulder.

"Why won't you tell me you love me, Cally?"

Her pulse thundered inside her temple.

"I know you do," he said softly. "I feel it."

She met his eyes. "I know what love can cause. I'm older than you. I've seen—"

His laughter rang. Pierre started, then flounced around. Ziggy Marley jumped from the end of the tub, raced to the rumpled mattress.

"Oh, yeah, girl. Older. But I am wiser. Wise enough to know you love me. Not wise enough to know why you won't say it."

He sat up, pulled her astraddle his lap, waited. His eyes were insistent, yet soft; he hardened beneath her. She kissed him, moved her mouth on his, pledging what he claimed to know.

He pulled back, held her face in his hands. "Two weeks, girl. That is all we have. Jessica's fine house is done. This grand party is almost over. Our life is going by, Cally. Say it."

Her voice divulged her thoughts, petitioned what she'd sworn not to ask. "Extend your visa. We'll go on working together . . . somewhere. Stay here until—"

"Until you don't ask me to extend it again?" He tensed, held her back from him. "Why would I do that, baby girl?"

The disappointment in his eyes soured in the pit of her stomach. His non-grasping nature had been a magnet in the beginning. Just waking up together should be enough to make them happy, but greed, instinctive and festering, had crept in, claiming their tranquility.

She eased his hands from her shoulders, stood, stepped over the side of the tub. She dried herself with the new blue bath sheet, a gift that must have cost him a day's wages. When he left the tub, she dried him, trying to ignore his rationale when he spoke.

"In your country I am black—not a good thing to be. And I am poor with little chance to change that." He took the towel, roped her waist, drew her to him, his voice and his eyes softening. "In my country I am not poor enough to notice. If I give up art and music and go back to school I can be anything. I will go home, Cally. I will do those things. When I am a fine pink Jamaican gentleman, you will come to me. You cannot love me more there, but maybe then you will tell me."

He braided her hair, erotically texturizing the six-hour ritual, just as before. He bathed her again and made love to her.

The pall of reality and their approaching separation hung over it all.

Chapter 20

That night Cally stood with Jessica and Alain at the front door to greet the party guests. One hundred invitations had been sent to Cally's friends and past clients, Jessica and Alain's new neighbors as well as acquaintances made in the two years they had migrated between Savannah and California.

Among the guests was a loud and colorful party of ten, whose authentic Jamaican attire and tans resembled the Renfros'. Jessica said that the group had "flown in." Cally pushed down images of wings and space ships and magic carpets.

She was presented with a flourish. "My designer, the illustrious Carolyna Sinclair. Connoisseur of Savannah chic."

"*Très magnifique*," Alain contributed.

An aging red-haired woman arched one brow. "Do you travel, darling?"

"At the drop of a check," Jessica snapped.

Cally smiled and shook the offered hands.

At dinner, the night of Cally's breakdown, Jessica had coerced her into sharing her financial apprehension, her quashed dreams of starting her own design firm. Cally surmised that Jessica had learned some Southern colloquialisms when she patted Cally's hand assuringly, concluding, "Well, sugar, there's more than one way to skin fat cats."

Cally was finding the woman's perceptive and avant-garde nature both comforting and disturbing. Paul Michael's introduction, when he had arrived early to help with the party setup, was amusing but disconcerting for her. For Paul Michael, she couldn't decide.

She had met him as he rounded the corner of the house in his pre-party uniform. Tank top, brief cutoffs, abused Nikes, no socks. The locket gleamed in the sun, matching his golden smile. Somehow, she managed not to touch him as she announced, "Jessica, this is

Paul Michael Quest."

Jessica's expression blended interest and amusement. Her eyes traveled over Paul Michael, taking in his hair, then Cally's, his sapphire stud, then Cally's ear. Tonight she wore one silver stud and two silver dangles, but recall, then comprehension, flicked across Jessica's pretty face. It seemed to Cally her client made no effort to curb a knowing smile.

"Paul Michael has been my friend and assistant throughout," Cally rushed. "He's the consultant who kept me authentic for this party and he's providing the entertainment."

Paul Michael offered his hand and a lustrous smile.

Jessica shook his hand, cocking her head. "Nice eyes."

"Deep-water blue." Paul Michael cast Cally a quick look.

Her throat tightened. She swallowed, glanced toward the caterers, back to Jessica.

"Nice earring," Jessica observed.

Paul Michael, with no guile or dishonesty, leaned to examine Cally's left ear. His disappointment was obvious when he discovered Cally's sapphire missing. She felt him sink into himself for a moment before he murmured, "It is an antique sapphire. Big-time nice."

Then he had turned to her, his voice lacking verve. "How can I help you with this fine party, little sister?"

The Steinbergs approached on the brick walk, forcing Cally's attention back to the party at hand.

"Olivia and Prentiss Steinberg, I'd like you to meet Jessica and Alain Renfro." Cally waited while they exchanged handshakes, noting Olivia's unguarded appraisal of Alain. "The Steinbergs and I are currently involved in an island project."

"With Hugh," Olivia interjected, surreptitiously adjusting a flounce on her brightly colored blouse. "It's . . . lovely . . . to meet you. Do you know Hugh Masters, Mrs. Renfro?"

"Jessica. I only know volumes about him."

Cally squelched a smile. She had confessed more than she'd intended last Sunday night, a result of Alain's gentle prodding and too much exquisite wine.

"Hugh's a fine man," Prentiss offered, his eyes sweeping the elegant interior behind Jessica. "I wouldn't want to tackle a project like this without him."

Cally's cheeks warmed.

Jessica shrugged her firm, tanned shoulders. "Why don't you get a drink from the bar in the parlor and see for yourself how well Carolyna managed on her own."

"Will I see you later, Carolyna?" Olivia asked. "I have some information for you about the dolls."

"Of course. Thank you." As the Steinbergs moved away, she whispered, "Here comes my family."

At the curb, Geneva, Lucinda, and Turner surrendered Geneva's Cadillac to the valet. Cally waited for the senator to appear. Instead, Hugh emerged from the front passenger seat, garish in a flowered shirt and a recent sunburn.

Jessica drew her to a position between Alain and herself. Cally sucked in new resolve. She kissed Geneva's offered cheek, then Lucinda's, attempting to ignore Turner's grin and Hugh's glare.

"Where's Daddy?"

Cally's quiet inquiry was ignored.

"How do you do? I'm Geneva Sinclair."

Alain took the extended hand, held it to his chest, beamed at her. Geneva stiffened for a moment, then helplessly, Cally noted, beamed back.

"Mother, these are the Renfros. Jessica and Alain." She turned to say, "My mother. My sister, Lucinda."

Alain appeared grieved to release Geneva's hand before grasping Lucinda's. Her delighted smile was instantaneous.

Taking a breath, Cally offered, "My ex-husband, Turner Cole." She paused, plunged. "And, Hugh Masters. My ex-fiancé."

Hugh's stare took in Cally's above-the-knee hot pink sarong, bare legs, braided hair, and flushed face.

Jessica scrutinized the group, her smile tolerant. "How . . . democratic."

Hugh's body jerked into rigidity. It seemed a lifetime before he accepted Jessica's hand, then Alain's.

"So this is where you've been hiding out." Turner's smile was brash, his observance reverent. "Cool, babe. You've mastered your trade all right."

"There is a bar in the parlor," Alain suggested. "Please enjoy seeing these lovely ladies' *pièce de résistance* before joining the party outside."

Visibly flustered by the scarcely veiled dismissal, Geneva murmured, "So nice to meet you at last and to see your lovely home." She turned her smile on Cally and elaborated, "It *is* lovely dear, just as you've been claiming."

They moved on, Turner leading the way, Lucinda attaching herself possessively to Hugh's arm. Geneva formed the rear of her entourage.

"She's never seen the house," Jessica summarized.

"No."

"Incredulous."

Alain circled Cally's waist, gave an encouraging squeeze. "This Turner Cole adores you, *mignonne*." Alain also knew the intricacies of the botched marriage. "Enough so, do you think, that you could coerce him to teach me golf?"

Turner's plan, to take Lucinda and rejoin the tour, gnawed at Cally. "I'll teach you, Alain. I had an excellent tutor."

As guests continued arriving, Jessica faithfully proclaimed Cally "solely responsible for this wonderful house" to anyone Cally hadn't pre-disclosed as a past or present client. Once the latecomers began to trickle down, Cally relinquished her co-hostess position at the door with a sense of accomplishment.

The Renfro house boasted a backyard only because Jessica had the wisdom and the wherewithal to purchase the decaying house behind her lot and raze it. The elegant yard and gardens had been transformed into an island atmosphere. Establishing the ambiance, a huge banner stretched across the back fence proclaimed, NO PROBLEM, MON. IS JAMAICA. Accordingly, the party had evolved in fine form.

Food stations positioned strategically throughout the area and around the pool featured varieties of island food. While balancing drinks, the guests sampled the fare and viewed the floor show staged by the Jamaica Jammers.

Cally stood with the Steinbergs when a member of the band

swallowed, expelled, and reingested fire while undulating to provocative music. A second band member walked on ground glass, then reclined on a bed of nail points while the guests grimaced and applauded. A girl, unseen on Cally's infamous visit to Jamaica Jam, coaxed a few male guests from their chairs to join her in a suggestive dance. Cally felt relief. None of the guests were opposed to having fun, other than Hugh, who stolidly refused. Nonplussed, the beautiful dark girl moved on to gamer ground. Turner.

Again, Cally observed how enthusiastically Lucinda grasped Hugh's arm, snuggled it against her upper body. She considered Turner's ambiguous new status in Lucinda's game, forced down her disquiet, and avoided conclusions, reminding herself she was not accountable.

"About the dolls, dear . . . ." Olivia claimed Cally's attention. "I have a date for you, more or less. Valerie will return from her trip next week. Would you like me to arrange an appointment?"

"Thank you. That would be wonderful." She couldn't resist, "Did you happen to ask—"

"The doll you wanted . . . Jumeau? She has one."

"Wonderful."

"I knew you'd be pleased. I'll arrange it, then."

Across the yard, Geneva engaged in animated conversation with one of Jessica's neighbors, a staunch advocate of the Historical Preservation Society. Geneva had been wise enough to cover her crepey arms and to conceal a good many of the liver spots on her upper chest with a wide organza ruffle that rimmed her ample breasts. She wore her hair sleeked back, her slightly-lined face a work of cosmetic art. Cally smiled inwardly. An Angels of Mercy recruiting session was in progress, but the history enthusiast would secure no commitment from Geneva other than a check.

"What's this?"

Olivia's question drew Cally back.

The band played softly, a repetitive, evocative rhythm. Paul Michael left his drums, joined the girl dancer to work with what appeared to be a prop.

"It's a limbo bar," Olivia announced then, her breath a little shallow. She elbowed Prentiss gently, jiggling Cally in her close

175

proximity. "Remember, Prentiss? We saw this everywhere in Jamaica." She turned to Cally. "Why, we couldn't even eat, dear, without being subjected to these native gymnastics."

Cally caught Prentiss's cajoling smile. "Try to remember what you see, Libby, until we get home."

"Prentiss!" The scolding was a ruse.

The steel bar rested in its highest position. The music increased in velocity. Paul Michael took off his tunic, dropped it to the ground, slipped his baggy pants off, revealing skin-hued Spandex trunks. His muscular body, obviously oiled, shimmered in the dancing light of the torches set up along the perimeter of the grassy area. A whisper moved through the crowd. Cally's breath caught with the fierce stirring in her groin.

Smiling enticingly at the girl, Paul Michael ducked his glistening head and body beneath the bar and danced into a position across from her. He waited, hips moving in erotic invitation. The crowd waited with him. With no need to duck, the girl walked beneath the bar. The crowd laughed softly, predictably. Together, Paul Michael and the girl lowered the bar. He leaned backward slightly, duckwalked his body beneath, repeated the provocative action of waiting as the music pulsated. The girl inclined her head slightly, danced toward him, her hips answering his call.

Olivia rolled her eyes, looked to Cally for confirmation, then nestled into Prentiss's arm about her waist. Cally adjusted her weight from one spiked heel to the other, ran a hand over her flushed bare shoulder, watched them lower the bar again. Making love with Paul Michael the night before, waking in his arms just that morning, the braiding, the bath, the sadness pervading it all, suddenly seemed illusory and long ago. Gradually Paul Michael progressed to traversing the bar almost prone to the floor, his braids dragging, his muscled body straining, the girl having long since dropped out. Cally excused herself, too impacted to watch further. To the backdrop of enthusiastic applause, she moved into the crowd, images of Paul Michael's lithe body wresting her mind.

"Carolyna."

Cally recognized her mother's voice and turned from rummaging in the boxes behind the caterer's screen for more rum. She straightened, rum bottles cradled against her breasts and in each hand. Geneva entered the shielded area.

"Having a good time?" Cally eyed the white-skirted refreshment bar across the terrace, where her cache was needed. "Where's Daddy tonight?"

"Where is he always?"

"I've never really known, Mother. My new aim in life is not to feel responsible." She offered a smile. "I don't appreciate your bringing Hugh, though. It's very uncomfortable for me."

Geneva looked triumphant. "That means you still care."

"That he's here, yes. For him, no. That's over and—"

"Who did you have in bed at the cottage, Carolyna?"

Cally's spine iced up. "The bartender needs this rum."

Geneva caught her arm, marched her further behind the screen. "Last Wednesday, when you picked up the chest? Mikela said—"

"Mikela wasn't there, Mother. Not within miles of there."

"This sounds like your high school days, Carolyna."

She wondered how Geneva would know, considering all the boarding schools.

"Where in the world did you get your devious, hot-natured— never mind. I know." Geneva grimaced, looked as though the mango dessert had been rancid. "You're a spoiled child, Carolyna Joy. You could never repair a mess decently. Of course Mikela knew you were there. If you've made your bed elsewhere, lie in it there. You can't have your cake and eat it, too."

Thoughts of Mikela remaking the bed incensed Cally. "Mercy, Mother. Too many clichés. You obviously never took a literary course."

Geneva's arm drew back. Cally's burden made dodging difficult. Geneva's palm caught Cally's lower jaw. A hot flame of shame and anger shot through Cally. Their eyes locked, held. Chests heaved in unison. Cally sucked in her lower lip, bade back tears.

"That's not all I have to say on the subject, young lady."

"What, then? What else? I want to know."

Geneva lowered her voice as if suddenly aware of a possible audience. "I should let you stew about it, Carolyna. But I just want you to know I've figured out the reason for your bizarre behavior.

177

There were hairs in those sheets. Not yours. Reddish-brown body hairs. Stiff. Curly. You are a slut, Carolyna Joy. Wain Sinclair's daughter."

Cally's stomach clinched. Her eyes sought the stage.

"Not a dime, Carolyna. Do you hear me? Not one more dime."

"I hear you. And in that context, please excuse me, Mother. Duty calls." Cally maneuvered around her, left her there.

At the bar area, a hand touched her arm. She stiffened, stilling the tremor rioting inside.

"Ms. Sinclair?"

The male voice turned her. She attempted to steady herself, to project her voice evenly. "Yes."

"My name is Morris Sheldon. I live—"

"Across the square. I know. I'm glad you came. Did you meet the . . . Jessica and Alain?"

"Interesting people. I'm sure they'll be an asset to the square." When she nodded, he said, "I'd like to talk to you."

"Of course." His somber nature piqued her curiosity.

"I've held property on Skidaway Island for years. Seeing this house has made me—"

Her disquiet eased somewhat, then her heart thundered, rattled her normal reserve. Skidaway was remote. Inconvenient. Still . . . she would have too much time with Paul Michael gone, time to utilize. "Is it old property? A restoration?"

"No. It's a deepwater lot. I want to build a home, a monument actually." His smile was sad. "My wife is ill. She . . . we have children and grandchildren out of state. A large family. I'd like something to accommodate everyone at once."

He stopped. Cally nodded encouragingly.

"I'll be honest with you, Ms. Sinclair—"

"Carolyna."

"I want to lure the children home. I'm not sure how much time my wife has. I need to do this in the near future. Actually, I have plans in the works."

"You have an architect, then."

"Yes. I understand from the—Steinbergs?—that you prefer to work with this fellow, Hugh Masters."

She had once relied on Hugh's expertise to put her in a favorable light. But she had accomplished the Renfro house without him, and going on alone challenged her. "Who is your architect?"

"David Mullican. He's out of Charleston."

"I know him well. I'd love to work with him."

His face mirrored her relief. "Do you do new construction? All your projects seem to be restorations, from what I've been told this evening."

She answered carefully. "I'd love to do new construction. It's such a pleasure to start from inception." At least she imagined it would be. "With your input, of course. And your wife's."

"Perhaps you could come for lunch tomorrow. You and Stephanie could meet. She's been collecting magazine tear-outs for years. And she's watched this house closely. From her room, I mean. Jessica tells me she turned this place over to you. I'm very busy, Ms—Carolyna. And Stephanie is housebound."

Geneva's angry face, her strident warning, descended on Cally again. She waited until she could master a matter-of-fact tone. "In the trade, my arrangement with Jessica is known as *carte blanche*, Mr. Sheldon. I prefer to work that way."

"Tomorrow, then. Lunch. And call me Morris. Please."

Near midnight, Paul Michael reached for the microphone. His voice floated over the slightly diminished crowd. "Ladies and gentlemen, it has been our pleasure to be here tonight. We hope you have enjoyed the party."

Applause.

Cally stopped talking to Lucinda and listened.

"I want to thank the beautiful lady who owns this splendid house and wish her much happiness here. Your hostess, Jessica Renfro."

Cally applauded resonantly, nudging Lucinda to do the same.

Paul Michael's hands stroked the drums before him gently, glided across their surface, stroked, glided. Cally's awareness rippled, her eyes riveted to his hands. The music softened.

As did his voice. "I have been in your fine country for one year.

The time comes, in only days, for me to return to Jamaica. My heart is light. My heart is heavy." He shrugged, smiled. "I have had many beautiful experiences in America."

He fell silent, his hands moving on the drums, his eyes searching the crowd.

Dread and knowing trickled along Cally's spine. Something both Paul Michael and she prized was now threatened in his innocence, his urge to love and be loved.

"The most beautiful of all has been my boss lady and friend, Carolyna Sinclair." He spotted her, nodded, singled her out. "I will go, but I will not forget."

A comprehensive hush pervaded the crowd.

She kept her eyes straight ahead, forced a smile. In her side vision, Lucinda's head jerked around. Cally felt the unguarded probe, felt awareness settle on Lucinda.

Paul Michael began to sing. "No woman, no cry. No woman, no cry. Oh, little sister, don't shed no tear. No woman, no cry."

Aching behind her mask of a smile, Cally endured the spell he cast. Then, with Jessica and Alain, she saw the last guests out, and all the while she knew that Paul Michael had led them across a bridge in danger of caving in behind them.

Chapter 21

Cally braced against the wrought iron table she and Paul Michael had unpacked the week before and watched the caterers clean, gather gear, and restore order to the Renfro residence. The sweet smell of jasmine, pinks, roses, blended with leftover food and spent kerosene wafting on the midnight air. So much had gone toward preparing for a celebration that played out too quickly, almost anticlimactically. Her emotions tangled, relief at having the party behind her raveling with discontent.

"Carolyna?"

The familiar voice raised the fine hairs at the back of her neck. Her pulse resonated in her ears as she turned reluctantly. "Hugh. I was under the impression you'd left with Mother."

"I came back."

"The party's over, Hugh." She folded her arms, witnessing the last of the Jamaica Jammers straggling through the back gate toward the street, instrument cases in hand. The van's starter cranked; the sound lay hollow and tinny on the placid night. Still rankled by Hugh's presence at the party, she asked, "Where was my daddy tonight?"

His eyes had the cold sheen of slate. "What kind of speech was that? What the hell kind of song was that?"

She concentrated on a lone paper cup bobbing in the azure pool. "Just let it go, Hugh."

"It was damned humiliating."

"It doesn't involve you."

"I told myself that it couldn't mean what I thought. But then I began to put the clues together."

He stepped closer, and she smelled the rum on his breath, accounting for the slight slur in his speech.

"We should talk about this some other—"

"When? When would you ever have time to work that in? Everyone is clamoring for you, now that—" He whirled in a wobbly fashion, his arm taking in the grandeur of the house, the yard being transformed back to formal elegance by the white-coated caterers. "This damned house. When you started running up the highway from Sea Island—that's when the trouble began, Carolyna. It's all falling into place now."

"You're wrong." She kept her reminder quiet, moved away, made an issue of straightening one of the terrace chairs in a perfect angle to its mate. "The real trouble began with the Steinbergs." The day she'd met Paul Michael, the day Hugh had foisted the Steinbergs on her, were one and the same . . . the day Hugh had been too busy to be bothered with them himself. He'd neglected to recognize her needs, that she was more than an extension of him.

She turned, suddenly weary. "We've been through all this. Nothing can be changed now. Jessica and Alain don't deserve to have this petty debate conducted in their backyard. They're tired. They're trying to—"

Hugh half lunged and lost his footing. Seizing her arm, he steadied himself. She tried to shrug him off, stepped backward. He held on, stumbling after her, his fingers biting her flesh.

"Damn you, Hugh. Stop this," she hissed.

He stared past her shoulder, his expression fixed, yet obscure. Rage, regret, fear? She stepped backward again, coming against hard, hot, human flesh, and knew.

"Hey, mon. Let go of this pretty girl."

Relieved and alarmed, Cally realized Paul Michael had not left. "I thought you'd gone," she said senselessly.

"He came back." Paul Michael nodded at Hugh. "So did I." He eased her to the side, one hand wrapping her waist as his other hand pried Hugh's fingers off her arm.

"Take off!" Hugh ground out.

Paul Michael only looked at him. Cally had never thought of Hugh as small. Paul Michael swamped him in height, in breadth, in demeanor. Cally was acutely aware the that caterers had stopped to watch and listen openly.

Hugh narrowed his eyes as he stared at Paul Michael. "You were in Darien that day."

"Yeah, mon. And you."

Anguish colored Paul Michael's tone again. The irony of these two men ever meeting, again, anywhere, the immediate effect on Paul Michael, the delayed effect on Hugh, seized Cally.

"Son of a bitch," Hugh swore hoarsely. Initial disbelief gave way to full comprehension. "You had been to the island."

"Yeah, mon." Paul Michael's hate welled up, so strong, Cally smelled it. His barely contained loathing and contempt approached rage. "Did you think me strange to look at that day? Too strange to be in your world?"

"Paul Michael, don't," she whispered. "Please don't do this."

Hugh regressed to his original grievance. "What the hell kind of speech was that tonight?"

Silence fell. She shook her head, implored Paul Michael with a look.

"Yeah, mon. It is true. I love this woman."

Hugh lunged. Paul Michael caught his shoulders, pushed him backward, caught his shirt front, righting him before he could topple. Cally clasped a hand over her mouth, eyes wildly searching Jessica's dimly lighted upstairs window. She tried to get between the men, but Paul Michael eased her aside with one arm. She shuddered, confronting his quiet strength for the first time, other than in the throes of passion.

"She does not sleep with you, mon, because she sleeps with me. She will not marry you because she loves me. Everything is going to be all right for you never again, Hubert Wilson Masters, A.I.A.' The triumph in his smile was lost in the futility only she understood. Still, he turned, urging, "Tell him, Cally. Let this big-time fool off your hook, girl."

Ragged breaths—Hugh's, Paul Michael's, her own—rivaled the crescendo of locusts in the oak trees. Paul Michael's eyes burned her.

"Jesus Christ, Carolyna," Hugh whispered hoarsely. "I'm trying not to believe this."

"Leave, Hugh. Take what you know—what you choose to think about it—and just go."

"Slut."

He made a move toward her for which she never knew the purpose. Paul Michael turned him like a toy, pointed him in the direction of the gate, and shoved him. Hugh stumbled awkwardly, then stalked away, his prim leather heels resounding on the tabby-paved terrace. The gate swung on its hinges, leaving nothing more than acrid air in Hugh's wake.

Cally hugged her upper body, trembled, visualizing the inevitable repercussions. "You shouldn't have done that."

"Dog run for him character; hog run for him life." Without invitation, he translated, "It means nothing to you, but everything to me."

"Damn you, Paul Michael."

"I love you, Cally. It makes me big-time crazy."

"That doesn't give you the right to manhandle my life. I won't have that. Never again. No matter how much I—" She whirled on her heel, eyes on the beckoning guest room entry.

He caught her arm, swung her around. "Why wouldn't you tell him you love me? Is it because I am black?"

She did not answer. Could not.

"And in your fancy white world you choose to sleep with a black man but won't allow yourself to love him."

"You want *me* because I'm white. What's worse?" She hated him for the ache choking off her tears, the grievous truth that was finally out in the open. She abhorred the caterers' soft, sad smiles, their pity and curiosity. "You want to take me home like a trophy. You call your craving love, when it's nothing more than a desire to control me. I've seen crimes committed in the name of love."

"And, I," he said softly. "The crime of my father grieving himself to death for a woman who didn't want him or me—as I told you, little sister, that day you wouldn't take no for an answer."

"We could have been—"

"Friends," he scoffed. "I ache for you. Every night. Every minute of every day we are together. Can you say you don't care?"

"I care. I hate the way I care."

He caught her shoulders, backed her against the shade tree that sheltered the terrace, held her there. She heard the back door open, a cue for the caterers to begin work again. Dishes clattered. Metal tables scraped on concrete. Cally heard distant footsteps, unhurried but purposeful, coming closer.

Paul Michael seemed not to hear or care. "Ebony was right."

"Don't you dare mention that name to me!"

"Either tell me you are coming to Jamaica with me—"

"No. I'm not coming with you. This is my life. If you want to be part of it—are you giving me an ultimatum?"

"Big-time, baby girl. Are you giving one to me?" If the light were stronger, she knew she would see his eyes narrow with emphasis.

"I'm not going with you." She wriggled, strained. His hands held her, his chest heaved. Seeing a figure approach, she said hoarsely, "Let me go, Paul Michael."

Alain's hand came to rest lightly on Paul Michael's big shoulder.

"*Petits enfants.*" The voice was quiet, kind. "It is very late. Perhaps you could duel at a different time, in a different place. I would be so happy to arbitrate. Or to furnish weapons and count the paces, if that is what you wish."

After an eternity, Paul Michael eased his hold and stepped back.

Suddenly cold, aching, Cally fought the urge to grasp him, burrow into their shared need.

"I'm so sorry, Alain," she murmured, cheeks flaming.

"Yeah, mon. And I."

"Peace, then? And good night?"

Paul Michael's blue eyes sought hers, then slid away, deep and stormy. He went through the gate, closing it with quiet finality.

<hr />

She sipped brandy listlessly, eyes fixed on a corner kitchen cabinet that displayed porcelain she'd collected from around the world for Jessica. Finally she looked across the scarred pine kitchen table into Jessica's fondly critical face. Alain wavered near the kitchen sink, eyes soft and sympathetic.

In her mind, Cally couldn't dismiss the determination on Paul Michael's face, or the defeated slope of his shoulders when he'd left, only minutes ago. She couldn't stop remembering that dissention had never existed between them once they'd passed the milestone that morning in his apartment when he tried to drive her away. Sitting here in the harsh reality of the fluorescent-lighted kitchen, she wished fervently that Paul Michael hadn't mellowed, hadn't followed her, but let her go down those rickety stairs and out of his life. Hurt she'd felt then, before she understood, was benign compared to the ache raging in her now.

Paul Michael, too, was hurting.

If only she had walked away from the dock that first day, called a delivery service, a real one—or insisted on paying him when he delivered the desk, rather than hiring him.

"Do you want to tell me about this, Carolyna?"

She jerked, shook her head. "I only want to apologize for involving you in my personal life, Jessica." A tear oozed out. She blotted it with a gold-imprinted cocktail napkin. "I'm sorry for acting unprofessionally."

"Darling, you haven't sinned."

Alain handed Cally a second napkin. "*N'importe, chérie*," he murmured before going to stand behind Jessica's chair. His smooth, delicate fingers massaged her shoulders through the magenta satin robe, then stole to the sides of her throat.

Jessica looked up at him. "Why don't you go to bed, Alain." She smiled conspiratorially, adding, "But not to sleep."

"But of course, *mignonne*." He gave Cally an amused glance. "*Bonne nuit*, Carolyna. Everything will look better with the sun."

He spoke her name with the same inflection Paul Michael employed. Eyes watering, she nodded.

"Now." Jessica spoke with finality as Alain moved away. She sipped her brandy. "What seems like a backyard riot to you, Carolyna, was nothing more than a lovers' quarrel."

Cally's mouth formed a denial, but Jessica's smile stopped her.

"I find this all very interesting," Jessica said. "Obviously, you find it tragic. I knew the two of you were lovers the minute I saw you together. I'd like to hear about it." Faced with Cally's dubiousness, Jessica added, "There's no shame in it. He's foreign and sensual and apparently quite passionate. Who could blame you?"

186

"I feel I've cheated you . . . somehow."

"How?"

"Your house. We would never have met or gotten to know one another if not for the time we spent in this house. Time I was supposed to be working, and nothing more."

"And never have fallen in love, if not for this house."

Quickly, Cally declared, "We never used the house to make love." Her conscience flared. "After the first time, and that . . . just happened."

Jessica laughed unguardedly. "Truth prevails."

"Never after I moved in. I've tried hard to be discreet."

"Apparently you succeeded. I don't see the scarlet letter on you anywhere."

"I feel so guilty." The brand was there, buried deeply. It colored her thoughts, threatened her serenity. "Because of Hugh, I suppose. If not for Paul Michael . . . if they weren't so different . . . ." She would have the invitations bought and addressed by now, a dress purchased—one Hugh would endorse—a church reserved. Heaven would be rehearsing to bless the union.

Her throat tightened, ached; she stopped trying to hold back the tears. "You don't want to hear this, Jessica. I'll just go to bed. I'm fine, really."

"I assure you I want to hear this. We'll approach from the angle of the house, if necessary. Since you used me, you owe me the story." She rapped her glass jauntily against Cally's, passed her yet another napkin. "Begin, darling."

Cally blew her nose, dabbed her cheeks. "I thought I was happily—suitably engaged to Hugh. Yet something kept me from finalizing the wedding plans."

"Something?" Golden brows arched.

"Vague discontent."

"Aha!"

"On a day of distinct discontent, the day I found your desk . . . I met Paul Michael. On the Savannah docks."

"And?"

Cally smiled at last. "Discontent evolved into intrigue."

"Understandable."

"That wasn't all."

"After the erotic eruption, you mean. I would hope not."

"*He* was complacent—happy, it seemed. He was kind. Gentle. Concerned for my plight. He offered help."

"He was intrigued, also." Jessica smiled wryly.

"Whatever his motives, he offered to deliver the desk."

The brows arched again. "He's in the delivery business?"

"No. He's an artist—and a musician, as you saw. He was drawing on the docks that day. Impulsively I agreed to have him take the desk home—he gave me his locket as surety—then delivered the desk the next day."

"You traded my desk for his locket?"

"Yes." Cally relived the day again. "The rest is . . . obvious."

"Not to me, dear."

Cally rose, crossed to the trash compactor, dropped the soiled napkins inside. She leaned against the counter, arms folded across her chest. The account suddenly seemed predictable, mundane. "You're sure you want to hear this?"

Jessica patted a chair bottom. Cally sat down. "Being with Paul Michael satisfied my soul. I hired him to deliver for me once a week. I began to live for those Wednesdays. When we were together he praised me, appreciated me, accepted anything I thought, said, or did. I'd never had a . . . friendship . . . like that. Going back to the island, to Hugh, I met with the opposite. As I grew more and more content being with Paul Michael, I became less enchanted with Hugh and the thought of spending my life with him."

Cally fell quiet, reaffirming memory. "Hugh sensed this. He increased his bid for control. I rebelled. Mother sensed that, and began to apply the pressure you and I discussed at dinner the other night."

Jessica nodded. "She knew then. About Paul Michael."

"She began putting the pieces together last week. After tonight, she'll know it's Paul Michael."

"And even more crap will hit the fan."

"Yes."

"Go on."

"As we worked, spending more and more time together, I could find nothing wrong with him. He's educated, broad-minded, wise. He's artistic, draws portraits at Factors Walk. He sells his art at Reggae Ruby's and—" Cally swallowed nervously. "I went to his home—an attic room filled with art, animals, and hand-me-downs. Junk in some people's minds, but more of a home than any space I've ever known."

She lingered a moment in the memory of the deep tub, the too-hot water, the mattress on the floor. "He helped me with this house, far beyond hauling furniture. I'd arrange a room. He would offer an option. So many times he was right. He hangs pictures by eyeing a wall space and nailing. This appealed to my creative nature." She smiled, confessing, "Most of all, though, he's very sensitive."

"And that appealed to your current need."

"One night we were working late. Hugh called. An especially disillusioning call. Paul Michael was . . . sympathetic."

"He *is* wise."

"I seduced *him*." When Jessica nodded, her eyes tender, Cally went on. "I realized my mistake and tried to right the wrong. Of course it couldn't be done."

"What is it you say down here? Something about the futility of closing the gate after the cows get out?"

"Yes. I never slept with Hugh again. Of course, that caused chaos. I moved in here shortly after that. Paul Michael and I began—he had all the qualities Hugh lacked, at first. Then, gradually, he started to display some of Hugh's traits. That was sobering."

"He was threatened. Acting out is a normal reaction."

Cally nodded. "His visa is up. I've known that almost from the start. Knowing was like . . . having a way out."

"A little calculating, darling."

"I know. But it didn't work that way. I began to wonder . . . began to want him to stay."

"Good."

"It's more complicated than that. He wants me to go to Jamaica with him."

Jessica tipped the brandy bottle, the golden-brown liquid coating the inside of her glass.

189

"I can't go with him," said Cally. "My independence is vital. I couldn't work in Jamaica. I'd have to depend on him. That's not the woman he knows. That would kill whatever we have." She wrapped her arms around her body. "If he stayed in Savannah, I'm not sure I could ever be with him openly. That would kill our—"

"Love, dear." Jessica smiled encouragingly.

"It would kill our love. Eventually. I know parting is the only answer. I just didn't want to face it . . . until he's gone."

"But he forced the issue."

"I wanted the memories to be sweet. Something we could remember. That's why tonight is so painful."

"Propriety is often hard to regain, Carolyna, once you've crossed the invisible line."

"I know," she whispered. "This isn't my first time."

Silence fell. The refrigerator hummed, seeming inordinately loud. The ancient foyer clock chimed the declining hour. Suddenly weary, hollow, Cally drained her glass.

Jessica's raspy voice interrupted the pall. "I'd be the last to subscribe to the 'happily ever after' theory, dear, but while love lasts, it's the most beautiful thing in the world. You've had a taste of that. Whether or not you choose to gorge yourself, or to go on starving in the name of what you deem proper, and in the hope of pleasing the world, only you can decide."

"I don't want to hurt him any more than I have." She stood, pushed in her chair.

"Commendable." Rising also, Jessica cocked her head to meet Cally's eyes. "How do you propose to avoid that?"

"Paul Michael gave me an ultimatum tonight. I refused it. We have another saying down here. 'Let sleeping dogs lie.' Thank you for listening—"

"For caring." Jessica frowned, her mouth pulling down at the corner.

"Thank you even more for that."

Sickened with loneliness, Cally made her way to what used to be her haven, the guest room.

Chapter 22

*D*espair, oppressive and glaring, settled on Cally the moment she opened her eyes the following morning. There had been no good-night call from Paul Michael, as had become their ritual. She had fallen into fitful sleep, cradling the phone. And now, in the pitiless light of morning, a second ritual had died. He had not called to wake her.

She forced herself to remember, first Hugh and then Paul Michael, exiting Jessica's gate. An era had passed.

If only it didn't hurt so much.

Cally pulled herself from the haven of the feather mattress and Porthault sheets and prepared to face her day, painfully re-embracing her ideal. Liberation.

⁂

Jessica was waiting when Cally returned from lunch with the Sheldons across the square.

"Were you successful, dear? Do you have *carte blanche*?"

"It seems so." Cally deposited her overstuffed bag and briefcase on a table. "I still have to meet with the architect, but that's a formality, more or less."

"Will you sign a contract after that?"

"I hope to. I need this job. Badly."

On the sofa with the medallion back rest, Jessica patted the seat beside her. How well Cally remembered the day Paul Michael had delivered it . . . . She jerked her thoughts back, her pulse quickening when she noticed the papers Jessica held.

"I found this on your desk when I borrowed a pen. What is it, Carolyna?"

Cally sat, slipped the papers from Jessica's plump, ringed fingers.

Her eyes caressed the realtor's tear sheet. "A town house on Taylor Street."

"That much I gathered. What is it?"

"A dream."

"And that's why you'll take on the Sheldon project, come hell or high water."

Cally nodded.

"To live in this town house, or to refurbish and sell it?"

"To refurbish and live there—not in that order. I'd have to live there during the refurbishing." The house came back to her, gloriously. The light filtering in fragile trails on the worn carpet, footsteps echoing on the original floors. "I'd never sell it. I could even fence the backyard if—" Her mind clamped shut.

"If you have children."

"If I get a dog."

Jessica's frame shook. Her laughter echoed off the marble floor. "Just because you're manless at the moment doesn't mean you'll never propagate. I want to see this house."

"It isn't right for me, really. I'd rather not see it again." She'd been driving by twice a day, to make sure it maintained its century-old-position on Taylor. "Actually, there's perfect space for my design firm . . . ." She smiled, cheeks warming. "Disregard that. I keep my design firm in that big canvas bag and in my briefcase. An efficiency apartment will be big enough, which I plan to find the moment I have the Sunday realty section. This Sunday."

She twisted one braid, tortured her scalp, tried not to think of Paul Michael and her fantasies that involved the townhouse. "You've been kind and I love it here, but—"

"I want to see this house, darling. And I want to take you to Windows for lunch to thank you for the wonderful party. We'll discuss the 'design firm in a briefcase' over martinis and salmon mousse."

Cally and Jessica stood alone in the room Cally had designated as the proposed office of her mythical but hoped for design firm.

Glancing out a window, she saw the realtor behind the wheel of her car, where Jessica had suggested she wait. Cally tried to visualize the surroundings objectively. Not having been here at midday previously, she was pleased with the light that flooded in the north window of the old servants' quarters. Track lighting wouldn't be crucial at first if—

"This would work out well," Jessica said. "Especially with the staircase to bring clients directly in here. The summer dining room, as you called it, could be used for a reception area. Ample seating, even a desk for an assistant."

"It would be a while before I'd need anyone."

"Not if I have my way. And I usually do." Jessica smiled. "You've checked the zoning, I suppose."

"Yes. The realtor even talked with the neighbors. No one seems to object. It's such an old-money neighborhood, I could hardly believe that, but—" She stopped, checked her enthusiasm, murmured, "I love all the tradition of this house."

Jessica crossed to the window, lowered, then raised a ragged vinyl shade. "But there's some stipulation, a rush of some kind? Or was that sales propaganda?"

"The bank has it. It goes on the auction block Monday."

"Let's go to lunch, dear. Martini time."

Cally gazed out the restaurant window at milling tourists on the ballast-stone street below. A tug passed on the Savannah River as she studied the old harbor on the opposite bank. The murmur of lunch patrons wrapped around her, the soft ping and clink of silver against china insulated her until the sudden patter of splotchy rain drops against the window pane reminded her of the rainy day when Paul Michael had braided her hair the first time. Her hand went to her head, then lowered.

Across from her, Jessica's form blurred. Dazed with the hurt of missing Paul Michael, Cally pushed crab fettucini around her plate and listened as Jessica speculated zestfully.

"All right, darling. This is the way I see it, from what you've told

193

me. A design firm, as opposed to a freelance designer, seems to consist of owning your own samples and having a place to store them. This eliminates constantly running to the Atlanta Mart."

Cally forced a smile. "That's a bit over-simplified. Going to Atlanta will always be mandatory for large items. The feasibility of having my own carpet, fabric, and wall covering samples . . . if I took on a new client I could just pull samples from my cache, which would be periodically updated. Investing in samples is costly. In order to do that I need credit. Money in the bank to guarantee it."

She tasted her martini, noted Jessica's rapt expression.

"Also, I've been taking cash deposits from clients to place orders, then collecting the balance to pay off the account when the merchandise comes in. That's not a professional image. I belong to the proper design associations, such as ASID, but I need to be underwritten by groups that verify my financial credibility . . . such as Lyons, Dunn and Bradstreet. I need a permanent mailing address, rather than a post office box. In short, all the props of any respected business."

"And the town house is a prop as well?"

"The town house, aside from being my home, would be like a showroom. It would give potential clients an idea of the quality of my work. In the reception area I'd display antiques, art, accessories, small furniture pieces they could purchase. I'd be able to write off a large part of the expense of living there, just as I'd write off a showroom or shop."

"You've done your homework."

"I learned all this in design school."

"I don't know if you're aware, darling, but Alain has a wonderful appreciation of fine things."

"I'm aware of how he appreciates you." Cally acknowledged an envious twinge.

Jessica smiled. "He has a vast knowledge of art. He could be useful to you if you attract the right clientele, which you seem to have a knack of doing."

"I would never impose on him."

"Am I being too tactful, Carolyna?"

"Did I miss something?"

"Alain needs to feel imposed on. He needs a purpose other than bedding me and mixing my drinks. He'd make an excellent procurer." She smiled again. "That sounds . . . *risqué*. In layman's language, 'a buyer.' He looks for any excuse to go to Europe. Alone. Am I making myself clear?"

Cally shook her head, not quite able to accept Jessica's insinuation concerning Alain, or her hint at . . . what? "Not exactly."

"I would finance your venture, Carolyna, if you'd be willing to drop Southern protocol and impose on Alain."

"That's . . . kind of you." Her heartbeat invaded her ears.

"Not totally, if you've heard me at all. You seem to be in a fog." Jessica frowned. "A casualty of last night's battle, probably. One thing I've learned, darling. Defeat in one skirmish doesn't necessarily determine the outcome of the war."

Hugh's face, then Geneva's, and at last Paul Michael's, flashed in Cally's mind. She put down her fork, sipped water.

She said, "Actually I have some money. Enough, probably, for the down payment on the town house. I've been saving to replenish the trust fund."

"Why, for God's sake?"

"To escape the guilt, I suppose."

Jessica rolled her eyes within her heavily mascaraed lashes. "Screw guilt, darling. You're spending too much time sorting your life into neat little categories when all life really amounts to is reaping all the satisfaction you can. Trust me."

"Replacing the money does seem foolish, now."

"Now?"

"Mother is going to take the rest of my inheritance unless I conform, which I won't. If I use the money I've saved to pay down on the town house, I'll have none left to finance the business, and then I can't depreciate the house. That amounts to living beyond my means, nothing more. So, I can either use the money for the town house and starve, or use it to hire an attorney. I know which choice is wiser. I'm just having a hard time giving up on the house. But I know what I *should* do."

"An attorney?" Jessica lowered her fork, seized the watery martini, rejected it. She flagged the waiter. "Two iced coffees and

195

two Remy Extra Perfections," she snapped, then allotted Cally her attention again. "An attorney?"

"I'm going to sue Mother for what Grampa Englander left me."

"On what grounds, dear?"

"I read an article about two adult children suing their father—a prominent athlete—for not being a suitable father to them. At least, the kind of father they wanted. They claimed he denied them time, attention . . . love. They won a healthy settlement. I'll use that case as a precedent."

The waiter brought Jessica's order. She poured the brandy into the glasses of cold coffee and motioned the waiter to take Cally's untouched fettucini away. Lifting her drink, she waited for Cally to follow suit, then clinked glass against glass.

"To a litigious society." Jessica sipped. "What's the case relevancy? If you know." To Cally's puzzled silence she reiterated, "Between lousy parents and withheld inheritances."

"I'm not sure there is one. That will be up to my attorney. I'm just angry at the moment for all the years I needed Geneva . . . Mother . . . and she was never there, other than to point out when I'd fallen from grace." Cally looked out the window. Rivers of rain, cloudy and cold looking, gushed down the curb sides, plunged into the grated gutter.

"All the time I wasted with Hugh, the subtle abuse I took from him, was to make Mother proud of me . . . at least, notice me. She controls my trust, as I told you. She cut off the income once, during the Turner era. The moment I crossed her by questioning my marriage to Hugh, she threatened to cut me out completely. Now that she knows I've slept with Paul Michael, she'll go through with it."

Jessica's face saddened. She looked ready to speak but only nodded, her mouth tightening.

"I've been depending on my inheritance to finance my career. I'm sure Grampa Englander put no stipulations on the money other than the age I'm to receive it. I wasn't wise enough to handle the first distribution at age twenty-one. Luckily it was small in comparison to what's coming to me—was coming to me—when I'm thirty. From what I've heard, Grampa Englander was a rebel, scandalous at times." Cally smiled. "My kindred soul, Mother has pointed out. He didn't stipulate my marrying Hugh, or loving someone of my own color, or conforming to Mother's wishes. I'm assuming he didn't, anyway. As I said, I've seen nothing in writing. She's been holding the inheritance over my head all these years. The right attorney can frame the legal wording, but those are the grounds I'll use to sue her . . . that it's not her money. She is only the trustee."

"Well, son of a bitch."

Buoyancy lifted Cally, like a freed helium balloon. She laughed, sipped her drink. "Daughter of a bitch, actually."

"You have my best wishes. Probably, dear, given your parents' high profile in Savannah, the suit will never pass the filing stage. To save adverse publicity, Geneva will have you in negotiations immediately. You might suggest that while hinting at press conferences. All kinds of malicious media interviews."

"I hadn't thought of that. I hope you're right. I hate to see Daddy suffer. On the other hand, if he were stronger, if he would stand up for me . . . ." She shrugged, her smile forced.

"Meanwhile, regarding the town house," Jessica said briskly. "Save your money. Use it to retain an attorney or whatever. We'll go to the bank tomorrow morning and I'll co-sign the note for the house. I'll demand rock bottom interest rates, and I have a feeling we won't need a down payment once you've pointed out the *exorbitant* repair needed." Jessica winked. "By convincing them they'd have to give the house away on the auction block, we'll most likely get the price lowered."

"We will?" Cally was breathless all of a sudden.

"I'll deposit funds into an operating account for the coveted samples, the furnishings and miscellaneous paraphernalia. You can begin work on the house whenever you like. How does that sound? I really want to do it."

"Because of Alain? It has to be more than that."

"Because of Alain, and because you remind me of myself once. No one helped me, darling. I came up the hard way, beholden to whatever man admired my assets enough to be willing to share his. These are new times. If a woman is beholden to anyone, let it be another woman. And not even that for longer than it takes to stand on her own."

"Thank you, Jessica. My independence—"

"Is vital. You told me that. And it's admirable, Carolyna. Just don't get tunnel vision."

"Concerning Paul Michael?" She read the answer. "Surely you wouldn't have me go to Jamaica with him."

"I'd have you look for a compromise."

"If I'm associated with Paul Michael, I can't promise you the business will survive in Savannah. I'm not sure how far Mother will go to see that it doesn't, if I alienate her further."

"Remember, there's more than one way to skin fat cats." When Cally smiled, Jessica said, "I won't have much local influence for a while, but I can direct a lot of California trade—Santa Barbara, L.A., the desert—your way. Enough to see you survive until I've conquered Savannah." She smiled coquettishly, a characteristic Cally was beginning to appreciate. "This town may be gossipy and class conscious, mannered and monied, and soaked to the soul in the finest bourbon, but I understand she folded without a scuffle during the civil war. How can she withstand me?" Head cocked, she eyed Cally. "California clients would involve travel, of course. Would you be opposed to that?"

"I have nothing to keep me. No, I wouldn't mind that." She looked away, speculating, knowing she should be elated. She should regard Jessica as deliverance. And she would, in time. "What can I say, Jessica, other than thank you?"

"How about, 'check, please.' This lunch is on Carolyna Sinclair Design."

That night Cally lay in bed, gripping the cellular to her breasts, feeling time inch forward, her hearing unusually acute, intensified by the darkness. Plumbing pipes rumbled quietly from the story above her. A dog whined in the next yard. A loving owner opened, then closed a door, and the dog's lament was soothed. Tires hummed as a car slowly circled the square. A clock ticked. Cally willed the phone to ring.

Examining Paul Michael's Thursday night schedule, she reasoned he'd be changing from Reggae Ruby's, about now, to Jamaica Jam. Ordinarily he would call. The silence of the cold phone left her ill. Some of her sickness stemmed from relief, the insanity of wanting something so badly yet being glad when it didn't happen.

A shrill sound pierced the night, vibrated against her breasts. She jerked the phone up, heart pounding. "Yes?"

"Yes? Have you ever tried just saying no, babe?"

She recoiled. "I can't talk, Turner. I'm expecting a call."

He laughed. "I'll bet. I hear you're in deep trouble with the general again."

"How did you hear that?"

"It's true, though, huh? Hugh told Lucinda, just before the sedation took effect—on him, not her. Actually, she's pretty damned wired."

"I have to hang up."

"The Rastafarian dude, huh? Well, you know what they say."

"I probably don't."

"Nothing's as beautiful as black skin against white sheets."

"Poetic."

"Most people want to dream in color. Not you. You go for black and white. But I'll say this, babe. He's a nice diversion from Hugh. And, yeah. If you haven't talked to Geneva, she's pissed. I just think you should know she has her war bonnet on. Expect anything."

She sat up, took deep breaths, then remembered her decision to launch an offense, rather than wait to be attacked. "Was there something you wanted, Turner? Other than to gloat?"

"Yeah. I want to go on record. I'm not prejudiced, and I don't keep score. Once Lucinda moves on to your latest discard— namely Hugh—I'll take you back, babe. Count on it."

"You'll have to take me, Tee. I'll never come peacefully."

He was silent, then offered, "Something just occurred to me, Cally. Once Lucinda's through with Hugh and you're finished with what's his name—Paul Michael Quest? That's colorful. Do you think baby sister will move on to him?"

Cally slammed the phone down, her insides churning.

⚜

At the bank the next morning, Cally peered through a glass partition of the empty office where they waited. A black woman with two children of obviously mixed parentage, a boy and a girl, visited a nearby teller's window. Feeling Jessica's eyes on her, Cally warmed under the scrutiny.

"Paul Michael would call those children pink," she said.

"They're beautiful."

"Yes." They were lighter than Paul Michael, their skin a paler caramel. Each sported a cap of loose curls, ringlets the color of hay after a rain storm.

"You know, Cally, mixed race children are highly fashionable, now."

Cally looked away, aching, anxious for the loan officer to materialize, or for those children to leave. "I don't usually let fashion dictate my life."

"Just prejudice and tradition."

Cally caught a hint of disapproval before Jessica's eyes turned kind. "I'm sorry," Jessica said.

"No, you're exactly right." Cally saw the little family leave, the woman holding each child by the hand. "We're all a product of our upbringing. Prejudice and tradition just happen to be a staple of the South."

"No, darling," Jessica corrected. "We aren't a product of our upbringing. We're what we settle for."

⚜

An envelope waited on the entry table when Jessica and Cally returned from the bank. Cally picked it up, read her name, turned the envelope in her hand. Lightly padded, it felt weightless. She ran her index finger beneath the flap. With Jessica's eyes on her, she unfolded a Kleenex and dropped the sapphire stud into her palm.

Jessica touched her arm, squeezed gently, her eyes soft. "He's just pissed, honey. He'll call and want it back."

200

Cally shook her head. "He's hurt." She closed her eyes. "It's all about his mother and his father . . . about a lot of things."

"A part of the story you've left out."

"Yes."

"And now it's all about you, you're thinking."

Cally put the earring back into the envelope, smiled at Jessica as she caught one errant tear with the back of her hand.

In the guest room, she dialed the phone.

"Curly Que Hair and Nail Salon. This is Yolonda."

"Hi. It's Carolyna. I need a special favor—today."

"You're in a conservative mode. You want to look like—"

"I want my cornrows taken out. Can you do it?"

"Cornrows. My God, Carolyna." After a long silence, Yolonda said, "It'll take a while to remedy a fiasco like that."

Cally breathed deeply. "Forever. But can you? Today?"

"Sounds decisive."

"Yes."

"Come on over. I'll order sustenance."

❦

Near dawn the next morning, Cally left for Atlanta to attend a three-day design seminar she had known about for weeks. She had even considered asking Paul Michael to go with her, but knowing he'd stand out like a raisin in Mikela's rice pudding, she didn't. But she had never considered leaving him to go alone, until he returned the sapphire.

All their bridges were caving in after them.

201

Chapter 23

$\mathscr{T}$he following Monday afternoon Cally sat across the desk from Lawrence Fulton, Esquire. Her eyes roamed over an abundance of framed diplomas and awards, just as they had done so many times in Philip Ballentine's office. The difference was, Lawrence Fulton was an attorney.

His cultured voice, saturated with Southern inflection, droned into a phone jammed between his collar bone and right ear. He took notes, shuffled files on his desk, shooting her an apologetic look now and then.

Cally surveyed her surroundings, the desk and floor scattered with files. A small conference table served as a catchall for more files, stacks of video tapes, a softball glove, a tennis racket, a can of balls. She considered a nearby pump designed to insert new life into those balls, a positive omen.

An oil portrait of a dark-haired beauty holding two Pug Bulls dominated an entire wall of family photographs. Poses of Lawrence Fulton with local and national political celebrities abounded.

Across the desk from Cally, Lawrence Fulton himself was a somber vision. Gray hair framed an unlined face punctuated by eyes so pale they seemed to effuse light. His charcoal and gray paisley tie hung loose and twisted slightly askew against the backdrop of a pearl-gray shirt. A gray suit jacket draped over a conference chair.

The phone conversation ended. He retrieved a file from the desk corner and studied it in silence until he glanced over half glasses. "So, what can I do for you, Ms. Sinclair?"

"Carolyna. I . . . want to sue Geneva Sinclair for . . . withholding the love a mother owes a child and for using the inheritance my grandfather left me as a tool to control my life."

"And Geneva Sinclair is?"

She'd assumed he understood that. "My mother, more or less."

She saw him wrestling with a smile.

"Interesting," he said. "A Biblical prediction, actually."

"Children will rise up against their parents?" When he nodded, she said, "I read it in Sunday school—where my mother sent me. I never thought the prophesy would apply to me."

He smiled, showing even white teeth. "Well, there's a story here. A good one, I'll wager. Why don't I just listen and then let you know if I'm your man."

Before Cally walked out of his office, near twilight, Lawrence Fulton had all the needed data to file what he called a "breach of parenting" suit on behalf of Carolyna Joy Sinclair.

❦

Late on Tuesday morning, Cally sat on the sand of Skidaway Island with Morris Sheldon and his architect, David Mullican. David, short, stocky, balding, quiet spoken, was Hugh's physical opposite. After inquiring about Hugh's health and a casual exchange of industry gossip, he got down to business.

While they sipped estate-bottled Pierre Jouet from plastic flutes and munched crusty, paté-laden toast squares, David explained the Sheldons' house plans. Cally listened, glancing periodically at the wind-ruffled plan and nodding dutifully. Much of the time, her eyes rested on the tumultuous, bluish-green water, her thoughts with Paul Michael.

Tuesday. The day would run into evening, the time when he once would have called—in the beginning—to get the delivery list. Would this occur to him, too? Stir his memory beyond pride and hurt, propel him to lift the phone and dial? Did a vacuum exist in his soul that only she could fill, a void that mirrored the ache raging in hers now? Tomorrow, a week would have passed since the party. She tried not to think of the few days remaining, even as she reminded herself that his departure was the only answer. When a short drive from the Renfro house to Paul Michael's, or a simple phone call to either Ruby's or Jamaica Jam would not tempt her . . . when he was gone, then they could each begin to heal.

In the car, crossing the Diamond Causeway back to Savannah,

203

Cally assured Morris Sheldon, "The house could be wonderful. I'm envisioning an eclectic design favoring contemporary. A lot of white with bleached wood, sparse almost, to allow your wife—"

"Stephanie."

"To allow Stephanie easy access within the rooms. David has already included extra wide doors in the plan and the elevator to accommodate the wheelchair. I'm thinking there should be no thick carpets, very little floor covering at all—sisal, maybe—so that she'll feel unhampered and encouraged to move around her home. To enjoy it."

She glanced at him, at his soft profile, the little pocket of excess flesh beneath his chin, the slight bulge above his belt line. She wondered what kind of man he was when not being polite and professional. "If I'm on the wrong track—"

"Stephanie is everything to me, Carolyna. She has been from the moment I saw her. I'd like you to keep that in mind, above all else— I take it you've decided to accept the job."

Her heart pounded. "*Carte blanche?*"

"Of course. Stephanie has some ideas, though."

"I'll be tactful. I've even learned to bend occasionally." She smiled. "I'll let her know it's her house. I'm only a tool to reach her goal."

"I appreciate that. I'll make it worth your while."

"Have you known each other . . . always?"

"No. The children are hers. We had prior marriages. Thank God, we found each other. Otherwise, I'd never have known what being loved is all about."

Cally stared out the window. "It's wonderful that you recognize that. I'm sure some people never do. Or even if they do, there's sometimes a reason . . . you're very fortunate."

"We can make our fortune, Carolyna, or just accept it."

❧

Driving to the island later in the week, Turner's warning about Geneva wound through Cally's mind like a cassette on continuous play. The cliché, "waiting for the other shoe to drop," gained sudden clarity. Lawrence Fulton had asked for a week to prepare the suit and serve Geneva. At that point, the "shoe" would become a steel-toed brogan and plummet with a thud. Cally's stomach reeled, then settled into a state of unrest that was becoming too familiar.

Olivia Steinberg waited with lemonade and cookies at her island house. The tired cooling system labored futilely against the oppressive heat that invaded sections of ripped-out roof, even though tarps covered the gaping holes designated as eventual skylights. Dusty draperies heaped here and there, discarded in favor of four-inch louvered plantation shutters. A compromise. Olivia would have her privacy, and Cally would savor the satisfaction of a flawless view of the third golf green.

Sipping lemonade, Cally toured the house, Olivia in her wake.

"Hugh did a nice job of sectioning this bathroom," Cally said. "You'll be able to talk to Prentice while you dress, but you'll feel you have some privacy."

"Yes. Hugh has done wonders. Of course, your touch combined with his expertise is incomparable. By the way, you just missed him. He knew you and I had an appointment, but he couldn't stay."

"Hmmm."

"Something is wrong between the two of you, isn't it, Carolyna? That bothers me."

"I'm sorry . . . bothers you how?"

Olivia clasped her hands tightly, her eyes anxious. "I'm not sure. I have this sense of guilt."

"It has nothing to do with you."

"But you didn't want to take this job. We forced—"

"No," Cally said quickly. "You didn't force me. I relented." She smiled. "And I haven't been sorry. When this house is done, it will be a feather in our caps—yours and mine. And please believe me, this . . . rift between Hugh and me won't affect your house."

Back at the kitchen table, they pored over wallcovering books while Cally made a substantial dent in the sugar cookies. "This pattern is nice." Pausing, she tilted a page for Olivia to consider. "It would go nicely in the—"

"That's Valerie Pennington's foyer paper. It's lovely, but I should choose something different."

"Pennington?" The name was familiar.

"Yes, dear. My friend Valerie. You do remember?"

"Your friend from Jamaica . . . the dolls." Cally closed the book, wrapped her waist with her arms, shivered in the heat. She didn't want to think of Jamaica. "I remember. I thought her name was Michelson."

"It is, now. I just lapse sometimes." Olivia reopened the book, turned a page. "When we were all in Jamaica, her name was Pennington. Stan Pennington, the gentleman posted with Prentice at the embassy, was Valerie's husband."

Cally remembered the dusty photographs she saw in the study that first night she'd come to this house. The three couples, two white, one black. The photographs had since been taken to the framer.

Olivia said, "Stan died a few years later—in Zaïre, of all places, of some horrible virus that now sounds like Ebola. Of course it wasn't called Ebola then. Anyway, Valerie remarried. A man named Michelson. I didn't see her for years, until she moved back to Savannah a few months ago."

"That recently?"

"Yes, and I still have trouble adjusting to her new name."

Olivia studied pages. Cally mimicked her action, absorbed nothing. An overhead fan whipped loose fabric samples, stirred the tendrils escaping her top knot, bathed her parched skin. She listened to the sound of a wall being ripped, gutted, altering the structure forever. But in her mind echoed over and over: Jamaica . . . Paul Michael . . . Jamaica . . . Paul Michael.

At last Olivia spoke again. "Valerie was never the same after the tragedy in Jamaica."

Cally looked up, waited.

"She lost a child there," Olivia said. "A stillbirth. Valerie's husband, along with mine, had already been dispatched to Nigeria. Valerie was in the last stages of pregnancy and couldn't travel. I felt badly for her, but, of course, I went along with Prentice. She assured everyone she would be fine. She had her classes to pass the time, and—"

"She was a student?"

"Valerie was the scholarly type. She was always enrolled in classes at the university. Literature and English."

Literature and English. Cally rose, stood quite still, struck by a sudden, outlandish notion. She tried to call up an image of the black woman in the photograph she'd examined that night, to remember if her features were blunt or . . . finely sculpted.

"Carolyna?"

"I just need to . . . wash this sugar off my fingers."

Cally stepped to the kitchen sink, let the water run. She stared out the window and listened to the stream gurgle into the drain. Surely she had gone mad to—

Slowly, she returned to the table. "How did the baby die?"

"A terrible thing. The cord was twisted. Stillbirth, as I said. Valerie buried him—she didn't want a service, she said later. I believe he was cremated . . . yes, that's what she said. And when she could travel, she joined Stan in Nigeria."

"Stan? The baby's father?"

Olivia nodded. "Valerie's husband, dear."

"He . . . Stan didn't go back for the funeral?"

"There was no funeral. Valerie simply wanted to put it—the baby behind her. It was her way of grieving, I suppose. And the distance was prohibitive. Transportation wasn't the same then as now. But when they divorced—"

"She didn't stay married to the baby's father? Stan?"

"For a while. Ten, maybe twelve years. We went on to different assignments, but we kept in touch. I always wondered if Paul's death was too difficult for her to accept. That perhaps it changed her—or if she somehow felt badly that Stan hadn't come back to Jamaica when it happened. We don't talk about it now."

Cally shivered. "Paul?"

"Oh, yes. He was called Paul from the moment she became pregnant. She named him after one of her professors . . . English, I think. Once you name a baby . . . in the old days, when I had mine, that wasn't done. Valerie is younger, though, and strong willed." Olivia fell silent, turned pages, then shifted the book around. "I like this. What do you think?"

Cally passed her a Post-It-Note to use as a marker. "It's very nice.

207

When did you say I could see the dolls? Did you arrange a time for me?"

"Not yet, but I'll do it. I know Valerie is back from her little trip. Jumeau . . . that's what you're interested in, isn't it? When would be convenient for you, dear?"

"Any time. Soon. I'll meet any appointment she has open."

Once the meeting was set for the following Sunday afternoon, Cally became irresolute, torn. She gave in to the craving to drive by the somber Victorian house on Pepper Street. Once there, only the van's absence from the curb kept her from racing up the stairs to share her rampant suspicions with Paul Michael. She would wait until she knew more before she involved him, gave him false hope, caused him indecision over returning to Jamaica.

Instead, she drove by the Michelson house. Olivia had given her an address in a modest neighborhood bordering a historical district gradually being integrated. Cally parked several houses down, across the street, and studied the neat yard, the lace curtains, the sturdy wooden swing suspended from a massive mulberry tree in the side yard. She tried to imagine Valerie Pennington Michelson, strove to understand what could cause her to desert her baby and live a lie for twenty-six years. Knowing the effect of that lie on Paul Michael, Cally attempted to imagine the effect on his mother. Then she rationalized that, had Valerie Pennington chosen not to desert her baby, had she taken him to Nigeria and foisted him on her unsuspecting husband, she, Stan Pennington, and Paul Michael would still have suffered a lie.

But all this was pure speculation, Cally reminded herself. Nothing but a crazy suspicion born from such small facts as a baby's name, a place, an English professor. Perhaps nothing more than coincidence. And yet she felt so certain . . . .

On Sunday, no longer able to sustain her original decision, Cally drove to Pepper Street. Again, the van was missing from the curb, and neither was it at Reggae Ruby's. It was nowhere near Jamaica Jam, a few blocks away. She drove back to the house and parked.

Ziggy Marley met her at the door. From behind the screen, he gave her a cold feline stare, then turned his topaz eyes away and flicked his tail. If he could speak . . . .

He could, in his way, and every line of his body spelled reproach.

She eased the screen door open, comforted by the familiar squeak and drag, the ripply flooring. Ziggy Marley slipped through. Tail vertical, its tip twitching, he descended the stairs and disappeared around the house.

She stepped inside, knowing even before her eyes adjusted to the interior, that no one was there. But there were signs of pending departure. Cartons, some packed and sealed, some half packed and gaping open, dotted the room. She spotted the puzzle box in an unsealed carton and turned away, aching.

Pierre and his perch were gone, also Major James Hewitt and Princess Diana. The huge pickle jar sat dry and barren on the windowsill. Drawn by a steady drip from the shower nozzle, she crossed the room and tested the blue towel spread across the side of the tub. Damp.

Stung by sadness, she turned and descended the rickety steps. Once more, she drove to Jamaica Jam.

The heavy door to the club stood ajar. Muted sounds came from the dusk within . . . guitar cords, blended voices stopping, starting again, the swish of a broom, the lazy clink of glass on glass. Soured perspiration, spilled beer, stale cigarette smoke assaulted her nostrils, stung her eyes.

A grizzled, stooped black man maintained his torpid pace with a shop broom, raising a small tornado of dust and cigarette ashes. Behind the bar, a red-haired woman eyed Cally wordlessly and dried glasses, placing them on a shelf. On the small stage, two young black men sporting shoulder-length dreadlocks, sandaled feet wrapped around stool rungs, kept rehearsing but stared at her. She recognized them from Jessica's party.

A fourth man squatted on the floor near the stage, his back to her. He was lean, light skinned with close-cropped curly hair, neatly dressed in khakis and a pink polo shirt. His bare feet were housed in soft loafers. He was dismantling a set of steel drums, his movements graceful, purposeful, exhibiting an economy of motion as he placed sections into an open wooden crate and carefully packed paper shavings around each part.

The singing and guitar strumming stopped. The men sat sullen, waiting. Cally moved a step forward, around a table stacked with chairs.

"Help you?" the woman behind the bar finally grunted.

"You lookin' for P.M.?" one of the singers asked, his eyes not quite meeting Cally's, but moving askance as he spoke, his head rocking sideways.

She nodded, approached the stage, catching the profile of the man on the floor. Breath lodged in her throat. She halted, chilled and startled when he turned in his squatting position. His eyes were hard, a frozen deep-water pond, the eyes of a stranger. An ache gathered in her. Awareness surfaced, an intangible warmth, a fluttery sensation she had come to associate with this stranger, Paul Michael Quest.

Chapter 24

A rash of emotion scuttled across Paul Michael's face. Surprise, anger, defiance. Then relief. He rose, caught Cally's arm, pulled her along with him into the three-sided cubicle that shielded the mens room entry from open view.

In the dim enclosure, their eyes searched, then held in silence. She fought to keep her mission in mind, but Paul Michael was like a child opening a Christmas present. His hands ran over her body, his mouth seeking her throat, her hair, her eyes, and finally her mouth, drinking her in, ingesting a revered treat. And his warmth, his sinewy body, his familiar aroma, stirred a longing that coursed through her like blood.

He looked at her. "Did you go back to Hugh Wilson Masters?"

"After knowing you, I'll never go back to Hugh Masters."

He drew her inside the pungent, littered toilet, closed the door, locked it with purpose. His hands at her waist lifted her to the sink counter, then pushed her skirt up her thighs. He moved between her legs as he loved to do, his eyes eager, daring.

"You came back to *me.* I had only to wait." He looked triumphant. "I waited in hell, Carolyna Sinclair."

She wound her arms around his neck, her long legs around his hips, and laughed for the first time since she'd last seen him. The ten days seemed an eternity. "You could have called," she whispered. "I waited in hell, too."

She touched his ear, naked without the sapphire and the gold hoop he used to wear. Her fingers trailed through his short hair. She raised a brow. "Curls?"

His shoulders rose in a shrug beneath her extended forearms. "From my mother." His face hardened. "Or so my *grand-mère* has told me."

"Has she?" Cally said softly.

Finally he smiled. "Are you coming with me, baby girl? Two nights from tonight—last flight to Atlanta. Then Jamaica!" He pronounced Jamaica with a theatrical flourish.

She moved against him, felt his heart pound against her breasts. Time was suddenly suspended; every sense quickened by a swift surge of memory. The sensation that swept through her wrenched like the grasp of a deep, internal fist. She understood wholly, for the first time, the magnitude of the impending pain of giving him up.

"I missed you, Paul Michael. So much."

"And I you. Come to my house. Let me show you. Then we will make our plan." He lapsed into stage language, his smile enticing. "Every little t'ing going to be fine."

She shook her head, dragged her refusal from a well of determination. She would wait until she saw Valerie Pennington. If it was as she suspected, as she prayed, then all would be viewed from a different aspect. He would feel compelled to stay, rather than to go.

"I have an appointment . . . to see a Jumeau doll. Come with me. I need you."

"And then you will come with me. I need *you*, Cally."

Paul Michael sat turned toward her in the car, one leg drawn onto the seat, watching her profile, his hand kneading her shoulder in a gentle promise that she savored deep in her soul.

As they rounded Lafayette Square, a car full of teenage boys skirted recklessly around them, hooted, made lewd gestures. First at Paul Michael and her, then to the girl scouts waiting in front of Juliette Gordon Low's birth house to worship at the shrine of their founder. Paul Michael smiled tolerantly at the boys, waved to the girls. His confident air permeated the Volvo.

Cally let the other car pull away, watched its back bumper drop as the car picked up speed. And felt just a little guilty that she had not told Paul Michael the true reason she wanted him to accompany her to the Michelson house.

"Where's the van? I looked for it."

"It is gone. To someone who needs it after me."

"And the license." She caught his smile in her side vision. "What about Pierre?"

"Gone with the van," he said quietly.

"Princess Diana and Major Hewitt?"

"You *have* been to my house. Awl *right*."

She glanced at him in time to see his triumph. "And that means you won." She granted him a smile. "And that's important to you." More important than she had known.

"I tried to have my visa renewed, to wait for you in this hell as long as it took. Did you know that, Cally?"

"How would I know?" She frowned. "What do you mean, you tried?"

"Some citizen of your fine diplomatic country filed a complaint against me—a dissident I was called." He fell quiet, then, "Finger nebber say, 'look here.' Him say, 'look dere.'"

She waited.

"People always point out shortcomings in others but never their own." His shrug didn't quite materialize. "No new visa. First I must go home, they say. Come back, maybe never."

She stole a look at him. "And you thought I might have interfered with your visa."

"Yeah, girl. Please forgive me."

As they rode in silence, she measured the meaning of what he'd told her, trying to quash the foreboding in the back of her mind. "Ziggy Marley was at your house," she said, pulling her mind away from the visa. "What about him?"

"My main man goes with me. That cat is Rastafarian, though. You know, girl? In Jamaica I will be a gentle man . . . like Jesus. No political uprisings. Get a good job. Sell my paintings on the sidewalk. I can only hope Ziggy Marley will not ruin my reputation there, too."

She swallowed furiously, stared out the window as they waited out a light.

The afternoon was closing down, the light waning from diamonds to old gold as they traversed the sidewalk approaching the Michelson house. Cally pressed the bell, and they waited on the

213

porch. The sun shone directly on Paul Michael's face, lit his hair like a copper helmet, a trick of the light making him appear guileless, invincible.

His hand brushed her shoulder, trailed down her back, across her buttocks. His smile was intimate, conspiratorial. She had come to him. She knew he believed she would go to Jamaica, have his babies, love him as he loved her. For now, he was content to humor her with dolls until he could take her to his attic room and make love to her. In turn, she held to her hope that after today all would change . . . somehow.

She nurtured speculation until the moment the door opened.

A woman, impressive of stature that echoed Paul Michael's proud bearing, stood framed in the dimness of the interior. Her eyes went immediately to Paul Michael. Her hair was his, thick, curly, brown with copper highlights—only hers was streaked with gray. Cally's skin chilled, then scorched.

Valerie Pennington Michelson was white.

Cally found her voice. "Mrs. Pennington?" She felt Paul Michael jerk, tense mightily.

The woman frowned, looked at Paul Michael again, and as Cally stared, she saw suspicion dawning in Valerie Pennington's eyes—eyes that were lighter in color than Paul Michael's, deep set splinters of blue ice, but the same fine shape. It seemed God had taken the ice blue hue, added a dash of burnt umber, and gifted Paul Michael with the result.

For a tiny second something flared in Valerie's eyes. Knowledge, perhaps even relief. "It's Michelson, now," she corrected. "Are you Carolyna?"

"Yes. This is my friend, Paul Michael. He's an authority on Jumeau." She smiled, caught Paul Michael's hand, drew him forward.

Valerie stood rigid, holding on to the door.

"Are we early?" Cally ventured.

She stepped back. "Come in."

The interior was cool, to the point of being chilled. It was deathly quiet, almost dark. In the corner of the parlor, a kind of museum-quality light fell on a table-display of dolls. They moved across the room, Valerie and Paul Michael on either side of Cally. She held firmly to his trembling hand.

For the moment, for the three of them, this meeting was no more than a game, a ruse that would endure unless Cally ended it. Paul Michael had waited long enough.

"Which is the Jumeau?" Cally addressed him quietly, touched by what she saw in his face. Shock, hope, triumph, understanding at last . . . and fear.

Boldly, he stared at the woman whose features were reproduced in his own, and Cally felt he no longer saw his surroundings, but was watching his own past. His breath came short and hard.

"Paul Michael?" Nothing. "Paul Michael?"

He extracted one doll, as carefully and gently as he would have held a child. "This one," he half whispered, his eyes on Valerie. "It is the twin of my *grand-mère's* doll." His Jamaican inflection and Valerie's audible intake of breath hung in the static air.

His eyes narrowed in that characteristic way Cally knew and loved. "Are you my mother?"

Valerie stepped back, her face crumpling. She raised her hands before her, palms out, as though to ward off a blow.

"Mrs. Michelson, my friend is Paul Michael Quest. We have reason to believe—to hope—"

"You must leave." Behind the curtness of tone could be heard a plea. Valerie cast a frantic look at a mahogany grandfather clock against the wall. "My husband will be home soon. Take the doll . . . a gift from me." She rambled, her words rising, then falling. One hand massaged a forearm frantically. The clock struck once, quieted. "Just go."

Cally felt Paul Michael go slack; he shrank into himself with an expression of pained bewilderment. Then he pulled to full height, dropped her hand. She sensed blame in the gesture.

"You don't understand, Mrs. Michelson. Paul Michael's been looking for you." She fought an urge to cry, to plead. "Your . . . his father . . . is dead now. No one ever told Paul Michael the truth. He's going home tomorrow. Unless—you *are* his mother, aren't you?"

She waited, wondered how the woman could stand not to touch Paul Michael, hold him, assure him, end the lie. Then Cally began to share the fear in his eyes, to read the denial in Valerie's. "Mrs. Michelson, I know this is a shock—"

"You're the one who doesn't understand." She seemed to muster strength, her voice purposeful now, indecision replaced by determination. She spoke to Paul Michael, ignored Cally. "I want you to go. I made a decision twenty-six years ago. I haven't changed my mind. You cost me one marriage and a life of hell. I have other children who don't know. I can't tell them now. And I won't lose another husband because of you." Her chin lifted, her face crystallized, slick hard.

Shock, fused with grief, surfaced, a vise around Cally's heart. The emotion melded into a staggering tenderness and love for Paul Michael. He resembled a simmering pot beginning to boil. Cally reached in two directions, grasping each of them, attempted to draw them forward. Mother and son stood their ground, eyes locked.

"You could have been a queen." Paul Michael addressed Valerie so quietly Cally wasn't sure she'd heard, or understood. Then she recalled hearing the words before. She hugged herself, warding off the pain. "You could have stayed with my father and blended our races. You could have accomplished something other than sleeping with a black man for your selfish curiosity."

Valerie trembled, her eyes glazed with desperation. Cally saw no malice there to back up her rejection.

"Mrs. Michelson, please. I'm sure your husband would . . . if you'd just tell the truth, it could end this—"

"No!" The cry came up through Paul Michael's soul, bereaved and inconsolable. His eyes fixed on Valerie, he thrust the doll into her arms and strode from the house, setting the door banging on its hinges.

The room loomed empty, defiled. Dazed, Cally stared after him. She felt Valerie's hand on her arm.

"Let him go." Valerie clutched the Jumeau to her chest, stared at the door. "It will hurt much less now than later."

"I'm sorry. You must hate me." Not waiting for an answer, Cally bolted through the door and across the lawn, intercepted Paul Michael on the walk.

"Please wait." She grasped his arm, planted her feet. "She doesn't mean it. She's hurting, too. Give her time to think."

His stare left her feeling that he'd reached out, rearranged her soul with fingers as icy as his eyes. He was a stranger now, capable of unreasoning anger, of hating intensely, even as he loved.

"Valerie Pennington has had my whole life to think," he said. "I have no more time to give her. She could have built a life with my father. A family. But, no. She had her pleasure and wanted no more of him. Of us." He looked at the *haint* blue house, his breath ragged. "My father hated me. I now know why." I cost him his white woman."

His hand rose to the neck of his shirt, grasped the heavy chain, yanked. The chain snapped, the locket came off in his clasped palm. Awed by his strength and anger, Cally saw him crush the locket in his fingers, splay it. He stared at the pictures inside, then turned them for her to see his father and Valerie Pennington. His bitter laugh edged on a dry sob.

"I knew you had white blood," she said, tears running down her face. "But I thought—you said way back in your family—I didn't know Valerie was white. Not until she opened that door. Don't hurt, Paul Michael. Please don't hurt."

She wrapped her arms around him, held onto his rigid body. "I'm sorry I brought you here. I should have come alone first, seen for myself. I'm sorry."

He peeled her arms away, flung the broken, jagged locket. It struck her cheek, clattered to the walk. Retrieving it, she thrust it back at him, sobbing, her vision blurred. He moved out of her reach. She stumbled, lost her footing, went down, striking her knee on the serrated edge of the walk. Blood oozed from the wound.

Panic and regret tangled in his eyes, then congealed in revived anger. She scrambled to her feet wiping tears; her hand came away bloody. She clasped the locket. Crediting his behavior to grief and shock, she strove for rationale, a way to reason.

"She doesn't matter, Paul Michael," she said quietly. "You have yourself. That's all anyone ever has. That can't be changed. It shouldn't be ignored, no matter how much we love. No matter how much we're loved—or not—in return." She held out the locket. "Please take it. Keep it." Into the silence she said, "I never wanted to hurt you."

His eyes burned. "You were never going to Jamaica. You brought me here to pay me off. You are like her! You can't love a black man. You can only bed him."

He took the mangled locket, cast it into the crimson stain where Cally's blood smeared the concrete walk.

She watched until he disappeared around a corner without looking back, then retrieved the locket once more—all hope dying.

Cally heard footsteps on the walk, felt a hand on her arm.

"Come back inside, Carolyna."

She looked into the face of a different Valerie Pennington Michelson. A woman who hurt. Searching for anger, resentment against her, Cally found only pity and curiosity.

❦

Valerie knelt on the kitchen floor and bathed Cally's knee with warm water, applied peroxide, then iodine as Cally held a piece of ice wrapped in a linen towel to her cheek.

"What if your husband comes home?"

Valerie's touch was tender, her motion as graceful as Paul Michael's when he had packed the drums away only an hour earlier, three changed lives ago.

"I'll tell him you're a doll client. You slipped on the walk. He'll be concerned only about a lawsuit. It won't really be a lie, even though I'm very good at those."

"I was nothing more than a doll client when I met Olivia." Cally fought the threat of new tears, laid the blood-stained locket on the Formica-topped table. "I didn't even know Paul Michael. And he was happy . . . before he met me."

Valerie taped a large gauze patch to the knee and rose, smiling faintly. "You won't have a scar." Touching her ample bosom at her heart she said, "Except in here."

She turned away, made tea, rejoined Cally at the table, placing a steaming cup before her.

"I would have raised him better." Valerie's voice caught, her smile was tremulous, forced.

"Someone raised him very well," Cally said. "What you saw today isn't—"

"Please don't." A single tear glistened. Valerie caught it, then raised her cup, sipped, her elbows braced on the table. "Knowing him would only make the hurt worse."

Cally nodded. "I know him. It makes it worse."

"How much did Olivia tell you?"

"She has no idea about Paul Michael. It's all a cruel coincidence. Fate, maybe. I don't know what to believe. Maybe it was only logistics. Savannah's not a large town, where this kind of thing couldn't—"

"How much did she tell you, dear?"

"Everything, I suppose." Cally sipped tea, relived the infeasibility of it all. "It started with the dolls. She knew I needed one and told me your collection was from around the world. She told me you were stationed in Jamaica together. About your attending classes there. About the baby being born . . . dead. No funeral. She said the dead baby had always been called Paul, named after a professor. Paul Michael had talked about his father being an English professor and about being abandoned by his mother the day he was born. That's why he's in Savannah. This was the last place he knew of her—you—living before you went to Jamaica. I just pieced it all together."

She paused, her body aching like an abscess. "He told me he had white blood but he thought it was from way back. I saw pictures at Olivia's house of mixed race couples. When I realized one of those women was you—please believe me, I never guessed that *you* were . . . ."

"White."

When Cally nodded, Valerie said, "I don't expect you to forgive me for what I did today, just as I hope he'll never forgive me. Hate will allow him to forget sooner. If it matters, I loved his father, but I was desperate all those months I carried Paul Michael, not knowing if he was black or white. God gave me an out when Stan left for Nigeria. I took it. The consequences have been hell."

Valerie fell quiet, took up the locket, studied the tiny scrap of a picture, then tried to close the trinket. The two halves no longer met.

219

She placed the battered object back on the table, coiled the heavy chain around it, pushed it toward Cally. If the locket hadn't been soldered . . . if Paul Michael hadn't promised his *grand-mère* . . . if only he had opened it before today . . . .

"Olivia has told me your background. You're a Southern woman. Born and raised. All I ask is that you understand I couldn't keep him, Carolyna."

Cally didn't bother quelling the hot fresh tears, the knowledge that she was no better than Valerie. She seized the locket, eased it inside her bra. The cold metal chilled and braced her.

"I understand," she whispered. "I can't keep him either."

At the door, Valerie handed Cally the doll. "Take this. It's the twin to Miriam Quest's doll, exactly as he said. I've never been able to part with it all these years. I kept it, I suspect, to punish myself for my indiscretion and for my lie. After today, I won't need a reminder."

Cally took the Jumeau, held it gently, as Paul Michael had done. She listened to the clock striking. She counted to seven, saw the light of the September evening had passed golden, seeped into gray.

Valerie said, "It was a foolish thing you did, but innocent. He has closure now, even if I never will. If you don't hate me . . . we could talk again."

Cally's mind whirled, judged her own ability for closure.

"Perhaps you could help me sell my dolls."

"I'll try." Cally could manage no more.

Valerie stood in the door as Cally went down the walk, carefully skirting the blood stain, and got into her car. At the stop sign, in her rearview mirror, she saw a late model Buick sedan pull into the side driveway of the Michelson house. She drove away quickly, not wanting to see the man whom Valerie had chosen over Paul Michael.

She clamped her mind against examining her own choices.

Chapter 25

$\mathscr{C}$repe myrtle, wild and faded, waning with autumn, banked each side of the tabby-paved walk at the Taylor Street town house. An overgrown loquat tree formed a jagged silhouette in the dusk. When Cally unlocked the old door, the essence of new paint and fresh carpet drifted out to her, along with the infeasible hopes and images she'd held concerning this house.

Wandering room to room in the darkness, she tried to form new visions, to replace those scarcely admitted hopes that had started when she had gone to the bank with Jessica to set up the loan, the day she'd seen the mixed race children.

Moonlight filtered through the open shutters of the window above the kitchen sink, spilled across the counter, onto Cally's folded arms. She pictured the food she'd prepare on Taylor Street, the wine she'd drink from a stash of her own choice, the serenity of consuming it all in independent, liberated loneliness. Strolling from room to room, she listened for the voices and footsteps she would never hear, envisioned the holidays and birthdays never to be celebrated. She was incapable of imagining the festivities this house *would* host some day.

In the master bedroom she sat on the new carpet, bathed in a sliver of light that spilled into the room from a corner street lamp. A water oak, massive and ancient, cast shadows at her feet. She discarded the image of a child's swing hanging from the lowest tree limb. She would have, instead, an old-fashioned porch swing, teak wood. She'd paint it yellow, crowd it with bright cushions, add color to a terrace where no hay-haired, caramel-skinned children would play.

Tears scalded and blinded her before they brimmed over and eased the ache somewhat. She tried to focus on Paul Michael's anger, but all that surfaced from the re-examined scene at Valerie's was his hurt. He had lashed out at Cally, the person nearest him, the least deserving. His chameleonic personality had always intrigued her. Sometimes like a guileless child, he was at other times a prophet, a seer, wise beyond his years. Today, in the face of rejection from a woman he had longed for all his life, he had been a man grieving beyond control.

In the last two days the closure she had sought and relied on had gotten muddled and lost in wanting a life with Paul Michael, believing it could be. Since childhood she had sought acceptance and security, fought a sense of not measuring up. The feelings had been prevalent in her marriage with Turner, in her relationship with Hugh. With Paul Michael, she had been peaceful, felt cherished, confident enough to love him back, even if silently. Today's grief and misguided blame had propelled him out of her life, but she understood grief associated with scars of a troubled childhood.

A different kind of memory whispered to her now, with faintly erotic breath, sending up images that stirred in the deepest well of her body, pained her. Paul Michael knew her so intimately. He had opened parts of her no other man had been granted access, and ultimately he had peered into her being. She closed her eyes and felt again the tenderness with which he touched her breasts, the gentle way he parted her thighs and loved her until she was able to receive him. She heard again their ragged breaths, their mingled cries. It was not just her eyes and ears that savored the memory, not just her body, but her heart and soul.

She would never have that kind of love again.

Cally looked up from Reggae Ruby's menu the next morning and anxiously surveyed the breakfast crowd. Dock workers, motel maids, businessmen with loosened ties, a few obvious street people. All genders, ages, and ethnic groups were represented. Chatter melded with the clank of dishes, the rattle of pans, and the steady hump-hump of Reggae music from the ceiling speakers. A fan above her head stirred her hair, flapped the menu in her hand.

A familiar figure approached.

"Well! If it ain't Miss Carolyna Sinclair."

She looked into Ebony's face. Black eyes stared coldly. The coffee-stained uniform gaped, hiked in front, revealing Ebony's bulging abdomen.

Cally's cheek smarted with the memory of the last time she'd seen her. She understood now, why she had been a threat to Ebony, why she fought so hard. Ironically, Ebony's protest and eventual abuse had created waves that thrust Paul Michael and Cally forward, pitched them together. Now, the sight of Ebony's pregnancy sickened Cally, awakened a tangle of envy, anger, and sympathy.

"I didn't know you worked here, Ebony."

"I bet you didn't." Her lips curled disdainfully. "Never mind, Miz Sinclair, honey. You ain't worth the trouble of whuppin' again."

"I'd like some coffee, please."

"Coffee make you black, woman, and stunt you growth."

"I'll take that chance."

Turning on her heel, Ebony swaggered away.

Cally surveyed the restaurant with anxious hope until Ebony slipped into the booth, facing her, shoving one of two cups toward her. Coffee splashed. A man behind the open window to the kitchen called Ebony's name as he jerked a food order from the revolving spindle. Waving him off, Ebony settled against the booth and turned her eyes on Cally.

"I'm looking for Paul Michael," Cally said. "I've been by—"

"No shit. When in your little honky life you ain't been lookin' for him? Or the likes of him?"

To keep calm was difficult, but Cally reconfirmed her purpose and continued. "I went by his house. I didn't know where else to go but here."

"P. M. don't live there no more, Miz Carolyna, honey," Ebony mocked. "He done gone out of your life. When you gonna let go?"

Cally's face stung.

"You must a wanted that, seein' how you canceled his visa."

"That's not true."

"I figure some of your people done it to get your white ass back to your own side of the tracks."

Cally flinched.

"And nice, trustin' little pink boy he is, P. M.'s figurin' he didn't get his hair cut quick enough. Dat da man done took a dislike to him."

"Are you going to tell me where he is . . . if you know?"

"Oh, I know. I ain't tellin' you nuthin. You think I like seein' him like he wuz yesterday, think again."

Ebony's mouth pulled downward, her eyes clouded. One hand went to her stomach, unconsciously, Cally thought, before both hands cupped the bulge in a protective gesture. When Ebony spoke again, her manner mellowed.

"P.M. gonna be gone outa both our lives tomorrow. I ain't lettin' you at him again. Guess it's time to let go . . . git on wid you nice white bread life."

The question whirling in Cally's mind fought its way to the surface. "Are you carrying Paul Michael's baby?"

Ebony shrugged, no mirth in her smile. "Who knows?"

"Are you?"

"What diff'rence that make to you, Carolyna Sinclair?"

Cally tried to control visions of Paul Michael and Ebony together, but her imagination sent up little scenes, little tongues and darts of flame. The thought of Paul Michael's seed in Ebony made her hot with anger and envy. She thought of the book she'd read that outlined the Jamaican man's propensity for a stable of women, his tendency not to accept responsibility for the lives he created. She'd been right to refuse to consider going to Jamaica with him. Ebony was proof. Then she remembered he had known Ebony before she came into his life, and after, while she vacillated in a state of denial. She tired to reason in terms of fairness, but the ache, the envy, was too deep.

Her mind raced to the lonely town house on Taylor, the barren yard. "If you're having his baby I want to know."

"Why you want to know?"

Why indeed? Would her longing for Paul Michael lower her to covet another woman's baby, seek that baby out after birth, beg to hold it, beg to be part of what she was too cowardly to take for herself?

224

As though reading Cally's mind, Ebony glared, all tolerance gone from her eyes. "This ain't nobody's baby but mine. Just like I was my mama's. No reason to be needin' no man now."

Ebony stared out the window onto the busy street, her fingertips gripping the table edge so hard they looked yellow. Sable eyes swam in the biggest, hottest looking tears Cally had ever seen. She felt them all the way to her soul.

Ebony said, "P.M. was always too fine to ever make a baby with the likes of me. That what you want to hear, Miz Cally, honey?" Her mockery carried no weight. "He gone, and you and me's losers. This baby is mine, no one else's, and don't get no fancy ideas."

"We aren't so different, are we? Each of us feels loss as deeply as the other. Blacks haven't cornered the market on hurting." Cally scavenged a smile from the depths of her own ache. "Even if they do sing the blues better. We don't have to hate each other, Ebony, but we will. It's the Southern way."

She saw Ebony's eyes quicken with the tiniest bit of agreement.

"With this baby you have a chance to make a difference. You can break the mold—"

"This ain't P. M's baby. I told you, girl."

Cally wanted to believe but could not. "It's yours. That's fine." Fishing in her bag, she passed her a card, then placed two dollar bills on the counter. "If you decide to tell me where Paul Michael is, call me. I never meant to hurt you, Ebony."

"I sure meant to hurt you. An' even after that nice speech, I still ain't tellin' you where he is." Clumsily, the girl slid from the booth, struggled to her feet, and looked down at Cally. "You never done him a bit a good, just like I knew you'd do. I don't see no reason you'd start today."

Cally watched as Ebony went to the wall phone. She talked on the phone, gesturing, her back to Cally. And Cally sat and waited, not knowing what the call would bring. When the coffee grew cold in the breeze from the overhead fan, she returned to Columbia Square and the Renfro house.

The next morning, Cally drove to the island. Turner was waiting for her when she turned into the security gate. His club-owned golf cart was parked on the median. He waved; she pulled to the curb. His spikes clattered on the pavement as he rounded the car, got in beside her, his expression glum.

"Drive somewhere, Cally. I have something to tell you."

She drove to a secluded cul-de-sac where the residents hadn't returned for the season. Shutting the engine off, she faced him. "I can't stay long. I'm moving this afternoon. I'm meeting a van to pick up my bedroom furniture at the cottage."

"Not anymore. Geneva won't let you."

Anger sliced her rationale. "That is *my* furniture. It belonged to my grandmother when she was a little girl. She gave it to *me* years ago. Mother can't—"

"Save it, Cally. I'm not the enemy."

She drew a long breath. "No, you're not. I'm sorry."

"They're waiting at the cottage for you, babe. I want you to be prepared—actually, you shouldn't go. You're outnumbered."

"They?"

"Geneva. The senator. Hugh and Lucinda. Jim and Pru, even the kids. Geneva keeps raving about—" He smiled, his eyes appraising her. "About that lawsuit you're threatening and about this being a family thing and—"

"And what, Turner?"

He took a perspiration-stained golf glove from his pocket, smoothed it on his hard thigh, looking almost reluctant now. "She's calling it an intervention. Even that doctor is there. They're waiting to pounce on you."

"Philip Ballentine?"

He nodded. "Geneva got the idea from some movie she saw about cults. You know. The parents swoop in and save the kids from a fate worse than—"

"Mercy!" Her first reaction was to leave. She was too vulnerable to face what awaited her at the cottage. When Paul Michael hadn't called after her talk with Ebony, she had relinquished the last of her hope for an amicable parting. The concession left her drained, defeated, feeling she'd been wrong all along about their relationship.

"Cally?"

"Just thinking, Tee."

"They're going to try and talk you into marrying Hugh."

She remembered the dreams she'd had for a conventional life. Dreams, polarized on Hugh. A staid, mildly content marriage, conformity in its most acceptable mold. She had stepped out of the traces again, with Paul Michael. Perhaps they were all willing to overlook that—if she conformed once more. But she wondered about Hugh's capacity to forgive, not to judge or remind her of past errors.

"Geneva had your friend's visa extension denied," Turner said quietly.

Her breath caught. She should have known! From the moment she'd learned of the denied extension, she should have known. Geneva had used the senator's political pull to track her down in an attempt to keep her from eloping with Turner. She'd seen the power used and misused often through the years. That political power still thrived.

Turner's hand covered hers, squeezed. "Geneva's a bitch. If not for her, you and I might still be married. I don't think I want to take her on again. Anyway, Lucinda is playing two ends against the middle, cuddling up to Hugh while she checks out the flights to Jamaica so she can pick up your discard."

Cally's shocked look made him grin and confess, "Just kidding, babe, but Lucy's kind of desperate, like a warm puppy looking for love. Both you girls got shortchanged pretty bad when you were kids, I guess." He studied her, his spaniel eyes soft and dark. "It's time to blow Dodge again, Cally. I'm out of here. My hand's all healed. One of the members is going to sponsor me for a year back on the Nike tour." He grinned. "One of the new members, that is. I'm not taking your little sister. Not because I'm a good guy. But she's a little bored already."

"I'm sorry, Tee."

"Hey! I wanted *you*, Carolyna Joy." He dragged her name through a mire of mock Southern inflection. "I love you, Cally. You never believed it for a minute, but—"

"You never acted like it. Not for a minute."

"Maybe you'd like to come with me for a while." His fingers picked at a loose thread on his khakis. He kept his eyes there. "We wouldn't live as high as before. That would be different, but I'd be different, too. I know how to treat you, babe. You're at loose ends right now. I'd like another chance."

"I'm *not* at loose ends. I haven't been since the moment I left you. I work hard, Turner, to take care of myself. I have a responsibility to my clients. It's my life. I can't—and I don't want to—walk out on that."

"Then finish that Steinberg fiasco Hugh got you into and meet me somewhere. From what I've seen of Geneva the last week or so, there's going to be hell to pay. In Savannah and on the island. You need a change of venue. She's pissed, babe." He clasped her shoulders. "I swear, it will be different. We might even have that kid you wanted. Go the establishment route. What do you say, Cally?"

Yes, she wanted a child. But not Turner's.

"You're well rid of the Sinclairs, Turner. All of us."

He was quiet for a long moment. Slowly, his hands slid off her shoulders. "Maybe you'll change your mind. I'll keep in touch."

"I won't change my mind. Save your postage."

A look of pain crossed his face. And relief, perhaps. He said, "Sorry about this thing with the Rastafarian. Are you going to follow him to Jamaica?"

"His name is Paul Michael. And, no. I won't follow him."

He leaned to kiss her, but she quickly turned her cheek. He grinned, his hand going for the door handle. "I'll just cut across the course to where I left the cart. You'd better go out the back way. Quick like. They were peeking through the curtains in high anxiety when I slipped out the back."

"Thank you for warning me about the intervention."

"Run, Carolyna," he said softly. "You aren't tough enough for them. You once told me you'd marry Hugh if it's the last thing you ever do. Trust me, babe. If you go to the cottage, you'll marry him at Christmas. Geneva hasn't—"

"Good-bye, Turner."

"Good-bye, huh?"

"This time for good."

She watched him disappear through a pyracantha hedge, then started the car and rounded the cul-de-sac. Relinquishing her plan to move into the town house, sleep in her own bed, she settled for going back to Jessica's to regroup. She could shop for new bedroom furniture . . . .

As she approached the back gate to steal away, the memory of being with Paul Michael in her childhood bed washed over her. She turned the next corner, back toward the cottage and the confrontation awaiting her.

Chapter 26

*C*ally pulled the Volvo behind a bob-tail van. The driver appeared anxious as he approached, a clipboard in his hand.

"Miss Sinclair?" She nodded, and he drawled, "They said this move was canceled."

"Come with me." Smiling was difficult, but she wanted to bolster him and herself. "Brace yourself, however."

"Is this a divorce case?" He looked wary.

"In a manner of speaking, yes."

He trailed her, his steps reluctant. The door popped open before they reached the porch. "Carolyna, I have told this gentleman to leave." Geneva fastened him in her gaze.

"This gentleman isn't working for you, Mother. I'm paying him by the hour. Please step aside and allow him to do his job. I've phoned Lawrence Fulton." She noted Geneva's quick intake of breath. "He's advised me to call the sheriff if I have to. That could prove expensive for each of us."

Geneva didn't withdraw but shrank back when Cally seized the driver's arm, drew him past her mother into the foyer. A mass of bodies, dressed to the nines, lurked in the parlor.

Cally addressed the driver. "Upstairs, third door to the right. Please start disassembling the bed. I'll join you in a moment."

Geneva blocked the stairs.

Cally and the driver exchanged looks; his mouth began to draw determinedly. She nodded toward the back of the house. "There's another set of stairs in the kitchen. Turn left at the top, count backwards. I'll call the sheriff." From the corner of her eye, she saw Geneva sidle off. "Well . . . maybe that won't be necessary."

The man clumped up the main staircase.

"Just because your grandmother let you use that furniture—"

"Gramma Sinclair *gave* me that furniture, Mother. I have a

230

birthday card upstairs with the handwritten note. If you insist, I'll produce it."

"Oh, hush, Carolyna. I see no reason to make a scene. Take the furniture. It isn't even valuable."

"Maybe not to you, Mother. Everything is relative." Cally looked toward the parlor, where everyone watched and listened. She was reminded of a prior family convention designed to bring her to her senses, wrench her away from Turner. That attempt had failed. "What is this all about?"

Geneva feigned innocence. "Why nothing, dear. Your loved ones have simply come to talk with you. Come in, please."

When Cally made no move, Geneva caught her arm to usher her along. Cally pulled away. The senator disengaged himself from Philip Ballentine, approached Geneva and Cally. His eyes looked weak, watery. Sad, Cally decided, but maybe she only wished that. She offered him her cheek.

"Hello, Daddy. What an honor."

"Hello, Carolyna, sugar. You're lookin' real pretty today."

Hugh lined up beside the senator. Cally stepped back, aborting his kiss, and caught a quick yellow-green flicker in his eyes. Lucinda, Philip, Jim, and Pru looked on. Pru's mouth seemed even more grim than usual.

"Let's all take our seats," Geneva directed. "Pru, if you'd just have the boys come in . . . ."

Pru slammed her cup and saucer onto a table and pranced off. Cally assumed the boys' involvement had been discussed before her arrival, with Pru objecting to their presence and Geneva insisting on getting her way. Cally caught her brother's eye. Jim shrugged and looked away.

Beside her, Hugh stood stone-like, breathing a bit loudly. Lucinda stole forward, tiptoed to kiss her cheek. "Hey, Cal," she whispered in her ear. "Hang tough, babe."

She sounded like Turner. Cally remembered how, as children, they had sworn an oath of absolute allegiance. But the stakes were too high now for Lucinda to honor that pledge.

Pru returned with the boys. Unnaturally quiet, they went to stand by their father.

"Would you like some coffee, Carolyna?"

"No, thank you, Mother. I won't be here long enough to enjoy it."

"Then why don't you and Hugh sit together on the love seat. Jim, take the sofa with Pru and the boys. Sit over there, Wain." Geneva indicated a wing chair banking the sofa, facing the love seat. "Lucinda, pull that little stool up by your father. Philip in the Carver chair—a good mediating position. And I'll just sit here." She placed her plump hand on the back of a pilfered dining room chair.

After Hugh had scrambled into position on the love seat, Cally took the only other seat in the room, an antique prayer chair.

"Carolyna—"

"I'll sit here, Mother." Her knees came up to her chest. She tucked them sideways. "So I can look up to all of you."

Lucinda scurried off her assigned stool and onto the love seat. Hugh made room for her, his face grim, his eyes on Cally. Silence descended. Cally looked around the circle. Only Phillip Ballantine met her gaze.

"I'm surprised to see you," she said. "But then, Hugh was paying you. Might makes right, I suppose."

"My being here doesn't indicate my opinion, Cally."

"Oh. You don't think I've taken leave of my senses?"

Philip smiled, started to speak. Geneva interrupted. "Let's not get off track. I have a few things to say, and then we'll turn the discussion back over—"

"No, Mother." Gratified, Cally saw Geneva grimace. "*I* have a few things to say."

Geneva's eyes darted to Philip, then to the senator who studied his watch. In the distance a phone rang.

"I want you to label this gathering for me, Mother."

"Why . . . this is an intervention."

"I neither take drugs nor drink to excess."

"You *are* excessively foolish, Carolyna Joy. I—your family—we're here to talk sense into you. This hideous lawsuit you've filed against me—what is it you hope to gain? Exactly what do you want?"

"Love."

A pained look came into Geneva's eyes. Her brow furrowed.

"I want your love, your understanding. Your approval, for once in my life. And, I want an apology."

A rustle issued from the sofa as Pru recrossed her legs, pulled at her skirt, her eyes averted. Cally saw Jim grin, exchange glances with Lucinda.

"An apology! Why, whatever for?"

"For denying me all the above. My attorney's research has revealed a precedent-setting case in which a judge ruled that a parent owes her child what I am asking for, a contract entered into at the moment of conception. An old-fashioned judge, maybe, but a precedent, still. You have withheld your love and dangled your approval in front of me from my earliest memory. I've tried every way between here and Hades to change that. To be worthy. Money talks with you, Mother. I've decided to seek money from you in lieu of love and approval. I have a far greater chance of succeeding."

"Wain," Geneva called across the room. "Say something."

The senator fished in his pocket for his glasses. He put them on, and Cally felt that *she* had better vision, for he suddenly looked like himself. His eyes were defined now, the weakness gone.

"Carolyna, honey, this could be very embarrassin' to your mother and me if word of this litigation should get out."

"I know, Daddy. Lawrence Fulton refers to that as leverage. I have every intention to go public if I don't get a legally sworn agreement from Mother that she will never again threaten to withhold my inheritance from Grampa Englander."

Geneva gasped. "Go public? What are you saying?"

"I'm calling a press conference this afternoon if I don't get your verbal compliance in front of these convenient witnesses until we can get the papers drawn and—"

"Hush that talk, Carolyna. We have never had one minute of scandal in this family."

"I think the press would also like to hear about that sheet and hood I found in Grampa Sinclair's closet when I was ten." She looked at her father. He returned a disbelieving look. "The . . . costume that Mother and Gramma burned in the bathtub."

"My God! Hush!" Geneva started to rise, sank back. "You are making that up." Her eyes darted wildly to Hugh, to Philip

233

Ballantine. "You have always had an affinity for story telling."

"Well, maybe I'll win an Oscar. From the local media first. Then on to wider exposure."

"You are testing me, Carolyna. Again."

"Yes. I am, Mother. You don't want to fail this one."

Geneva smoothed her skirt. "We have other issues at hand—more important than money. Dr. Ballantine, would you speak to this girl?" Cally had never heard her call him doctor before.

Philip Ballantine asked, "Concerning what, Geneva?"

"You know perfectly well, concerning what. Her broken engagement, of course."

"Cally and I have discussed the engagement. Cally, Hugh and I, actually. I'd be beating a dead horse."

Elbows on his knees, Hugh pulled forward on the love seat. "I never wanted the engagement broken. Cally knows that. I was baffled. Then at that party I learned why she wanted out."

Despite his outward calm, Cally recognized anger, like burning ice, at the back of Hugh's mossy eyes. His ire brought thoughts of Paul Michael, their angry parting . . . .

She struggled to stay expressionless. "Please go on, Hugh."

"Anyone can make a mistake. Get confused." He looked directly at her. "You created a lot of pressure for yourself. All the work, driving back and forth, then living in Savannah with those . . . liberals. You don't do well under pressure, sweetheart."

Cally said nothing, fighting down flaring irritation.

"You stopped seeing Philip, and that was a mistake," Hugh said. "I'd like to see you reschedule a series of visits, get back on track. There's no reason we can't have that Christmas wedding."

"I thought you wanted a Thanksgiving wedding so we could go into the Christmas social season married."

"That was important politically. I'll have to sacrifice. But I don't mind. I'll—*we* will get mileage from the wedding."

In Cally's side vision Geneva nodded, and Cally gave in to the inner spiral of pain and anger. "What about the fact that I've been sleeping with Paul Michael Quest? I love him. Can you overlook that, Hugh?"

His body stiffened. A uniform gasp rose, rustled around the

circle. Philip Ballantine sat on the edge of his chair. Cally could feel the doctor's eyes on her, shoring her up.

"I'm going to try," Hugh said. "It will be difficult. If he were more your class—"

"You mean if he weren't black?"

"I'm willing to forgive you, Carolyna." Hugh's voice was cold, clipped. "If I can."

Her skull imploded. "You sanctimonious bastard."

Philip sank back in his chair. Surprise and shock swirled wave-like across the faces of her loved ones.

Cally rose, faced Geneva. "I gave you my terms, Mother. Are you going to comply with them?"

"You won't be thirty for a year and half." Geneva's voice shook. "We'll see what happens."

"Is that a threat?"

After an eternity, Geneva murmured, "No more threats."

"Fine. The lawsuit stands, however. And I can assure you what *won't* be happening. There will be no wedding." She turned back to Hugh. "Anything will be better and less painful than years of a loveless marriage."

Lucinda reached for Hugh's hand, gazed into his livid face.

Cally said, "Maybe you haven't noticed, Mother, but Turner is gone. Look at Lucy. It's all coming out your way, just one daughter later. Maybe you'll forgive me now for Lucy's mimicking me all her life."

Sudden comprehension played across Geneva's face.

"I've added a condition to the press conference," Cally said, looking directly at the senator, then back at Geneva. "I want the blight taken off Paul Michael's visa, if you have to call the president to do it. I want Paul Michael free to come and go when he wishes. Is that understood?"

Geneva stared, speechless.

"Thank you, Mother. I'll go up and get my furniture now."

Jessica and Alain were waiting for her when Cally returned from the town house later that afternoon. Their expressions showed anxiety, relief, and elation.

Cally closed her umbrella, brushed the cold autumn rain from her pant legs. "Hello," she ventured, offering a smile. "I'm moved in, for the most part. I'll sleep there tonight. I just need to get my things from the guest room." She sensed more anxiety. "Is something wrong—or right, by some miracle?"

Jessica kept smiling, like a cat stuffed with guppies.

"*Oui, mignonne*," Alain said. "Something right, we believe."

"Something I should know?" She set her bag on the hall table.

"We'll make you a drink." Jessica took her arm, drew her along.

"Sherry, please. Will I need a double?"

At the antique armoire that served as the living room bar, Alain fixed drinks, passed one to Cally. The party proceeded to the kitchen. Jessica nodded toward the desk where the answering machine flashed more rapidly and redder than Cally had ever seen it. Her heart pounded a furious, similar rhythm.

"You have a call, darling."

Jessica's gentleness spawned a fleeting image of Geneva's austere face. Cally pushed it away.

"Would you like privacy?"

She shook her head, her finger jabbing the button.

The machine rewound and then ground forward, blank for a moment. She heard breathing. Then, "Please forgive me, Cally. I know you wanted only to make me happy by finding Valerie Pennington. I hurt you, baby girl. I meant nothing I said. I would die if that would take it back. But I do not deserve to forget so easily. I will go home and remember there."

Another long silence in which she willed him to speak. A dog barked, a car honked in Paul Michael's background. Cally closed her eyes.

"I love you, Carolyna Sinclair."

An eternity passed before the line went dead.

She moved from the desk, leaned her forehead against the cold glass of the french door. Paul Michael was leaving. She'd never see him again.

As she watched the rain puddling on the back terrace, her pain suddenly melded into a clear-cut decision. She turned, touched by the concern on Jessica's and Alain's faces. She seized the phone, dialed information.

"The airport, please."

Her new loved ones' faces erupted in smiles as she wrote down the number. Cally pushed the disconnect button. "I know he's taking the last flight to Atlanta this evening," she explained. "I need the flight time. I want to be there."

❦

Savannah International Airport was quiet. Cally's heels echoed on the pink and gray marble squares as she made her way along the nearly empty concourse toward gate eight.

She picked him out instantly in the waiting crowd, even though his short, kempt hair still surprised her. Wearing the same khakis, the pink shirt, the brown loafers from two days before, he slouched on his spine at the end of a bank of black and chrome seats. A large black duffle bag and a small kennel sat on the floor beside his chair. One ankle rested on the opposite knee, forming a casual well for his sketch pad. Eyes fixed solidly on his work, his hands moved quickly, as she'd seen so often before, to shape forms from inside himself, tap his memories, and tug an empathetic cord within her.

Conscious of the time, yet hesitant to forsake her view of this man in innocent repose, Cally slowed her step. He lifted his head as if sensing her presence. She walked faster now, with purpose. Unmoving, he stared through her like a stranger. At last he put the pad aside and stood. She threaded her way through strollers, feet, and bags and walked into his arms.

She relinquished the lonely, disjointed feeling she'd had since leaving the cottage that morning and felt she'd reached journey's end. Paul Michael, now schooled in prejudice, was hesitant, his wariness easily sensed.

She took his face in her hands, kissed him, her mouth working his with purpose and promise. As he had that night on Jessica's floor, he abandoned resistance and gave in to her. Those around them stared as his arms tightened and he held her, her head tucked beneath his chin in that special way she'd loved and missed.

237

Finally, she pushed back a little, looked around. "Let's go over there." She bent for Ziggy Marley's carrier. "We'll talk."

His anxious glance took in the plane arriving outside the window; he cocked his head to the announcement. She caught his hand, drew him to a closed gate area across the corridor. They found a bench, stashed his bag and sketch pad and Ziggy Marley. Paul Michael straddled the bench, and she faced him, reached out for a moment to test his curls. They sprang back in precise coils, tightened by the rain, she supposed. His eyes, wary still, focused across the way, then came back to her when she picked up his sketch pad. A pencil sketch of a man and woman walking hand in hand in gentle surf, the man's pants rolled up, the woman's skirt fluttering in a breeze.

"It's us," she said, and his eyes answered. "It's beautiful." She placed the pad on the floor, caught his hand. "I saw Ebony."

He nodded, his face solemn, a little closed, wary.

"I was looking for you. I didn't want you to leave with things the way they were. She wouldn't tell how to find you."

His blue eyes quickened. "Ebony is a hard woman."

"Is she carrying your baby, Paul Michael?"

He frowned, his body coming alert as though warding off a punch. "No, Cally. I swear, girl. I have never slept with her, and if I had, I would not be so irresponsible as to make her pregnant. Ebony has no idea who the baby belongs to. She knows only that it's not me."

Cally looked away from his soulful eyes, away from the masculine beauty tugging her soul. She willed, then allowed herself to believe, to trust him. And now she understood the hurt and sorrow in Ebony's eyes.

Paul Michael touched her shoulder. "We have very little time, girl," he said softly, anxiously.

She faced him fully. Smiled. "We have the rest of our lives."

His eyes darkened past the deep-water hue for a moment, then glistened.

"I love you, Paul Michael Quest," she whispered. She brought his hand to her face, pressed her mouth into his cinnamon-creased palm. "I never knew I could love a man the way I love you."

"All *right*," he said quietly, his voice husky, tremulous.

"I've loved you from the first moment, even before you knew you loved me—"

"No way, baby girl." His fingers cupped her cheek.

"I should have told you. I didn't want to give either of us false hope. I know that was wrong, now. Please forgive me."

"I knew. I only wanted to hear you say it."

"I love you," she said again, tasting the relief of it. "I want to live with you, wake up in your arms every day for eternity." She smiled. "I want to make pink babies with you."

He caught her in his arms; she moved against him. His kiss was deep, stirring, his reticence gone.

"I want to lie forever with you, Cally Sinclair. To make love to you. Never to hurt you again," he whispered against her mouth. "Feed you and give you a bath and braid your hair. I want to take care of you. It will be fine, girl. In Jamaica we—"

She sealed his lips with her fingers, shook her head. "Listen to me. Try to understand." His brows knitted and she rushed on, aware of the little time left. "I don't want to be a queen. I want to be a woman and face life with the man I love, make a difference, change the part of the world that needs changing. Not in Jamaica. In Savannah, with you."

Disappointment and doubt clouded his face, along with a resolve that scared her. "How can I take care of you here?"

"By loving me. By working with me. We'll build Sinclair Design together. I need you—not to haul furniture. You have skills I'd never find in anyone else. You're an *artiste*. No one can draw renderings like you, or choose colors and fabrics." She raced to share all the dreams that had lain in the back of her mind. "Alain is opening a gallery. You can hang your work there." She smiled. "No need to show your paintings on the sidewalk."

His brows knitted. "I would be a kept man."

"No, Paul Michael. We'll be a team. We'll take care of one another. You can get your citizenship, work alongside me. We'll make a statement in our community, raise our children with the love you and I missed. Maybe someday Valerie's grandchildren will heal her pain, and yours."

He turned away, stared across the concourse toward the departure

239

she knew he had anticipated and dreaded for so long.

Passengers lined up, juggled bags, children, and illusions of their own. A tiny girl toddled toward Cally and Paul Michael, her hands outstretched toward Ziggy Marley's box. Cally caught Paul Michael's chin, turned him to face her. "This didn't have to be your leaving. My mother tampered with your visa."

His eyes quickened.

"I'm sorry. I've spoken with her. The visa will be reinstated whenever you want."

"Rockatone at ribber bottom no know sun hot."

Her heart was heavy. "Mercy. A proverb covering visas."

He translated somberly, making her throat ache, "The person in easy circumstances never cares for the suffering of the needy." Then he added, "Or the suffering of a man in love with a woman he cannot have. My own proverb, Cally."

She rummaged in her jacket pocket. Catching his hand, she pressed the sapphire earring into it, folding his fingers over the tiny gem. She drew the back of his hand against her breasts, cradled it there. Warily his eyes shifted to the crowd, came back to hers.

His hand warmed her flesh beneath the cold silk shirt. She said, "I have the locket. Do you—"

"No," he said quickly, firmly.

"Go see your *grand-mère*, Paul Michael. Make peace with her concerning Valerie. But come back to me. I don't know what will happen to us . . . what our lives will be like. I only know a life with you is what I want."

The errant child reached them, patted Ziggy Marley's cage. "Dead kitty," she said solemnly.

"He's sleeping," Cally said. "Resting for his adventurous life."

The mother caught up. Not quite smiling, her eyes on Paul Michael, she grasped the girl's hand, led her to the shortening passenger line. Paul Michael's eyes followed, a part of him slipping away as well.

He looked at Cally, hesitated. "I love you, Carolyna Sinclair."

She heard the tentative quality in his declaration, nodded, and tried to smile, her hope beginning to fray.

"I am not sure, baby girl, if I can love you enough—"

"To live here with me . . . as difficult as it will be?"

"Yeah, girl. Do you understand?"

"I don't want to believe your love can be measured, but I understand your doubts about Savannah."

He looked away again, a muscle in his jaw pumping. Cally held her breath, ached, tried to believe he would make the decision she craved, prayed for ways to convince him. At last he turned back, his eyes solemn.

"I will try very hard to do what you ask, Cally, but under one condition."

Her heart thudded, caught in her throat. "Tell me."

"You will come to Jamaica with me, meet my *grand-mère*, let her know you and love you as I do. We will be married there. A big beautiful wedding with my aunties and my friends, a wedding that deserves a queen for a bride." He fell silent, measured her. "Will you do that? Will you marry me in Jamaica, Carolyna Sinclair? Do you love me that much?"

She raised his hand to her mouth, pressed her lips into its smooth warmth, consumed in memory and need. "I do, Paul Michael Quest. And I will."

"Awl *right*," he whispered.

She smiled. "There's more to this condition, I assume."

"No more. I will make preparations to change my life, come back here. I know you have obligations with the Steinberg house, Cally. You can return. I will follow when—"

"I'm never leaving you, Paul Michael. No house in the world would be worth that." The truth of it settled peacefully onto her. She looked at the thinning, straggling crowd of passengers, back to him, her mind whirling with the pressing moment.

"And I will not leave you, Cally. Come, we will change my ticket to a later time, get one for you."

Her life was changing with tornado force. Yet the changes felt destined from that first day on the dock, scary but more right than she could believe.

"And my clothes . . . ."

"A bathing suit, pretty girl. You will need little else."

She leaned, whispered in his ear, "*Awl right.*"

Paul Michael caught her in his arms, kissed her. The gate attendant watched brazenly. Cally met the woman's curious stare over his shoulder.

"I love you, Paul Michael," she whispered urgently. "I've never been more certain of anything in my life. No matter what happens."

"I know now, baby girl. No matter what happens in this new life together, your love I will not forget."

Paul Michael picked up his bag and Ziggy Marley's carrier. Cally took the sketch pad, hugging Paul Michael's depiction of lovers against her breasts as they walked up the concourse together.

The End

We hope you enjoyed *Forbidden Quest*, the first release in our Love Spectrum line. Be sure to look for Dar Tomlinson's next Love Spectrum release, *Designer Passion*, coming in June, 1999.

Genesis Press

ORDER FORM

Mail to:
Genesis Press, Inc.
315 3rd Avenue North
Columbus, MS 39701

Visit our website for latest
releases and other information
http://www.genesis-press.com

Name _____

Address _____

City/State _____ Zip_____

Telephone (_____)_____-_____

Ship to (if different from above)

Name _____

Address _____

City/State _____ Zip_____

Telephone (_____)_____-_____

Qty	Author	Title	Price	Total
	Gloria Greene	Love Unveiled	$10.95	
	Rochelle Alers	Reckless Surrender	$ 6.95	
	Beverly Clark	Yesterday Is Gone	$10.95	
	Gay G. Gunn	Nowhere to Run	$10.95	
	Mildred E. Riley	Love Always	$10.95	
	T. T. Henderson	Passion	$10.95	
	Robin Hampton Allen	Hidden Memories	$10.95	
	Sinclair LeBeau	Glory of Love	$10.95	
	Kayla Perrin	Again, My Love	$10.95	
	Vicki Andrews	Midnight Peril	$10.95	
	Donna Hill	Quiet Storm	$10.95	
	Rochelle Alers	Gentle Yearning	$10.95	
	Beverly Clark	A Love To Cherish	$15.95	
	Donna Hill	Rooms Of The Heart	$ 8.95	
	Donna Hill	Indiscretions	$ 8.95	
	Gay G Gunn	Pride And Joi	$15.95	

**Use this order
form or call
1-888-INDIGO-1
(1-888-463-4461)**

Total for books _____

Shipping & Handling _____
($3 first book, $1 each
additional book)

Total Amount Enclosed _____
MS Residents add 7% sales tax